The Lost Chalice

ALSO BY ANITA CLENNEY

Awaken the Highland Warrior

Embrace the Highland Warrior

Faelan: A Highland Warrior Brief

Angus: A Highland Warrior Brief

Heart of a Highland Warrior

Jamie: Shadow of a Highland Warrior
(Here We Go Again Anthology)

Guardians of Stone (The Relic Seekers)

Fountain of Secrets (The Relic Seekers)

The Lost Chalice

The Relic Seekers

ANITA CLENNEY

Montlake
Romance

Text copyright © 2015 Anita Clenney

Published by Montlake Romance, Seattle

www.apub.com

Amazon, the Amazon logo, and Montlake Romance are trademarks of Amazon.com, Inc., or its affiliates.

ISBN-13: 9781477821572
ISBN-10: 1477821570

Cover design by Anne Cain

Library of Congress Control Number: 2014949394

Printed in the United States of America

This book is dedicated to my wonderful friend and sister-in-heart, Sandy White, who has encouraged me along every step of this writing journey.

RELIC SEEKERS
CHARACTER INDEX

THE PROTETTORI—an ancient brotherhood that protects powerful relics

NATHAN LARRABY—handsome billionaire and relics collector with a dark secret; it is believed he may in fact be the long-lost Adam Whitmore

KENDALL MORGAN—human bloodhound with a nose for mystery and a sixth sense for the history of relics and sometimes people

JAKE STONE—sexy ex-mercenary; hired by Nathan to protect Kendall

ADAM WHITMORE—Kendall's childhood best friend who she thought had died when she was ten

MARCO—ancient member of the Protettori; the relic keeper

RAPHAEL—ancient member of the Protettori; the guardian

FERGUS—Nathan's butler

BRANDI—Thomas's sister; their parents were killed by the Reaper and their relic collection stolen

THOMAS—Brandi's brother, who went undercover to find and destroy the Reaper

THE REAPER—a master criminal of the antiquities world, once an ancient member of the Protettori, also known as Luke

JOHN WHITMORE—Adam's father; rich relics and antiquities collector

WILLIAM MORGAN—Kendall's father; archaeologist; ancient member of the Protettori

GREGOR—ancient member of the Protettori

HANK—Nathan's head of security

THE BACKSTORY

MANY CENTURIES AGO, A SECRET BROTHERHOOD WAS BORN to protect powerful relics, some religious, some thought to be myth. Four of these relics were so powerful they had to be separated to ensure no one could use them together and gain the power to rule the world. The first relic is the Spear of Destiny. The second is the Fountain of Youth. The third, the Holy Grail. The fourth remains a mystery.

The brotherhood made their home in Glastonbury Abbey in England until the abbey's destruction, after which they relocated to Italy upon discovering a portal connecting the two locales. There, they built a castle to conceal the relics and continued their work, becoming known as the Protettori. Throughout history, men searched for these relics and lusted after the power they held, but the Protettori had guardians to keep the relics from falling into the wrong hands. Guardians who included legendary men such as King Arthur and his knights. Unfortunately, the wrong hands belonged to one of the brotherhood. Luke, a powerful guardian, wanted the relics for himself, so he betrayed his brethren many centuries ago, earning a reputation as a nefarious, evil entity—the Reaper.

The brotherhood cast him out and surrounded their sacred places with sentinels to ward off the betrayer, statues that had once been living men, guardians of the Protettori.

After centuries of working in secrecy, the brotherhood has been infiltrated by a team of relic seekers who also want the relics. The team has three members: Nathan Larraby, billionaire, who has been driven to find the relics but who hasn't been truthful about his reasons for the quest. He believes he has a curse that only the relics can cure, a curse that's connected to his past.

Kendall Morgan is Nathan's relics expert. She has a sixth sense for relics and sometimes people, and she knows her boss is hiding something important. She feels a connection to him that's much deeper than attraction.

Jake Stone is an ex-mercenary who Nathan hired to protect Kendall, but he's watching more than just her back. He's never met anyone like Kendall, and all his crude efforts to keep his heart safe have failed. Both men are falling in love with her, and would die to protect her and win her heart.

The relic seekers and the Protettori join forces to keep the Reaper from finding four powerful relics he believes will make him invincible. Now that he's discovered the Fountain of Youth, he needs the Holy Grail so he can drink from the fountain and complete his quest for immortality.

The story weaves its way through legends and myths as the relic seekers work alongside the Protettori, facing danger and mystery as they uncover connections to the past that could only be the result of destiny.

CHAPTER ONE

*D*IRT COVERED HER BODY, FILLING HER MOUTH AND NOSE. SHE *clawed at the darkness as silent screams tore from her throat.*

Kendall woke but she couldn't move. Something heavy covered her. Her first thought was that she'd been buried alive, but when she pried open one eye, she saw light. A noise rumbled over her. A groan? There wasn't enough air in her lungs for even a breath, much less a sound. Someone was lying on top of her. Jake? Nathan? It didn't smell like either of them. She shoved at the body, and the weight shifted, allowing her a tiny gasp of air.

Her oxygen-starved brain lit up like a switchboard, and her memories came rushing back. She wasn't in a grave. She was lying on the bathroom floor of her room in the Abbey House in Glastonbury, England. She, Nathan, and Jake had found the Fountain of Youth hidden inside a mountain called the Tor. Raphael, the ancient guardian of the Protettori, had attacked the Reaper there, and both had disappeared into thin air.

Raphael wasn't missing anymore. Kendall had opened her shower curtain and found him passed out in her bathtub. What he was doing there was a mystery. Before she could ask, he had opened his eyes and lunged at her, but his feet got tangled in the shower curtain, causing him to land square on top of her, which explained her current predicament.

It had happened so fast it was like a flash of her sixth sense, but she knew it was Raphael. She saw his memories, pieces of his life—some he'd probably even forgotten. And some she couldn't quite believe. That's what happened when you could touch objects and people and know things no ordinary person could know. Except when your sixth sense wasn't cooperating, and that was usually when you needed it the most. Paranormal abilities had a way of not being there when you needed them and popping up when you didn't. At least for her.

Footsteps pounded across the floor and a boot moved into view. Her fuzzy gaze traveled up a long, muscular leg to a fit body and the gorgeous face of Jake, her bodyguard, and lover—at least twice. Her blurry inspection was interrupted by a familiar British curse.

"Bloody hell!" That was Nathan, her handsome billionaire boss, who was also her newly discovered best friend, Adam, who she'd thought had died when she was a kid. He wasn't sure he was Adam. But she was. "Get him off her." The weight lifted and her lungs whooshed in a gulp of air.

"What's he doing here?" Jake asked.

"He was in the bathtub," she croaked. "He lunged at me." Another hard gulp of air. "Got tangled in the shower curtain."

"How the bloody hell did he get there?" Nathan asked.

Kendall looked up and saw the ceiling swirling, similar to how it had inside the Tor just before Raphael and the Reaper had vanished. If Raphael was here, maybe the Reaper wasn't far behind. "The Reaper!"

Jake and Nathan dropped Raphael, and the room filled with curses as they went into fight mode. Through the tangle of Raphael's hair, still covering part of her face, she saw Jake

4

and Nathan whirl toward the door, Jake with his knife drawn, and Nathan . . . Nathan didn't need a weapon. His eyes were like flames, his body tensed for attack. When it was evident the Reaper wasn't there, they looked back at her.

"Ceiling," she mumbled. "Swirling . . ." Like the portal in the temple room. Then she noticed that Jake was swirling. So was Nathan. And the walls. "Everything's swirling. It must be my head."

Jake's gaze ran over her body, the half that wasn't covered by Raphael's muscular arm. Kendall's hand grasped for something to cover herself and found only the thin cloth of the shower curtain that had fallen with Raphael. She dragged it over her naked parts and tried to sit up, but the room was still spinning, and Raphael's arm was as heavy as a log.

When they finished dragging Raphael off her, Jake removed the shower curtain and covered her with a towel. Kendall saw his eyes moving together across his forehead. They settled into one wide eye above his nose and then everything went black.

She woke in the bedroom to shouting and opened her eyes in time to see Jake sail across the room. Raphael appeared to be the thrower. His eyes were glowing like Nathan's, but even brighter. *Bad*, she thought, trying to clear her head. *Very bad.* Jake bounded to his feet, his body a mass of fury, but he didn't attack Raphael. Nathan did. The two men rushed at each other, eyes burning, and collided in the middle of the room.

Kendall pulled herself up and slid off the bed. "Stop it!" she yelled from the floor. "What do you think you're doing?"

The men turned. Nathan and Raphael's eyes slowly began to return to normal as all three men gaped at her. Kendall looked down and saw the towel had slipped. She adjusted it and tried to stand. Still unsteady, she leaned against the bed. "Why are you fighting?"

"I was trying to stop him," Nathan said. "He woke up as we were moving him."

Jake wiped a drop of blood from his lip. "He wasn't happy."

"I thought you were the Reaper," Raphael mumbled. His eyes rolled back in his head and he started to sway.

"He's going." Nathan grabbed for Raphael. Together with Jake, they caught the guardian before he fell. "Get him to the bed," Nathan said, grunting as he and Jake carried Raphael between them. "He looks pretty bad."

"He just went through a portal and fought with the Reaper, who's probably nearing a thousand years old," Jake said. "Raphael's insides could be mush for all we know."

Kendall dragged herself out of the way and watched their progress. "He should be in a hospital."

"I can't see Raphael confined in a hospital," Nathan said as the men maneuvered Raphael onto the bed. "I don't think he'd like being examined."

Jake made a sarcastic grunt. "Yet a few days ago, you kidnapped him and locked him up like a lab rat."

Nathan's mouth tightened. "I was desperate."

"Not sure how we'd explain what happened to him anyway," Jake said. "I wouldn't want to tell them he followed an ancient villain through a portal."

"We'll get Marco and see what he suggests," Kendall said. "Don't move him. He'll need rest."

"There go the sleeping arrangements," Jake said. He turned to Kendall and looked her over, his eyes concerned. "Do you feel OK?"

Kendall pulled a robe over her towel. "Like I got hit by a train."

Nathan moved behind Kendall and examined her head. "You've got a nasty bump."

"You need to start wearing a helmet," Jake said, joining Nathan's inspection. "Maybe you should see a doctor."

"I'll be fine," Kendall said. "My head's tough." It had to be to deal with Nathan and Jake. "How's Raphael?"

"Still out." Jake bent down and shook him. "Raphael, can you hear me?"

The tattoos covering one side of Raphael's face were dark against the paleness of his face. His eyes fluttered opened, and he muttered something.

"What did he say?" Nathan asked.

"Sounded like *water*," Kendall said. "I have a bottle here." She got it from a nearby table and carried it back to the bed. Gently, she held it to Raphael's mouth.

He shook his head. "No," he murmured, fumbling inside the pocket of his robe—a wicked ninja-looking outfit. He pulled out a metal vial like the ones she'd seen in a room at the castle containing relics and priceless artifacts.

"Is that water from the Fountain of Youth?" she asked.

Raphael nodded and shakily brought it to his lips. It started to spill, and she steadied the guardian's hand. He drank a few sips and then his head fell back against the pillow.

"How'd you get into Kendall's bathtub?" Nathan asked.

"I was thinking about the fountain. Needed water to heal."

"And you landed in Kendall's bathtub?" Jake shook his head. "Your gifts seem about as stable as hers."

Kendall rolled her eyes. Raphael's gifts were far superior to hers. He could make a person fall asleep, read their memories, walk through walls, and as evidenced by his surprise appearance in her bathroom, he could also teleport.

"Where's the Reaper?" Nathan asked.

"I lost him." Raphael's voice was weak. "But he's injured."

"If he's injured, it might slow him down," Nathan said.

"How did he just disappear like that?" Kendall asked.

"He opened a gateway." Raphael grimaced. "I don't know how he found out where the fountain was hidden. We can't let him find the chalice." His eyes closed. "Or his child."

"Child?" Kendall swallowed. "The Reaper really does have a child?"

CHAPTER TWO

RAPHAEL MADE A MOVEMENT THAT MAY HAVE BEEN A NOD, or just a twitch.

"Raphael, what do you know about the Reaper's child?" Kendall held her breath, waiting for the answer. After learning that her father had been a member of the Protettori, she was afraid she was in fact that child.

"He's unconscious," Jake said. "We'll have to wait until he wakes up to question him."

"Give him more water," Kendall said. She had to know.

Nathan shook the vial. "It's empty. Maybe Marco has some."

"He doesn't drink from the fountain," Kendall said. "That's why he's aged and Raphael hasn't. One of us is going to have to go back to the Fountain of Youth. I'll go. You two stay here and keep an eye on him. And someone can get Marco."

"You're not going alone," Jake said. "Besides, you're injured."

"I'm fine." Kendall didn't like being told what to do, but she knew Jake was just being protective, and understandably so after everything they'd been through. He and Nathan both believed the Reaper wanted her for her sixth sense so she could help him find the relics, which was in part what Nathan had hired her to do.

Nathan frowned. "He's right. We know the Reaper has a portal there. He could come back. I think I should go. I'm better equipped."

"Are you forgetting my new power?" Kendall asked.

"You don't have a clue how your *power* works," Jake said. His voice sounded sharp, but his eyes were worried. "You're not letting this relic keeper stuff go to your head, are you?"

"No, but the fact that I'm the one in charge of the relics, or Marco seems to think I am, might give me more protection. You know the fountain can be dangerous, and I can also sense things."

"She has a point," Nathan said.

"She's not going alone," Jake said. "There'll be no way to contact her. There's no cellular signal inside the mountain. I'll go with her."

"I didn't mean she should go alone," Nathan said. "I'll go with her. She might need me . . . my abilities."

"You're really playing the superhero card now?" Jake shook his head. "So leave a powerless mortal here to fight off a man who can walk through walls and move like a streak of light?" He motioned to Raphael, who was unconscious on the bed. Or just asleep, Kendall thought, as the guardian sounded like he was quite possibly snoring.

Kendall touched Jake's arm. "You're anything but powerless, Jake, but I think he's right. Nathan and I are both connected to the Protettori by the vow."

Jake's frowned deepened, and Kendall felt his frustration and insecurity. Her hand slid from his arm to his chest. "I don't want anything to happen to you."

His muscles relaxed. He wasn't pleased, although he did give Nathan a glance that smacked of gloating before it quickly faded. "I'm worried about the Reaper. He must be pissed as hell at you for tricking him."

Nathan nodded. "And assuming he's still alive, he'll need the real Holy Grail more than ever to heal his injuries." He looked at Kendall.

Jake's face tightened. "And you're the one person who may be able to find it."

Kendall held her hand steady over his heart. "We have to do this, Jake. Raphael could die."

Resolve flickered in his eyes. "Go on then. But hurry back. You have your cross?"

The Protettori crosses they wore functioned as amulets that allowed the wearer to pass the statues that guarded the Fountain of Youth and other treasures. They were also keys that opened some of the Protettori's secrets doors.

"Yes, but Nathan doesn't." Kendall touched her head, still tender from smacking the floor. "Remember, the Reaper said we're safe as long as we're touching someone with a cross."

Jake lifted a derisive brow. "So you're gonna hold hands and trust the Reaper, the one who's trying to kill us?"

"Brandi got past the statues with Marco, so it must work," Kendall said. Brandi's parents had been killed by the Reaper. She was as determined to find the relics as Nathan was, but whereas he wanted to protect them, Brandi wanted them destroyed.

Nathan rubbed his chin, something he did when he was puzzled. "But how did Marco get inside the temple? Jake had his cross."

Kendall looked at the outline of Marco's cross under Jake's shirt. "Maybe he doesn't need a cross."

"I think Marco is hiding more than just his memory," Jake said.

"Nathan, you should take Jake's cross, just to be sure."

"I'll take Raphael's," Nathan said. "He won't need it for a bit."

Jake scoffed. "I'll try explaining that to him when he wakes up."

Nathan eased the cross over Raphael's head. "He shouldn't be too pissed since I'm trying to save him."

Jake's sarcastic manner turned solemn as they prepared to leave. Nathan walked out first, and Jake caught Kendall's arm, pulling her aside. His steel-gray eyes looked almost black. "Be careful." He touched her cheek, and in that moment his thoughts were as clear as her own. He was scared that Nathan was Adam, that he would take Kendall away from him.

Jake wasn't afraid of much, certainly not of anything that she'd seen, other than maybe her safety, so it was troubling to read fear in him. More troubling to know she was to blame. "I will."

"Hurry back to me," he said, touching a finger to her lips.

Kendall was still thinking about the look in Jake's eyes as she and Nathan drove past the abbey and the Chalice Well. "You haven't heard anything I've said," Nathan said as he pulled the car into a space at the base of the Tor.

"Sorry. I was thinking."

He turned off the engine and gave her a searching look. "About Jake?"

She blinked, hoping he didn't see that he'd hit the target. "About lots of things."

"I know you have a thing for him." A muscle twitched under his eye.

They'd avoided talking about it, and she wasn't sure what to say. "He's not the arrogant jerk he pretended to be. But you knew he had another side, didn't you? You know everything about the people around you."

Nathan rubbed his chin. "Not everything."

"What about me? Did you have any idea you already knew me when we met?"

He frowned. "I still don't know—"

"For the sake of argument, pretend you're Adam. Did you know me?"

"I felt something when I saw you. I just thought . . ." Half a smile hovered over his lips. "I thought it was because you were beautiful." Heat flared in his eyes. "You are."

"Thank you, but you're avoiding my question."

"And you aren't? We were talking about Jake."

Touché. She glanced at her watch. "We need to get moving. We don't know how badly injured Raphael is."

Nathan reached over her to open the glove box for the flashlights, and his arm brushed her breast. He pulled back. "Can you get the torches . . . flashlights?"

Kendall found them and handed one to Nathan, and then they started up the path to the Tor. The mountain—more like a big hill— was a central part of the history of Glastonbury, England. The Tor was considered a mystical place, connected to many legends. King Arthur, Christ, and the Holy Grail . . . even fairies, ghosts, and UFOs. According to Marco, some of those legends intertwined. She didn't know about all of them, but she knew the mountain hid one of the world's most sought-after treasures. The Fountain of Youth. And she knew there were ghosts here. She'd seen the ghosts of King Arthur and his knights as well as her father in the abbey ruins below.

Her father. Just thinking about him stirred her fears. Could he be the Reaper? Could the man who had raised her, loved her, tended her wounds, taught her about relics, and sometimes played dolls with her, be an ancient madman who would kill to possess the relics that would give him unlimited life? She'd just learned that her father was several centuries old. If he had hidden something that shocking, could he have also hidden the fact that he was evil?

"We're here," Nathan said.

She had been so preoccupied with her thoughts she hadn't realized they'd reached the hidden entrance in the side of the Tor.

"You were thinking again."

"I was thinking about my father."

"If you're still worried about him being the Reaper," Nathan replied, with a quick glance that clearly said he was afraid she was still thinking about Jake, "I don't think he is. The Reaper was cast out centuries ago. Your father was part of the Protettori just before you were born."

"He could have changed his appearance and come back into the brotherhood. You saw him in the temple. His face is constantly changing."

"I think the statues would recognize him even if he changed his appearance. Their purpose is to keep him out."

"I wish I was as certain."

Nathan stroked her cheek. "I don't blame you for worrying, but I don't think he's your father. Even if he is . . . it doesn't matter." His expression was open and warm.

The Reaper wasn't the only one who could change. Her rich, reclusive billionaire boss was almost unrecognizable now. She saw more of Adam in him now than Nathan. Jake had changed too. He didn't pretend to be a sarcastic womanizing jerk anymore. He had a caring, serious side that made Kendall's heart ache. What about her? Had she changed as much as they had?

Nathan's hand dropped. "Come on. I'll go first," he said, just as he always had, even when he was Adam.

The entrance to the tunnel was so well disguised it looked like part of the hillside unless one knew where to find the opening. The Tor was rumored to have mystical elements, including a labyrinth inside, and now that they had found the Fountain of Youth and the portal connecting England and Italy, Kendall knew the myths held some truth. And the tunnel didn't just contain a portal to another place. Time was affected inside as well. During their first trip inside the tunnel, Kendall, Nathan, and Jake had lost an entire day.

"I hope the entrance works the same way going in," she said. "The Protettori love booby traps. She, Nathan, and Jake had encountered several and nearly died.

"Can't blame them," Nathan said. "The priceless relics and treasures the Protettori protect are a matter of life and death."

"I don't blame them. I just don't want to get caught in them."

"If it doesn't work, we'll have to go back to the Protettori castle in Italy and come through the maze."

As far as they knew, this entrance and the one from the maze provided the only access to the tunnel. Kendall shuddered. "I'd rather face a booby trap."

They stepped inside the narrow passageway and used their lights to follow the path to the main tunnel that led to the hidden room housing the Fountain of Youth. "This reminds me of when we were kids," Kendall said.

Nathan nodded, and then hesitated slightly. He still wasn't sure he was Adam.

"Do you remember when I fell through the broken boards of the tomb in Egypt?" she asked.

Kendall couldn't see his face clearly, but she could feel his mind grasping for the memory. He wasn't blocking her now. Before she had found out he was Adam, his thoughts had been beyond her reach, as if he'd put up a wall.

"I'm not sure."

"You just don't want to admit it," she said. "Why?"

Emotions mixed with the shadows on his face. "I'm not certain I'm . . . him."

"I know you remember some things. For God's sake, I saw one of your memories. It was of me as a girl. How is that possible if you're not Adam?"

He shrugged, his handsome face conflicted, and as usual, she found herself searching for traces of the boy she'd loved. "I don't know what to think," he said.

"Nathan, you know you're Adam. You have to be."

"I want to . . ." He stopped and frowned. "I'm just not sure yet."

Kendall patted his arm, noting the muscles under his shirt. Adam hadn't had those. "Sorry I'm pushing you. Let's just focus on getting water for Raphael. He must have the answers we need."

Like the identity of the Reaper's child.

Kendall and Nathan walked through the main tunnel until they found the wheel etched on the stone wall. "This is it," Kendall said.

"Sure you have your cross?" Nathan asked.

"Yes."

Nathan touched his chest. "I hope Raphael doesn't wake up until we get back." He pushed the wheel and the door grated open. A soft light emerged from the widening crack. They stood together, watching as the room was revealed. It had only been hours since they'd left, but Kendall was still amazed at the sight. The room resembled a Roman temple with white columns lining the edges and polished stones covering the floors and walls. The painted ceiling could have graced a cathedral, but the hum of the statues that surrounded the temple and the soft glow radiating between the stones in the floor reminded her that the real beauty of the room lay beneath them, where the Fountain of Youth was hidden, born of two holy wells.

Legend said one well had sprung from the spot where Joseph of Arimathea had buried the Holy Grail containing Christ's blood, which he'd caught at the foot of the cross. Whether it was truly the start of the well, she could only speculate, but she knew the cup of blood existed. She had seen it in a vision that felt as real as if she had been there.

Nathan glanced at the closest statue, one of many surrounding the inside of the temple. "You ready?"

Kendall nodded.

Nathan slipped his hand into hers. It was warm and strong. She felt a lump in her throat. Adam was back. Kendall's heart thudded as they stepped past the nearest statue. All that stood between them and death were the silver crosses hanging around their necks. She didn't know how they worked, but she had witnessed the horrifying consequence that occurred when someone tried to pass the statues without a cross.

As they moved farther into the room, their gazes were immediately drawn to the golden light seeping through the floor above the Fountain of Youth, as if mere stone couldn't contain its glory. "I always wondered if it really existed," he said. "I guess every treasure hunter and collector has."

"Even we did, when we were kids. You said if we found it we'd drink from it and never grow old. We would search for relics forever."

Nathan stared at the light, his expression hopeful. "You think it really works? Eternal youth and all that?"

"You're not still looking for a cure for your *curse*?"

He shrugged.

"You know you have a gift, like Raphael's."

"What if I don't want it?"

Kendall didn't know what to say. She had a gift. It was frustrating, but she'd had it for so long she couldn't imagine being without it. It was part of her. She tried to imagine how Nathan must feel, having it appear out of the blue. Sensing things was a lot different than having your body physically change. "Marco said you're a guardian. You've sought relics all your life, whether you admit you're Adam or not. It's in your blood. I don't understand it either, but what better way is there to use your abilities than to protect relics?"

"What if Marco's wrong about what I am?" Nathan sounded uncertain, like he had when he first admitted to her and Jake that he believed he had a curse.

"You've got eyes like Raphael's," Kendall said. "That must mean something. You wouldn't walk away from this, would you?"

"Not as long as you're part of it." And though he didn't say it, wouldn't even admit it, she knew that inside he was thinking, *I'll never leave you again.*

She wanted to forget everything and wrap her arms around Nathan and cry. Cry for the lost years, cry that she'd found him again, but there were more important things to attend to. It was time to start acting like a keeper, or a keeper in training. If someone would take the time to train her. With Marco's wandering mind, that task may be left to Raphael, and if he didn't drink more water, he may not be around to do the job.

"If people find out the fountain is real, the world will become a dangerous place," Kendall said. The lure of eternal youth would bring out the greedy and ugly side of humanity. There was no telling the lengths people would go to to find it. The Reaper already knew, and he had almost destroyed his brotherhood to secure the fountain.

Nathan's face grew somber. "Maybe Brandi's right about destroying the relics so no one can use them."

"That's a conversation for another day. For now, we have to save Raphael. He's probably the key to this puzzle. If anyone can sort out the Reaper's motives, it's Raphael."

"And he should know better than anyone what the chalice looks like. He's the one who hid it. Wait. What's that noise?" Nathan turned his head to listen.

"I think it's the statues," Kendall said, turning to look at the stone guardians—sentinels, Marco called them—that stood along the edge of the temple. "Hard to believe these were once alive."

"Sounds like they're whispering."

It did sound like someone softly whispering. "Maybe they are."

"You think . . ." Nathan walked closer to one. He was a tall man, but the statue was taller and broader. If Marco was right about the statues once being alive as guardians, then they were essentially living tombs. Guardians in life, sentinels in death. "I don't see how they could have once been alive," Nathan said. "Maybe Marco was confused again."

"I don't think so. When I touched them before, I sensed pieces of their lives."

"What did you feel?" Nathan's eyes sparked with excitement, reminding her of the dust-covered boy who'd stood on a cliff above her, his enthusiastic grin urging her to hurry and see what he'd found. How had she missed this similarity between Adam and Nathan? Or had she known subconsciously all along, and that was why she'd felt so connected to him?

"You want to see?"

Nathan's eyes flared. "Yes."

"Put your hand over mine. I'm not sure this will work, but sometimes it does. It did with Jake." She felt Nathan stiffen and wished she hadn't mentioned Jake's name.

Nathan put his hand over hers, and she slowly reached toward the statue. The sentinel's stone eyes were open, his hand grasping his sword. Kendall touched the hardened fingers gripping the handle of the blade. The humming sound that the statue emitted flowed into her fingers and up her arm. Colors flashed, and she saw a man with short auburn hair and green eyes. He was outside a house, not the Protettori's castle in Italy, but a simple house with a thatched roof. He was leading a horse and smiling as he talked. To the horse, she guessed, since she didn't see anyone else there.

Nathan yanked his hand away.

Kendall pulled back too, and the images disappeared.

"Bloody hell. What was that?"

"That was the sentinel before he was a statue. When he was a live guardian."

"He was talking to his horse," Nathan said, his voice hushed with awe.

Kendall looked at the hand that had held the reins, now stone, and the mouth set in a straight line instead of a smile. "Yes," she said softly. "He looked happy. I wonder what his name was." If she spent a little more time with him, she may find out. Sometimes her senses were so sharp she could pick up small nuances in addition to larger details. Other times she couldn't sense anything at all. And she had no idea why or what controlled it.

Nathan's face wore a troubled frown.

"What's wrong?"

"I can't let anyone find out about you, about what you can do. I've got to keep you hidden. Do you know how valuable your gift is?"

"Enough for you to hire me," Kendall said, making light of the matter. She was comfortable with her gift, but didn't like feeling different from everyone else. *Guess you'd better get used to it, Miss Relic Keeper.* Even her subconscious was starting to sound like Jake.

"You know what I mean?" Nathan said. "People would kill to use your gifts. Governments, politicians, criminals. You're as dangerous as the fountain. Makes me want to lock you up in a vault."

"Don't even think about it. We'll just have to keep it a secret. I've done that most of my life." Only her father and Adam had known what she could do. Not even Aunt Edna knew.

Nathan brushed her cheek with his thumb. "But now the Reaper knows. He's the one I'm worried about."

"We're going to beat him, Adam . . . Nathan." The slip surprised them both. His eyes locked on hers, and something passed between them. Nathan wasn't the little boy she had adored. He was a man. A handsome, powerful, and very sexy man.

Jake.

The name whispered through her mind, as if he were beside her, glaring at her thought. "All three of us, you, me, and Jake. Five of us, including Marco and Raphael, unless they're retiring or something, which I hope they're not, since we don't have any idea what keepers and guardians really do. We'll stop him. We have to."

"Let's get the water and get out. The sooner we can get some answers from Raphael about what happened in that portal, the better." They walked to the stone wheel on the wall, which controlled the opening in the floor that led to the fountain. It was similar to the etching in the tunnel and the tattoo on Nathan's arm. "Do you want to open it?" Nathan asked. "Or shall I?"

"I will." Kendall stepped up to the wall and placed her hands on the wheel. The sensation hit her with the force of a storm. *He had to find the Holy Grail. It was the only way to save her.* Kendall's head swam with the intensity of the strange thought, and her body felt as if it weren't hers. A raw burst of energy caught her off guard and flung her aside. The sensations worsened, as if her body were separating from her head. She heard Nathan calling her name, and when she could focus, she saw him reaching for her, but he seemed to be fading. He cursed and lunged for her, wrapping his arms tight around her.

"Bloody hell. Not again."

CHAPTER THREE

J AKE TOOK ANOTHER SIP OF SOUP AND STARED AT RAPHAEL. No doubt about it. He was snoring. It was comforting in a way. Made him seem ordinary, not like the centuries-old being he was. Better have him snore—even fart—than walk through walls. What was a normal guy to do with that? How was a normal guy supposed to stand a chance with Kendall when Nathan was around? Adam. Jake grunted and moved to take another sip, hitting his tooth on the spoon. He frowned and put the soup down. It was bad enough when Nathan was just a handsome billionaire. Now he was a handsome billionaire who was the lost love of Kendall's childhood, and he had superpowers. Don't forget the damned superpowers. And here Jake was sitting in a room drinking soup while they were off exploring like they had when they were best friends. Rekindling old feelings . . . and who knew what else. This would bring them closer than ever.

No way in hell he could beat that. What did he have in his corner? Good sex with her. Really good sex. Amazing sex. That wasn't enough. He'd acted like an ass when he'd first met her, doubting her, coming on to her like a pervert to keep her at a distance. Which hadn't worked. She'd seen right through him. But he still didn't stand a chance. Kendall would probably start acting awkward and distant, and then she'd dump him. Dump him? They weren't even dating. Not really.

"Damn it." What was wrong with him? He was acting like a lovesick teenager. He wished Raphael would wake up and get mad again just so he could fight someone and get this bullshit out of his head. Women were nothing but trouble.

But Raphael didn't wake up, and Jake sat and thought about Kendall while his heart twisted in his chest. After a couple of hours, he was getting worried, stir-crazy, and bored. So bored he was leaning over Raphael, close enough that he could have counted his eyelashes, wondering whether to hit him and wake him, when someone knocked on the door. It wasn't Fergus's knock. Kendall. Maybe they'd forgotten the room key.

He hurried to the door, but it wasn't Kendall. It was the irritating little boy who'd gotten tangled up in the search for the Fountain of Youth. The kid had found a dead body, gotten stuck in a priest hole, and witnessed a kidnapping. Apparently he was back for more. "Art."

"Hey."

"Shouldn't you be in bed?"

"I can't sleep. I'm excited." Art stuck his hands in his pockets. "I wanted to talk to somebody."

"I'm kind of busy." Jake felt bad for the kid. He was annoying as hell, but Jake remembered what it felt like to want someone to talk to. He'd been lonely and closed off until he'd met Lilly, his friend at the orphanage in India.

"Oh." Art's face scrunched up, making his freckles look like they were moving. "I thought you were alone. I saw Guinevere and the other knight leave."

"Guinevere?"

"The blond woman. I guess she's Guinevere, not the redheaded lady like I thought at first. Guinevere wouldn't steal the chalice."

Brandi was the redheaded lady, and she had stolen the Blue Chalice in hopes it was the Holy Grail. But it wasn't. "They should have been back by now. So what were they doing, the knight and Guinevere?"

"Their heads were real close."

"Kissing?"

"Yuck. No, talking. I think. Then they got in the car. The red-haired lady was watching them."

"Did she follow them?"

"I don't know."

Jake felt a twinge of panic. Brandi knew the location of the fountain, and she wanted it destroyed like the other relics. If she followed Kendall and Nathan, she could steal one of their crosses and get inside the temple. But Jake couldn't see Brandi taking on Nathan and Kendall with their Protettori abilities. Nathan still freaked her out. Still . . . she had said she'd kill anyone in her way.

Jake rubbed a hand through his hair. "I've got to go do something."

"Can I come?" Art asked.

"No. Go to sleep. Your mom must be worried."

"She took a sleeping pill. She'll be out for hours."

What about Raphael? He couldn't leave him alone. He'd called Fergus earlier, but he hadn't answered. He and Marco were probably exhausted after their narrow escape from the Reaper. Jake looked at Art. No way. Kendall would kill him if he let Art babysit Raphael. "I changed my mind. I need your help after all."

Art perked up. "What do you want me to do?"

"You know which room the older men with us were staying in?"

"You mean Merlin and the man in the suit, Fergie?"

"Fergus, not Fergie."

"I like Fergie better. It reminds me of Frankie."

Frankie was Art's pet snake. "You can take that up with Fergus, though I'm not sure he'll like being nicknamed after a snake. You know which room they're in?" Art nodded, and Jake suspected the kid knew who was in every room. "Ask them to come here and keep an eye on Raphael."

"Is Raphael another knight?"

"Uh, yeah. He's hurt. Remember your promise," Jake said. "Secrecy."

Art held up his fingers in the Scout's salute. "I'm not gonna tell anyone but Frankie."

Jake returned the salute, and at the last second, he clapped Art on the shoulder. "Camelot is depending on you. Hurry."

As soon as Art left, Jake checked on Raphael, grabbed his pack, and drove the rental car to the Tor. Nathan's car was still parked there. Jake couldn't think of any good reason for that. Maybe Brandi had kidnapped them. Or killed them. Or the Reaper had come back. Or maybe Kendall and Nathan were reacquainting themselves in private.

Jake ran so fast up the long path, he was out of breath by the time he reached the hidden entrance to the mountain. Moving quietly, he followed the passageway to the engraved wheel marking the door to the secret temple that housed the Fountain of Youth. After checking to make sure he had his cross, he pushed the catch. The door opened, and Jake stepped inside.

The place reminded him of a Roman temple, with stone floors and walls and columns throughout. The only light came from a faint glow in the floor, where hidden steps led to the Fountain of Youth. There were three rooms, the large central room, the smaller room where Nathan had been held captive by Raphael, and the room containing the three marble tombs.

Statues were spaced evenly around the perimeter of the temple like an elaborate version of Stonehenge. But according to Marco, these weren't just chunks of stone. They had once been living men, ancient guardians—like Raphael—but had been turned to sentinels. Jake didn't know if that were true, but he knew they could kill a man.

How they could be turned from flesh to stone and why they hadn't died were more questions on the growing list of things Marco and Raphael hadn't fully explained.

"Kendall? Nathan?" No one answered. Where were they? Jake approached the wheel that opened the floor to the fountain. Kendall's scent still lingered, so he knew she'd been here. How could he have missed them? He hadn't seen anyone on his way here. Had they gotten trapped down by the fountain? He grabbed the wheel. It was cold against his fingers and palms. As the wheel turned, a section of the floor began to open, and the light grew brighter as the Fountain of Youth was revealed. Jake hurried down the wide steps to the pool of water, which was fed by two streams flowing from the wall into a bowl that overflowed into the pool. One stream was stained red, the other white. The light was strongest in the bowl, but otherwise it was ordinary looking. Simple. But this bowl wasn't ordinary. It was the Fountain of Youth.

Jake was more concerned about what wasn't here. Kendall and Nathan. Jake went back up the steps to search the rest of the temple, and he noticed something that made his heart wrench with fear.

Raphael's vial lay behind a table near the wheel.

CHAPTER FOUR

THE THIN METAL CONTAINER LAY ON ITS SIDE AS IF SOMEONE had dropped it. Was it the same vial, or did Raphael keep others here? Jake picked it up and turned it over. A single drop of water ran out, and he knew in his gut that it was the one Kendall had brought to refill.

Jake checked the rest of the temple, putting the room with the tombs off until last. There was something about the room that made him sick. There were three tombs of black marble, which most likely held the remains of King Arthur and Guinevere, whose bones had disappeared along with the treasure that the monks of the abbey protected. Legend said their tombs were made of black marble. The third tomb was a mystery. Merlin's? A knight's?

Jake felt the same twisting in his stomach and head as he had the first time he'd seen the room. Bones, that must be it. He hated them, and tombs this old must contain bones. Kendall and Nathan weren't in this room either. There must be another room, or rooms. The Protettori loved secret rooms. And booby traps. Kendall and Nathan could be trapped somewhere.

He searched every square inch of the place, but didn't find them or any secret rooms. Either they'd gone exploring somewhere else, been kidnapped, or vanished into thin air.

Vanishing into thin air didn't seem likely, so that left exploring or kidnapping. Jake couldn't see them exploring when Raphael was lying injured, waiting for the water. That narrowed it down to kidnapping. Nathan had enemies, as any man in his position of wealth and power would, but there were only two who knew this location. The Reaper and Brandi. The Reaper was the most likely candidate since Brandi didn't have a cross to get her past the statues. Of course, she wouldn't need a cross if she touched Kendall or Nathan as they passed. Jake didn't see Brandi taking on Nathan and Kendall so soon after they had all escaped the Reaper. Brandi was scared of Nathan. Had the Reaper come back through the portal?

The thought had just crossed Jake's mind when he heard a whisper coming from the main room of the temple. Pulling his gun, he slipped out to see who was there. The temple was empty, other than the whispers, soft at first, growing louder and faster until they created a hum like the statues made. It gave him an eerie feeling, as if the statues were talking to each other. He took the vial and walked down the steps to the fountain again. Raphael needed water, and right now he was Jake's only source of help, since Marco was out of his head half the time.

Jake filled the vial and closed the opening to the fountain. Carefully holding the precious water, he started to leave the temple. As he passed the statues, he heard a sizzle. Pain shot through him like a bolt of lightning, flinging him across the floor. He lay there, unable to move as blackness descended and the smell of ozone filled his nostrils.

When he regained consciousness, it took him a minute to figure out he was still inside the temple. His head and body felt like they were on fire. Near the doorway, the closest statue watched him with stone eyes. The statues. They must have zapped him when he tried to pass. Why hadn't the cross protected him? He lifted his hand, the only part he could move, to his chest. The cross wasn't there.

He should be dead. He tried sitting up, but he couldn't, so he lay still, gasping for breath. Something warm ran from the corner of his mouth. He touched it with his tongue. Blood. That's why his insides felt like they'd been fried. They had. He coughed and felt another trickle of blood. He was hemorrhaging internally. He was going to die.

He'd survived war and countless enemies, only to be killed by statues? Kendall's face filled his mind. Her lovely green eyes, her smile, the catch of her breath as they'd made love. He'd finally tasted love and lost it. Dammit. He couldn't leave her alone. His throat worked, and he started to choke on the blood.

Kendall wasn't alone. She had Nathan. He would protect her. But Nathan needed him too. They were both in trouble. Jake put his hands against the floor and tried again to push himself up. He felt something hard in his left hand. The vial of water. Moving stiffly, he raised his hand to his mouth and did the only thing he could think of. He opened the vial and drank.

He didn't know how long he'd been out, but he wasn't dead. Jake sat up and moved his legs. They worked. What the hell? He even managed to stand. Something rolled across the floor. Raphael's vial. Drinking the water must have kept him alive. But without a cross, he was trapped.

He gathered his backpack, which had been knocked off when he fell, and retraced his steps, but didn't find the cross. Impossible. It couldn't have vanished. He looked at the statues watching in silence. "Don't suppose one of you has an extra cross?" he asked. Then he was struck by a thought. Assuming the tombs contained the corpses of knights, they must have had crosses. Perhaps they were buried with them.

He dreaded going into the room again, but he had to get out of this temple so he could search for Kendall and Nathan. He looked at the first two tombs. King Arthur and Guinevere? Jake was hesitant to open those. He'd idolized King Arthur when he was a kid. It didn't seem right to desecrate his tomb. Nor Guinevere's. Mentally Jake was drawing a comparison to her and Kendall after the visions he'd had of the couple from Camelot while he and Kendall were making love. Since Kendall had called him Lancelot afterward, Jake was pretty sure the woman in the vision had been Guinevere. He had no concrete explanation, but he assumed he must have tapped into Kendall's vision when he touched her.

Swallowing his dread, he walked back into the room and looked at the first tomb. Now wasn't the time to be courteous. If anyone would have a cross, it should be King Arthur.

The black marble was still shiny, which was surprising. He couldn't imagine Raphael polishing the tombs. The covering was heavy. Pushing and tugging didn't work, so he decided he must be going about the process wrong. Using his knife, he slid the blade around the edges, searching for a catch. The Protettori loved secret catches. He was surprised when he heard a click.

This time when he pushed the covering, it slid back without a sound. Jake looked down at the corpse inside. It wasn't King Arthur.

It was Nathan.

CHAPTER FIVE

J AKE STARED AT THE BODY IN SHOCK. NATHAN WAS WEARING
some kind of strange clothes. The Reaper must have caught them
here. Where was Kendall? Pulse drumming in his ears, Jake hurried to the second tomb and, with trembling hands, used his knife
again to find the catch. When the lid slid back, his heart stopped.

Kendall's eyes were closed, but she didn't look dead. He
pressed his fingers to the cold skin of her neck in search of a pulse.
Nothing. A harsh cry rose in his throat. "No, dammit. You can't
be dead." He started to lift her out of the tomb when he noticed
her fingernails. They were long. Kendall's nails weren't long. And
these clothes weren't right. He scoured her face and body and
noticed other things that were different. The corpse's lips weren't
as full as Kendall's. Her eyebrows were thicker. It wasn't her.

He felt light-headed with relief. But who was she? He looked
at the first tomb again, and felt the same shock at seeing Nathan,
or his likeness. This time Jake recognized the corpse's clothes.
He'd seen them on King Arthur in a vision.

How could that be? Unless it was one of the Protettori's traps, a
mental one to make trespassers hallucinate and go insane. Kendall
had mentioned myths about men getting trapped inside the Tor

and losing their minds. Or maybe he was dead and this was hell. If it was, he wasn't planning on staying here. He needed a cross. A quick search revealed that there wasn't one on Nathan's or Kendall's—he didn't want to think of them as corpses—likenesses.

He stepped over to the third tomb, and his stomach rolled with waves of nausea. Swallowing, he opened the tomb and looked inside. His jaw dropped. "Why the hell not?"

It was him.

He was so well preserved he didn't even look dead. Like the corpses in the first two tombs, the clothing was old, but the face was enough like Jake's to be him, or at least a brother. There were slight differences. Haircut, scars that Jake didn't have. Was this a joke? The closer his fingers got to the body, the higher the contents of his stomach climbed up his throat, but he didn't stop. By the time he finished searching *his* corpse, his stomach felt like he'd dived off a cliff. He stepped back and pulled in a hard breath. The search hadn't helped. There wasn't a cross in any of the tombs. He'd have to find another way out. Stomach churning, he closed the tombs. Later, after he escaped, he would figure out who the hell the corpses were.

He searched the temple one last time, but he didn't find the cross. Logically, he knew it couldn't have vanished, but he also couldn't have just searched his own corpse. Logic didn't seem to matter here.

He couldn't pass the statues, so he had to go up or down. He looked at the ceiling. The Reaper had used it as a portal, but Jake had no idea how it worked, or if anyone could open it besides the Reaper. That left the floor. If he could dig down far enough, it should be safe to pass the statues, considering that people walked all over the hillside above the statues and didn't get electrocuted. But how the hell could he dig his way out from under the Tor?

He found a loose stone and started working with a small tool from his backpack. It took a while to remove it, and he was disappointed to find rock underneath. He chipped away at the granite, and after several minutes, the rock underneath cracked. A few more strikes and he was able to lift the broken rock. Dirt. That was good. But after an hour, he knew this was never going to work. He'd starve to death before he moved enough dirt to get out. The Tor wasn't a huge mountain, but it was a mountain, and there was a good possibility that the temple was right in the center.

Jake stopped digging. He was so thirsty he decided to risk taking another drink of water. He did, and he felt refreshed. Then a plan occurred to him. It was insane, and might kill him, but he couldn't just sit there waiting. He'd passed the statues before and nearly died, but the water had healed him. If he drank the water as he was crossing . . .

He refilled the vial from the fountain, but didn't drink any more until he would need it. The water was powerful, and he didn't know enough about it. Overdosing on the Fountain of Youth would be a hell of a way to die.

He walked back to the door leading from the temple—the only exit, as far as he knew. The statues stood a few feet inside the temple wall, so if he could just get past them, he'd have some time and space to recover—which he was sure he'd need—before getting out into the tunnel. He opened the vial of water and moved as close to the line of statues as he dared. His skin tingled as the fingers of electricity reached out for him. He pictured Kendall in his mind, lying underneath him, her face glowing, so that in case he didn't make it, she would be the last thing he saw. Then he took a long drink and leaped.

The ringing in Kendall's ears settled into a low rumble, but her body was tingling all over. She was wrapped in Nathan's arms, and the rumbling sound was coming from his chest. She scrambled out of his arms and saw his eyes glowing the most beautiful shade of amber. He looked frightening and terribly beautiful.

"Nathan. Calm down." But his fiery gaze didn't fade, and his chest was moving in and out too fast. He hadn't tried to stand, which worried her. He stayed on the floor, arms tensed, body curled like a wounded animal. Kendall swallowed and eased toward him. Kneeling, she touched his arm. His skin was burning hot. He had taken the brunt of their fall . . . but where were they?

Glancing around, she saw a room with large stones covering the walls and floor. The former was decorated with pictographs illuminated by candelabras lining the walls. In the center of the room was a rectangular object like an altar. It would be a fascinating place to explore at any other time, but now she was more interested in finding a door.

Nathan's body was thrumming with energy, and his gaze hadn't left hers, like a tiger watching its prey. Then his eyes rolled back in his head and his body slumped. She checked his pulse. Fast. "Nathan? Can you hear me?"

He didn't open his eyes. His heartbeat was erratic and his skin felt dangerously hot. She tried her cell phone, but there was no signal. Not surprising. There wasn't a signal in the temple either. She touched his cheek and brushed her hand over his light-brown hair. "I'm going to look for a way out. I'll be back in a few minutes." She had no idea where she was—under the Tor perhaps—but she had to get help.

She left him there and quickly searched the room for a door. The pictures on the walls reminded her of some Egyptian tombs. The altar in the center of the room had writing along the edges, but she couldn't read it. Latin perhaps? There was a large, round shield-looking stone on one wall. But there wasn't a door. Panic started setting in. She had to get help. Nathan could die, and Raphael needed water.

There wasn't an obvious door, so she started searching for a hidden one. She examined the stones in general, and spent a good amount of time studying the round stone on the wall, but found nothing. Someone had built a lovely room here that required materials and labor. They weren't here now, so there must be a way out. She glanced at the altar. Maybe it wasn't an altar but a tomb holding the body of the last person who'd built this room. It was large enough. That was a morbid thought, and highly unlikely. Nonsense. Maybe the only way back was the way they came.

The best she could tell, they had fallen from the ceiling. Had she activated a trapdoor? She couldn't see any sign of an opening from here. Giving up for the moment, she went back to check on Nathan. He was still hot, heartbeat still too fast. Alternating between checking on him and searching every stone for a way out, she finally grew exhausted. Her head felt strange, from the portal, she guessed.

Nathan was calmer and not quite as warm now, but still unconscious. Kendall sat down beside him, and when her eyes grew too heavy, she lay down, listening to him breathe. She thought about Jake. He would wonder where they were and come looking for them. But would he find them? She concentrated on his face, his steel-gray eyes and those dark lashes, as if trying to conjure him. *Help us, Jake.*

Her scent filled his head, the sweetness of Kendall's warm, female flesh. Since his *curse* had come into effect, Nathan's sense of smell had intensified, making nearness to her sometimes like torture. It was all he could do to keep his hands off her. Through the pleasant drowsiness, he realized her scent was very close and there was a firm bum pressed against his groin.

Nathan opened his eyes. Kendall was lying in his arms, her blond hair tickling his nose. He couldn't recall how they'd gotten in this position. The last thing he remembered was seeing Kendall fall and him reaching for her. Then that awful light-headed heaviness, as if his head were being separated from his body. They must have fallen through another portal. Damn the Protettori.

"Kendall?" He touched her shoulder.

She sat up with a start and turned, her startled eyes soft with sleep. "Nathan. Are you OK?" she asked.

He sat up beside her. "You?"

"I think so. You scared me. You got stuck in your adrenaline mode."

He felt a shiver of fear. "Did I . . ."

"No. You weren't dangerous. I was just worried for you. You felt so hot." A blush started creeping across her cheeks. "Warm, your skin felt too warm."

"The monster was trying to come out." What if it had? What if he'd hurt her?

"You're not a monster. Raphael is like you. He's not a monster."

"We don't know much about what Raphael is or isn't, and whatever he is, he's had a long time to learn to control it. Where are we?"

"I don't know. Under the temple, maybe. I touched the wheel." Kendall said. "Maybe I accidentally opened a trapdoor. Remember the rumors about a labyrinth underneath the Tor? It would make sense for the Protettori to have something to stop a person if they got too close to the fountain."

"My head feels like it did when Jake and I fell through the portal in the maze."

Kendall looked dismayed but nodded. "Mine too. I would rather it be a booby trap."

Nathan stood and helped Kendall to her feet. "How long was I out?"

She glanced at her watch. "It's not working. A couple of hours, I think."

Nathan glanced at his beat-up watch. He could afford a thousand Rolexes, but he couldn't part with this watch. It was the only link to his father. It wasn't working either. "Blimey."

"Are you sure you're feeling OK? I've never seen you like that before. I was afraid I would lose you . . . again."

A thrill went through him to know she cared, that Jake didn't consume her thoughts. "I feel OK, other than my head. But we do need to find a way out. Raphael needs water."

Kendall touched her pocket. "The vial's gone. I must have lost it when I fell."

"Or else it's floating around in some kind of time warp." Nathan pulled his cell phone out and cursed. "No signal."

"I already checked."

He put it back in his pocket. "There has to be a door out of here."

"I checked that too. I couldn't find one."

"There's always a door." Nathan looked back at the ceiling. "Unless we just fell through the only one."

"Don't say that."

"Do you sense anything? Any clue to where we are?"

"No."

"We'd better start exploring." *They were good at that.* The quick memory didn't startle him as much as the earlier ones had. But he didn't tell her. She was already sure he was Adam. He still wasn't certain he hadn't gotten the memories from Kendall and Raphael. They both had the ability to share things they sensed with others, and most of Nathan's memories of Adam had come when he was touching one of them. He needed more proof.

He conducted his own search, briefly admiring the amazing paintings and sketches on the walls, but Kendall was right, there wasn't a door. "Did you light the torches?"

"No. They were on when I woke up," she said. "Someone must have been here recently."

They checked the room, carefully prodding each stone. They fell into a rhythm, methodically tapping and listening, studying surfaces. Occasionally he would turn and catch her looking at him. "Is something the matter?" he finally asked.

"No," she said, smiling. "Nothing at all. Other than falling through a portal and getting trapped."

Nathan smiled in return. "Business as usual."

Kendall looked as if he'd said something impressive. "You're different now," she said. "You smile, and you're more . . . open. I can sense more about you. You were blocking me when we first met, weren't you?"

He took a moment to answer. "I didn't want to frighten you off with my thoughts."

"You were worried that I'd sense your curse?"

He was worried that she would see herself in his thoughts. *Bloody fool*, he chided himself. How could he not be Adam if he'd had memories of her as a child before he even knew anything about Adam? She hadn't been touching him then. Why the devil was he fighting it so hard? He didn't want to explain, so he nodded.

As they searched the room, Nathan grew more concerned about Raphael. Kendall's wrinkled brows indicated that she was having the same thought.

"What will we do if we can't find a way out?" she asked.

"Jake will find us." God knows he wouldn't let Kendall out of his sight for long. That relationship wasn't something Nathan had expected. If he'd known, he never would have hired Jake to guard her. Nathan looked up at the place from where they'd fallen. "We should check the ceiling for a catch. The Protettori are good with their traps, and someone has obviously been taking care of this place, as they have the temple. This could just be a booby trap." Though it hadn't felt like one when he and Kendall had fallen. It hadn't felt like anything normal.

"It's got to be ten feet high," Kendall said, still kneeling where she'd been checking a stone on the floor. "We'll never reach it."

Nathan reached out a hand to her as she got to her feet. "We might, if you sit on my shoulders like you did in that Mayan pyramid—"

Kendall squeezed his hand. "You remembered?"

"You're touching me. It could be your memories I'm sensing," he said. "I bet you were thinking about that time, weren't you?"

"Yes, but I don't think that's what's happening." She looked at the ceiling. "Let's give it a try. We're running out of options."

Nathan bent down so she could climb onto his shoulders. When she didn't move, he turned. "What's wrong?"

"Nothing. It's just . . ." Her gaze went to his mouth, and moved quickly down his body. "We're not kids now."

"You think I can't lift you?" he asked, knowing full well that wasn't her concern. He knew exactly what she meant. She wasn't a little girl either. She was a grown woman, a beautiful, sexy woman, and she was getting ready to wrap her legs around his neck. "Come on. Let's do this. Raphael's waiting."

She put one leg over his shoulder—a very nicely shaped leg—which made him remember the nickname Jake had first given her . . . Legs. He frowned, but the irritation didn't last a moment, as he was distracted by her other leg settling over his left shoulder and her crotch pressed against his neck.

He was feeling overheated, and not from exertion or his bloody curse. "Ready?" he asked, hoping to get this done before he did something stupid.

"I suppose."

He stood, but Kendall was still a few feet from the ceiling. "I can't touch it."

"Try standing. Can you manage that?"

"I'll try. Back up to the wall so I'll have something to balance against. I don't want to rip out your hair." She ruffled his head. "It's nice hair."

"My hair thanks you." He put his back a few inches from the wall, enough for her to maneuver into a standing position. "Will that work?"

"I think so." Holding on to his head and using the wall for balance, she pulled one leg up at a time, until she was standing on his shoulders. "I can touch the ceiling," she said. He balanced her weight while she checked the area for a catch or an opening. They slowly worked their way around the corner, wobbling as they searched, until it was apparent they were wasting their time. "I don't see anything. I don't think there's a door." She sighed. "Which means . . ."

"It was a portal," he finished.

"I think so. That may explain why you were so affected by the fall."

"You ready to get down?"

Without warning, she jerked, causing him to lose his balance. She teetered for a moment before slipping. Nathan grabbed her and they ended up on the floor again. "Kendall?"

"I'm OK," she wheezed.

"What happened?" he asked, rolling off her.

"Something hit me."

"A loose stone?"

"I don't think so."

"I don't see anything," he said, looking around them.

"I think I'm sitting on it." Kendall moved aside and saw a cross on a chain.

Nathan picked it up. "Your cross? You must have lost it in the portal."

Kendall touched the cross under her shirt. "It's not mine."

Nathan frowned and pulled his cross from under his shirt. "Not mine either. Then who does it belong to?"

Kendall's eyes widened with fear. "I think it's Jake's."

For a second Jake felt like he was on fire. He heard sizzling and smelled ozone again, and then he fell hard. For the second time in the past hour, he thought he might be dead. Then he caught his breath, and it hurt so much he knew he was alive. Unable to move, he lay there for a minute, trying to concentrate on the cool stones of the floor to get rid of the burning pain in his body. It didn't work. Water. He needed more water from the fountain, but he didn't know if he had drunk all the water in the vial or if it had even made it past the statues. He tried to move, but it came out as a twitch. After a minute, the pain eased enough that he pulled himself up and leaned against the wall. He'd done it. He'd passed the statues without a cross.

His gaze fell on the vial lying near his feet. He picked it up and shook it. There was a little water. He needed it, but so did Raphael. At the moment, the guardian's survival was more important to Kendall than Jake's. Raphael had answers. Jake didn't know what the hell was going on.

He put one foot in front of the other and took a few lumbering steps. He wasn't sure how he made it outside the mountain or down the long path to where he'd parked his car. Nathan's was still there. Where were they? He caught a blurry glimpse of himself in the rearview mirror as he started his car. His hair was standing on end, and his skin had a slightly smoldered sheen as if he'd been cooked. He managed the drive back to the Abbey House without crashing, though he couldn't see anything but large shapes. He saw one car, and quickly realized he was driving on the wrong side of the road. Swerving, he held on to the steering wheel to keep from collapsing.

He parked as close to the house as he could and stumbled out of the vehicle. His vision was fading in and out. He didn't know if he had enough strength to make it inside, so the figure standing before him was a welcome one.

"Have you been fighting?" Art asked as he hurried toward Jake.

Fighting statues. "Art . . . get Marco. I mean Merlin. Get Merlin."

"You look kind of scorched. Are you dying?"

"I might be if I don't get help."

"I'll help you." Art was surprisingly strong for his age. He put a stout arm around Jake's waist and took on some of his weight.

Jake was embarrassed by how much he was leaning on the boy. "What are you doing out here anyway?"

Art was heaving with exertion. "Waiting for you. I thought you'd never get back."

"Did you find . . . Merlin and Fergus?"

"I did," Art said, looking offended that Jake would even question that he had. "And they went to check on the wounded knight."

"Did they say how he's doing?"

"They don't know. When they got there, he was gone."

Art and Jake were both gasping as Jake opened the door to his room. Marco and Fergus were inside looking very confused. Their faces lit when they saw Jake, but their relief was replaced by alarm as they took in his appearance.

Fergus hurried over to him, tsking like a parent. Jake felt a lump in his throat that he hoped came from being nearly cooked and not because the butler was worrying over him like a father. "Did you have an accident?"

"Statues." Jake stumbled to the bed that, as Art had said, was minus Raphael.

Marco's worried blue eyes studied him. "The statues did this?"

"Whoa!" Art's eyes were round as marbles.

"Art. I'm fine now. You can go."

Art didn't look like he wanted to leave, but Jake was worried that he knew too much already. "But I want to hear about the statues."

"We can talk later. I need rest. So do you. You have done well." And it was damned late. Or early.

"I am kind of tired."

"Get some sleep, and don't tell anyone what happened tonight."

Art gave them the Scout's salute. Marco and Fergus returned it, looking very confused again. If Jake could have formed his burned lips into a smile, he would have.

Art left, and Marco and Fergus hovered over Jake like nurses, asking what had happened as they checked him over for injuries.

"I lost my cross." Jake explained that he'd also found Raphael's vial.

Both men looked alarmed, but there was a look in Marco's eyes that made Jake nervous.

"You're sure you had the cross with you?" Fergus asked.

"Obviously," Jake said. "Or I would have gotten fried on the way in. I searched the whole place and couldn't find it. It's like it vanished into thin air." His worried gaze met Fergus's and Marco's. The cross had vanished, just like Kendall and Nathan had.

"Marco, how is it possible?" Fergus asked, turning to the older man as if he had all the answers. Squinting, Marco leaned closer, studying Jake's face. He pushed his hair off his forehead, inspecting him from every angle like a sculptor looking at a lump of clay. He closed his eyes briefly and seemed to be humming under his breath. Marco's eyes opened, wide with surprise. He pulled back his hand and held it, as if he'd been burned. The hand was shaking.

"Marco, can you explain?" Fergus asked again. Fergus was patting Jake here and there as if checking to see if his skin was still attached to his body.

"It's a mystery," Marco said, staring at Jake. "A mystery."

"We must find Nathan and Kendall," Fergus said. His voice was strong and determined, but he looked frightened. Nathan was like a son to him, and the butler was very protective of Kendall, not just because she meant the world to Nathan. It was apparent in the way Fergus treated her that he adored Kendall. The cooked feeling inside Jake felt a little soothed knowing that Fergus was also fond of him. Jake rarely inspired affection in people. Women liked him, but that was just lust or misguided thoughts of romance. He kept them, like everyone else, at the distance that suited him. The men on his team and his grandmother had been the only real family to him since Lilly.

"I assume Raphael hasn't come back?" Jake asked.

"No," Marco said, still giving Jake a bewildered stare. "I wish he would. I'm worried about him. We don't know what happened when he followed Luke . . . the Reaper." Marco blinked several times.

Jake was starting to get nervous. Had the old man sensed something terrible about Kendall and Nathan?

"He must have been feeling better if he left," Fergus said.

"Or desperate," Marco whispered.

Jake rubbed his chest. He still hurt like hell. "Can we call him? Does he have a cell phone or does he just fly around and walk through walls?"

"He does have a cell phone," Marco said. "But he doesn't like it. He rarely keeps it charged. I've left him a voice mail."

"If he's strong enough to leave, I'm drinking the water." Jake pulled out Raphael's vial and opened the cap, but then he found he couldn't drink it. Raphael could have crawled off somewhere like a wounded animal. This sip of water might be the only thing to save him.

Marco rubbed his beard, his eyebrows moving together in a worried frown. "This is all very bad. We must think."

"Perhaps Raphael woke and went to find the water on his own," Fergus suggested.

"I hope," Jake said. "We need him to help find Kendall and Nathan."

"Maybe Kendall and Nathan are somewhere talking," Fergus said. "They've made some startling discoveries, and they have many years to catch up on."

As alarming as that thought was, it would have been a relief to Jake. The other options were terrifying. "I'll go search the tunnel."

Fergus's arms stiffened at his side. "You will not. You need medical attention." The butler's mouth was firm. "You are very ill."

"I don't have time to get medical attention. We have to find them now. They could be in terrible danger."

"I'll call Hank and have him bring some of the guards," Fergus said. "They can search the tunnel."

"We need boots on the ground now," Jake said. "Call the castle and send some guards through the maze. I'll start at this end, and we can cover more area."

"No." Marco shook his head. "We can't let outsiders know about the maze."

Jake shook his head. Even his brain felt fried. "Kendall and Nathan's safety is more important than hiding Protettori secrets."

"I cannot allow that," Marco said, sounding less like a frail old man and more like an ancient keeper of a secret brotherhood.

Jake sighed and rubbed his head. His hair was still sticking up. He tried patting it down. "They could have been taken deeper into the tunnel. We need to search now."

"The secrets are too important to reveal," Marco said.

"Damn Raphael. Why did he leave? When I see him, I'm gonna knock those tattoos off his face."

Fergus cleared his throat and took a step back, his gaze focused on the wall behind Jake. "I believe you now have your chance."

Jake turned and saw Raphael standing in the room, as if he'd been summoned. He was a terrible sight—face pale against his tattoos, hair so wild it looked like he had dreads, robes like the Grim Reaper. Glowing, amber eyes locked on Jake like a laser. "Who took my cross?"

Fergus edged closer to Marco. "What on earth happened to you?"

"Someone stole my cross," Raphael said, keeping his eyes on Jake.

"Nathan took it to the fountain so he could refill your vial with water," Jake said.

Raphael's expression relaxed some, but he still looked like a wild animal. "Give me your cross. I need water."

"Mine's missing too. I went to the fountain to look for Kendall and Nathan, and I lost the cross."

Raphael's eyes—almost normal now—narrowed in disbelief. "How did you get out?"

"I drank some of the water as I leaped past the statues."

The guardian's singed eyebrows shot up. "You passed the statues without a cross?"

"Didn't have a choice. What happened to you? You were unconscious when I left."

"I woke up and everyone was gone. I went to the temple to get water. I didn't realize my cross was missing until my foot touched the sentinel boundary." He moved his mouth in something resembling a snarl.

"Tell me about it," Jake said. "At least you're alive. How were you going to drink without a vial? Won't the water harm you otherwise?"

"I have another one hidden there."

Could that be the one he'd found? "Where?"

"I won't say."

"I need to know," Jake said, gritting his teeth. He was tired of their secrets. "I found a vial on the floor near the wheel that opens the fountain steps." He pulled it from his pocket and showed Raphael.

"That's not the one I hid."

"Then it's the one Kendall took. Damn." He handed it to Raphael. "There's some water left in it."

Raphael opened the vial and drank.

"I think Kendall and Nathan dropped it," Jake said. "They're missing."

"Missing?"

"They've vanished."

Raphael leaned against the wall, and Jake wondered why he didn't fall through it. "He must have come back."

Jake's heart thudded. "The Reaper?"

"Who else?"

"Maybe Brandi grabbed them. The little boy, Art, he saw Brandi following Kendall and Nathan." Jake hoped like hell it was Brandi and not the Reaper. "The Reaper can't drink from the fountain without the chalice. Why come back without it?"

"To get Kendall."

"Kendall?" Jake's insides felt worse now than they had from his encounter with the statues. "Is she his daughter?"

Raphael frowned in confusion, which in his present condition was both comical and terrifying. He seemed steadier after the drink of water, but he still looked like he'd been struck by lightning. "I don't understand."

"She still believes the Reaper could be her father, that he's changed so much he wouldn't be recognizable now."

"The statues would know," Raphael said. "But she needn't worry. I believe his child is a son. The Reaper will want Kendall, but it's for her sixth sense so he can find the Holy Grail."

Of course. Just like Nathan did. "Do you know who the Reaper's child is?" Jake asked.

Raphael glanced at Marco. "No."

Marco must know something. Jake turned to the old man. "Do you?"

"He could be anyone," the old man said.

Jake didn't have Kendall's gifts, but he usually knew when someone was lying to him. Or at least not telling the truth.

"Jake needs rest," Marco said, giving Raphael a strange nod that seemed more of a command.

Raphael's hand moved toward Jake, and the room disappeared.

CHAPTER SIX

FERGUS HELPED RAPHAEL MOVE JAKE INTO A MORE COMFORT-able position on the bed. "He looks terrible." He turned to Raphael. "You look quite ill yourself. You should rest before you pass out."

"I have to search for Kendall and Nathan," Raphael said. "I think I know where—" The guardian's eyes fluttered. "Marco, what did you do . . ." Raphael's eyes rolled up in his head and he fell onto the bed on top of Jake.

"Very impressive," Fergus said, staring at Marco's outstretched hand. "I didn't know you could do that too."

"Yes." Marco looked proud of himself. "Raphael forgets sometimes that I'm still capable of many things."

"I don't suppose you could teach me how to do that."

"I'm afraid not," Marco said. "Now, help me move Raphael over. He won't be happy when he wakes up."

"Neither will Jake," Fergus said, pulling at Raphael's arm. "My, he's heavy."

"Yes, but we must move them apart or else they may kill each other when they wake."

They worked at separating the two men and making them comfortable. "Move Jake's arm," Fergus said. "It's touching Raphael's dagger. On second thought, perhaps we should remove the dagger and put it somewhere else."

"Very wise." Marco took the dagger and placed it on a table across the room, while Fergus continued arranging the bodies like a funeral director.

He moved Jake's arm, made a few more adjustments, and then stood back, studying the two men lying side by side on the bed. "There."

Marco nodded and tugged his beard. "Very nicely done. I do hope they don't hurt each other when they wake. Come now, we have much work to do."

"We're leaving? But . . . Raphael and Jake?"

"We'll leave them a note. There is something I need to do," Marco said.

"We're going to find Kendall and Nathan on our own?" Fergus asked. Marco's abilities were remarkable at times, but he was still an old man. They needed young people with muscles and strength. And weapons.

"We're going to find the Reaper." Marco's eyes narrowed under his white brows. "I'm afraid he has Kendall and Nathan."

Jake opened his eyes and saw something in front of his face. He cursed and jumped, thinking it was Raphael's hand, the last thing he'd seen. But it wasn't the guardian's hand. It was a note stuck to his forehead. He pulled it off and turned it over.

Fergus and I will meet you at the castle,
Marco

Even more distressing than the note was the fact that he wasn't alone in bed.

Raphael sat up, his face red with fury. "Marco!"

Jake glanced at Raphael's dagger sheath, glad to see the weapon wasn't there. "They've gone to the castle." He handed Raphael the note. "I assume he did the same thing to you that you did to me. Not as much fun when the shoe's on the other foot."

Raphael jumped out of bed, staggering only a bit, and looked at the window where the sun was shining behind the curtains. "It's afternoon."

"We need to get moving. We've lost too much time. Do you feel up to searching the tunnel?" Jake asked. That was the logical place to start. He still felt fried, but not as bad as he had before.

"Yes. Let's go."

"You gonna walk around looking like that?" Jake asked. "You look like a burned rump roast."

Raphael scowled. "I don't have anything else here."

Jake walked back to the dresser to get his bag. Kendall's lay next to it. *Where are you?* He glanced at the bed where he and Kendall had made love, and his heart ached. He had to find her. He rummaged through the bag and pulled out some pants and a shirt. "You can borrow these," he said, handing them to Raphael.

The guardian held them up. "You want me to wear these?"

"They're sweats. They'll grow on you." Jake had bought them in the gift shop near the abbey after he, Kendall, and Nathan had fallen through one of the Protettori's damned portals and ended up in England, dirty and tired, with Kendall still in her pajamas.

"I doubt it." Raphael grimaced at the clothing and disappeared into the bathroom. He returned a moment later wearing the sweats. Jake struggled to keep his face blank. Raphael was a big dude, probably thirty pounds heavier than Jake and a good three inches taller—definitely bigger than the sweats. He looked kind of like the Hulk, except he wasn't green and his pants weren't as short, and the Hulk didn't have singed hair and a sweatshirt with

"Glastonbury, England," straining across his chest. But even in the odd getup, he still looked like a badass.

"If we don't find Kendall and Nathan, we'll take the maze to the castle," Raphael said. "I need more water." He ran his gaze over Jake. "So do you. A lot more."

"You have water there?"

"Some. We keep it for healing and ceremonial purposes."

"We can't risk losing more time. There's something wrong with that tunnel. We lost an entire day in there the first time."

"I know where I'm going."

"Then you search the tunnel, and I'll look for Brandi. The boy said he saw her. I'll find out if she knows anything about their disappearance." Jake paused, feeling the bite of fear. "If she didn't, we'll know the Reaper has them."

"We should stay together."

This was odd coming from the mysterious guardian. "Why, you need my help?"

"I think you need mine. You're wounded."

"It's not the first time. If we're sticking together, let's get a move on. We have a lot of ground to cover. Do you have something to pull your hair back?" Jake asked. "You look like Attila the Hun pretending to be a tourist."

Raphael's face darkened. "No. And don't ever call me that again."

Jake found a hair tie in Kendall's things. A blond hair was still attached. His throat tightened as he pulled the strand of hair free and gave Raphael the tie. "Let's go then." Tucking the strand of hair carefully in his pocket, Jake walked toward the door.

The drive to the Tor was tense, not only because both men feared for Kendall and Nathan's safety, but also because Raphael criticized every turn Jake made, every tap on the vehicle's brakes. "Do you want to drive?" Jake asked.

"No."

"Then shut up. A man who can walk through walls shouldn't be so intimidated by a rental car." He probably shouldn't bad-mouth the guardian, but Jake was too worried about Kendall to fear what unspeakable things Raphael might do to him. Luckily, all Jake got for his tirade was a frown.

Jake and Raphael searched the entire tunnel, but there was no sign of Kendall or Nathan. "Maybe they went through the maze." Jake didn't know why they would have with Raphael waiting for them to get back. "Should we try it?" Jake's head already felt like mashed potatoes, but he was willing to try about anything.

"Not in our condition. We're both weaker than we realized. I'm afraid we'd never make it. You have to be strong to use the gateways. We'll have to get to the castle another way."

They exited the tunnel the same way they had come in. The trip was much faster with Raphael than it had been when Jake was with Kendall and Nathan. "I wish you'd been here when we fell through the maze. It felt like we wandered in circles."

"You probably did. The tunnel is . . . unusual."

No kidding. "How does it work?"

"I don't really know."

Jake hadn't expected more than stony silence or a grunt in reply. Even this short admission was a surprise. "You didn't build it?"

"No. It was already here. We found it when we moved the treasure from the abbey to the Tor."

"And the maze?"

"It was already there too. That's why we moved the brotherhood to Italy and built the castle there. With the maze as a gateway connecting the two locations, we were hidden but could still watch over the fountain."

Raphael must be sick. He never talked this much. Or maybe he was distracted by the sweats.

"Are there other portals?"

"Gateways? That's what we call them. There are some."

"Where?"

"That information is secret."

There was the Raphael he knew. "We're up to our eyeballs in this. Seems to me you could be a little more helpful."

Raphael sighed, but it sounded like a growl. "The maze is an ancient gateway. We don't know how it came to be."

"But there are others? I mean you travel around, popping in and out of rooms, landing in strange bathtubs."

"Traveling as I do requires good physical and mental condition. I was injured. I needed water. I was thinking about the fountain and Kendall."

"Kendall?"

Raphael's mouth tightened. "I was hoping she was all right after her encounter with the Reaper."

Something about Raphael's explanation didn't feel right. Then again, it was Raphael. "Wait a minute. You don't use portals?"

"Gateways? Not always."

Hell. Portals were eerie enough, but just popping up anywhere was something out of a science-fiction novel. "How do you do it?"

"It's all in the mind."

"You can move your body through space with your mind?"

"To some degree."

"Anywhere you want to go?"

"Not anywhere. It's complicated."

Was there anything about the Protettori that wasn't? "Kendall's gift is complicated too. It just seems to work when it wants to."

"She and Nathan need to drink the water. That will help them focus and control their powers."

"So that's why Kendall's sixth sense is so quirky. Does she have your traveling gift?"

"Perhaps. I don't know her well enough to say."

"Something strange happened to us when we were in the tunnel under the Tor. She saw the ghost of a black knight." He paused, feeling like an idiot for even talking about such a thing.

Raphael scoffed. "The black knight. Serves him right to be stuck as a ghost."

"You know about him . . . knew him?"

"Yes. He was a good knight, but a hateful man."

"Holy . . ." Jake shook off his shock. "When the knight ran at us, Kendall touched Nathan and me, and we ended up in Camelot."

"Camelot? You mean a vision?"

"No, I think we were really there. The black knight came after us. Nathan stopped him, scared him off."

Raphael looked disturbed. "Very strange. You're lucky you made it back. As I said, he was a powerful knight."

"So Kendall might be able to walk through walls too?"

"It's hard to say. She needs training to learn to control her abilities. So does Adam. Nathan, I mean."

"You believe he's Adam?" Jake asked.

"You don't?"

"I don't know. Kendall seems to think so. Nathan's not sure."

"You hope he isn't?"

"I didn't say that."

Raphael shrugged. "You didn't have to."

"So you read minds too? This Protettori stuff sucks sometimes."

"You're jealous because they have abilities and you don't."

Jake grunted. Hell yeah, he was jealous. All the odds were in Nathan's favor. "I wouldn't mind being able to run like the wind and walk through walls."

Raphael gave Jake a dark smile. "Careful what you wish for."

They drove back to the room to see if by some miracle Kendall and Nathan had arrived. They hadn't.

"I'm going to look for Brandi and see if she knows something," Jake said.

Raphael stayed in the room in case Kendall and Nathan showed up. Jake secretly thought the guardian was planning to get more rest. On his way out, Jake arranged to keep the room for another few days since he didn't know if Kendall and Nathan were nearby, and they still had to wrap up things with the police regarding the stolen Blue Chalice and the death of the Reaper's man.

Jake asked around the local hotels and found that Brandi had been seen by several people. Her hair made her noticeable, and it didn't seem as if she was trying to hide. Another indication that she wasn't responsible, but he could still wish. He could deal with Brandi. The Reaper was a different ball game. A taxi driver remembered dropping her off at a hotel. Jake found out which room she was staying in, but she had already checked out. Alone.

When he arrived back at the room, Raphael was eating an apple. Jake hadn't seen him eat before. It was a relief to see him do something human. "Any sign of them?" Jake asked.

"No. Did you find Brandi?"

"No, I found out what hotel she was staying in, but she's checked out. Desk clerk said she was alone. She's got her faults, but for all her talk, I can't see her hurting Nathan or Kendall. Where the hell are they?"

Raphael frowned at the apple and then put it down. "I've been thinking. I don't believe they're in England."

Jake's gut tightened. "Where do you think they are?"

"When I followed the Reaper through the gateway, I ended up in a city. An old city. I was too injured to search for him. I could hardly move. I needed to get back and drink from the fountain."

"What's this got to do with Kendall and Nathan? Oh hell." Jake's stomach dropped down to his balls. "You think they fell through the Reaper's portal?"

"I'm afraid they must have."

"You don't know where you were?"

"The language was strange, but I can't quite recall it." Raphael's eyes sparked with a memory. "Czech. I think someone was speaking Czech."

"The Czech Republic?"

"Perhaps."

"Hell. How are we going to get to the Czech Republic? We can hardly walk."

They decided to go to the castle in Italy first to get more water in hopes that they would recover from their injuries and that Raphael's memory would improve. The jet wasn't close enough, so they booked a commercial flight. Considering how old Raphael was, and the fact that he could travel without a car or an airplane, Jake was surprised that Raphael possessed a current ID. Raphael replied that he'd had many identities over the centuries.

Flying with Raphael wasn't fun. Everyone stared at him. With half his face tattooed and his large physique, what could he expect? And there was the attitude. He was sullen, he took up his entire seat and part of Jake's—unfortunately they had to fly coach, with the seats already too small—and the guardian snored.

Jake closed his eyes and tried to drown out Raphael's snoring with thoughts of Kendall, but that made him so tense and uptight that he had to focus on the snoring to keep from worrying. He needed his head clear and his mind focused if he was going to help Kendall and Nathan.

CHAPTER SEVEN

"A RE YOU FEELING WELL, MARCO?" FERGUS WAS WORRIED about the old man, who had been resting in his quarters. Marco had hardly spoken on the way back to the castle. He had pretended to be sleeping, but Fergus had caught him several times staring ahead with a look of anguish on his face. He hadn't mentioned finding the Reaper again. Thank God.

Marco bent with a flurry of robes and put something underneath his bed. He looked flushed when he stood. "I have been better."

"Shall I get some food brought up to you?"

"Not now, thank you, Fergus. I owe you much for all you've done."

"You've paid me well." Of course, he hadn't known until recently it was Marco paying him to raise Nathan. There had just been automatic deposits into a bank account, which covered anything Nathan could want and paid for the best education a boy could have. Fergus had mailed quarterly reports on Nathan to a post office box in Italy. It had all seemed unusual, even sinister, but Fergus had been under the impression that Nathan's father had been a powerful man who died in a witness protection program. Fergus's only task was to care for Nathan, see to his well-being, and keep his identity a secret. Keeping Nathan's identity concealed wasn't hard, for Fergus hadn't known the boy's true origins.

"Should you drink some of the water, perhaps?" Fergus asked.

Marco's white head moved slowly from side to side. "I can't."

"Why do you believe you don't deserve the right to drink Fountain of Youth water?"

"I've done terrible things."

Marco? A gentle old man. "What could you have done that's so bad?"

"I betrayed the brotherhood."

"How? By protecting a boy from an angry group who might have killed him to protect their secrets? Surely that wasn't enough to lose the privilege of drinking the water."

"There were other lies. Other secrets."

More than one lie? What could the old man be hiding? "Well, I think you should rest. Raphael and Jake will find Kendall and Nathan." He hoped. Fergus couldn't bear to think of losing Nathan. Or Kendall either, for that matter. He had grown very fond of the young lady.

Marco didn't answer. He seemed to have drifted off again. Fergus sighed and stood. As he left, he noticed the corner of a suitcase sticking out from under Marco's bed.

Marco's bones creaked with age as he walked down the winding staircase to the round door in the bowels of the castle. It took a moment to remember how to open the door. So many things slipped his memory now. He should have been strong and full of vitality instead of a senile, doddering old man. He finally got it open and stepped inside, terrified at what he was about to do.

He didn't see any other options. The Reaper was too close. If he found the chalice, the damage would be irreparable. He felt a rush of pain, one that he had tried to numb himself to over the centuries. It was said that time healed all wounds. Not all of them. Some remained until the grave.

He approached the room and stood for a moment, thinking through his plan again. There would be consequences for his actions, but this was his mess. He was the one who had betrayed the brotherhood. He was the one who had lied, even to Raphael, his most trusted guardian. If he hadn't, perhaps they could have stopped the Reaper before so many lives had been lost. Raphael was angry with Marco now. He would be angrier if he knew the whole truth.

After he finished his task, he waited there for several minutes before realizing it was hopeless. It wasn't going to work. He would have to take care of matters himself. How could he take care of this mess in such a weakened state? Would such a cause justify a small drink?

Kendall stared at the cross lying on her palm. "How can it be Jake's?" she whispered.

Nathan was quiet, looking at the necklace. "He must have gone to search for us. I guess it came through the portal."

"Then where is Jake?" Kendall touched the cross again. Her fingers tingled, but she didn't feel the same shock she had before.

Nathan's jaw tightened. "The chain's broken." His worried gaze met hers. "Maybe he lost it."

Or maybe he was floating around in a portal. "If he lost it in the temple, how will he get out? We have to get back. He could die in there."

"Do you love him?"

"Jake?"

"Yeah, Jake," Nathan said softly. "Don't act like you don't know what I'm talking about."

"I care for him."

"You didn't like him before."

"That wasn't really him. He puts up walls to keep people out. Or to keep them at a safe distance." Nathan should know a lot about that. He used the same trick. "Probably something to do with being raised in an orphanage. I'm sure it's made him slow to trust."

"He trusts you. He loves you." Nathan's voice wasn't so much bitter as it was sad. "I didn't expect that."

Kendall felt as if she should apologize. She didn't want to hurt Nathan. She adored him. If she was honest with herself, she was even attracted to him. "He's not the only one who puts up walls. You do it too. You've both had sucky childhoods. I'm sure it wasn't easy. At least I can remember mine."

"I get glimpses of my father. At least I think he's my father. When I try to remember, my head starts pounding, and everything changes like I'm standing in a room of warped mirrors."

"I'm sorry, Nathan. Really sorry. I loved him too. I thought he was my real uncle for a long time. He liked it, I think. He was adventurous, intense, like my dad. I think everyone involved in relics and archaeology is."

"I wish I could remember, but sometimes I'm afraid to."

"Why afraid?"

"I don't know."

"You blocked everything . . . assuming you're Adam," she added, seeing his frown. "You may have seen something that's too frightening to remember."

"Like?"

"Like who killed your father."

"You think he was murdered?" Nathan asked.

"I thought about what Fergus said, about the witness protection program. I don't think that was true. I think that was something Marco made up to justify keeping you hidden and changing your name. Uncle John was too much in the public eye to have been in a witness protection program. But he did have enemies. He had one of the greatest collections in the world. Thieves and other collectors would have stolen or killed to get their hands on it. And who's the one person who we know killed to obtain collections?"

"The Reaper."

"The Reaper. My guess is that he killed your father like he killed Brandi and Thomas's parents."

"My father's collection was astounding."

Kendall stilled. "You remember it?"

Nathan look rattled for a moment. "I think I saw it because I was touching your hand."

"I don't think so. I saw your eyes. You were remembering. What other glimpses do you get?"

"You, as a girl. And places that I don't remember visiting. I've traveled to some of them, hoping I would find answers, but it's like having pieces of two different puzzles floating around in my head."

"What kind of places?"

"The pyramids in Egypt."

"We were there," Kendall said. "A lot."

"I spent three months in Peru. I'm not sure why. The place drew me."

"We were there too, Nathan." She turned over her hand and showed him a small scar on her palm. "I got this there."

He brushed his fingers over the small, jagged line. "You were climbing a tree and fell."

"That's right." Adam had hurried over, laughing, because the fall hadn't been far and she'd landed with her butt in the air. He was the one who'd put antibacterial cream on the cut so it wouldn't get infected, and then bandaged it in a way so that her father wouldn't notice it and get upset. He'd told her not to climb that tree. "Face it, Nathan. You're Adam."

Please be Adam.

He nodded toward their joined hands. "It'll take more than some memories that may not even be mine to convince me." He dropped her hand. "If we don't get out of here, it won't matter who I am."

He was still afraid, she thought. "How? We're in a room without a door." Nathan rubbed his chin and Kendall could see him thinking. "You look like you have an idea."

"Maybe we didn't travel through a portal. Remember how we went from the tunnel in the abbey to . . . uh . . ."

"Camelot?"

"Yeah, Camelot, and then we came back to the tunnel. I don't think that was a portal. I think you transported us there and back. If we can figure out how it happened, maybe you can do it again."

"I don't know how I did it. I saw the black knight riding toward us, or his ghost. I grabbed you and Jake, and I think the knight went . . . through us, and we ended up in Camelot with the real black knight, like Alice down the rabbit hole. We could have died there if that knight had gotten hold of us."

"He didn't."

"Because you scared his horse out from under him. You have to admit, that was cool. Terrifying, but cool."

"His horse recognized another creature," Nathan said.

"It recognized something stronger. Did the knight say anything to you?"

"No. He just looked at my cross and backed away."

"He bowed first," Kendall said. "I wonder why."

"Probably thought I was one of the Protettori. We got back to the tunnel by thinking about it. What if we try thinking about the fountain? Maybe we'll go back there."

"It can't hurt. We need to get back to the temple for Raphael's water anyway. How did we do it? We were sitting down, holding hands, I think."

They did it like they had before, sitting cross-legged, facing each other. Nathan reached for her hands. His were warm and strong.

"What if we get separated?" she asked. She had lost Adam once. She wasn't going to risk losing him again. She'd rather stay here and find another way out.

"I'll hold on to you," he said, holding her hands tight. "I won't let go."

A rush of tears stung her eyes as she realized this was Adam sitting across from her, vowing to protect her, just as he had when they were kids. She blinked so he wouldn't see her eyes glistening. "We should think about the same thing. Something safe. Not the fountain." The fountain could kill them if misused.

"The room with the three tombs," he said. "That should be safe. Are you ready?"

Kendall closed her eyes and thought about the black marble tombs. Probably King Arthur's and Guinevere's. And the third tomb . . . maybe Merlin—if he existed—or another knight? Jake appeared in her head as clearly as if he sat in front of her, but his eyes were closed, his skin pale. Kendall gasped, and Nathan's eyes opened.

"What's wrong?"

"I saw Jake. He looked like he was dead."

"I'm sure he's fine. You know Jake can take care of himself."

"I don't think this is working." She let go of Nathan's hands. He stood and then helped her to her feet. "We have to get out of here."

"Come on," Nathan said. "Let's look again."

"Where? We searched the walls."

"We didn't check the floor."

This was Adam, leading the way, being strong for her. She nodded and followed him, holding on to Jake's cross. She couldn't lose him either. They searched the floor until Kendall's knees ached from kneeling. Why couldn't she just sense the way out? Her gift had let her down again.

"I've got something."

Kendall hurried over to see what Nathan had found. It was a stone along the edge of the floor that looked different from the rest. Thicker. After some examination, Nathan did something, and a small section of the wall started to move.

"I think I found the catch." Nathan put his arm in front of Kendall. "Stand back. We don't know what—or who—is on the other side." When the section of wall ground to a halt, they saw a metal door with a heavy lock. "I don't think this is a way out. Looks more like an entrance to another room. And I'd say it's to something they don't want found."

"Maybe there's an exit on the other side. Can you get it open?"

"I don't know about this lock."

"Forget the lock. Knock it down."

Nathan gave an astonished glance. "That's a metal door!"

"You can . . . you know . . ."

"You want me to change?"

"Yes. If it'll get us out of here."

"I'm not a Transformer," Nathan said.

"I'm surprised you know what Transformers are."

"I go to movies. Sometimes. I went to see the last Transformer movie the day it came out."

"So did I."

"I know. I was there in the back of the theater."

"You followed me?"

"No, but I was afraid you would think I had." He smiled. "I wanted to ask you to go."

"Why didn't you?" She would have gone with him.

"I couldn't." He shrugged. "I thought I had a curse."

What would have happened if he hadn't held back his feelings? Would their relationship have been different? Where would that have left her and Jake? "You're different than I thought."

"How?"

"You . . ." She hesitated to tell him he wasn't as uptight. "You have a tattoo."

Nathan gave her a sideways glance. "You don't like tattoos?"

"I don't mind them. I just didn't expect to find one on you." Her cheeks warmed. That had sounded way too intimate and reminded her how good he looked without a shirt. "I would have expected a tattoo on Jake. Not you."

Nathan's expression tightened. "Does he have tattoos?"

"No. Kind of surprising—" She stopped when she saw Nathan's expression, alive with emotion. She had as good as admitted that she'd seen every part of Jake, and she had, but she didn't want Nathan to think about that. She didn't want to hurt him.

Nathan turned toward the door, his shoulders stiff. "If you want me to get this opened, you'd better stand back. Way back."

Kendall went to the other side of the room and waited. Nathan just stood there. "What are you doing?"

"This isn't easy. It's like trying to go to the loo when someone's watching."

"I'll turn my back if it helps. Or I could offer to hit you, since Jake's not here." She said it to lighten the tension, but realized it was a poor choice. *Please be all right, Jake.*

Nathan's muscles began to tense. Kendall watched as his body started to change. It was still him, but there was a difference in his stature. He turned and looked back at her, dark eyes lightening to hazel, and then fading to amber. In seconds, the color started to glow, increasing until his eyes looked like flames. It was one of the most amazing things she'd ever witnessed. When he'd fully changed, he grabbed hold of the lock and, with a roar, yanked it out. She didn't go to him yet, letting him change back first. No use tempting fate. But his eyes were still amber when he turned to look at her. He was so beautiful, her Adam. She walked toward him and reached for his hand. "You did it."

"You shouldn't come near me when I'm like this," he said, his eyes still amber.

"I trust you."

He didn't respond, but a muscle in his jaw twitched. "Let's get out of here." He threw the broken lock on the floor and pushed the metal door. It creaked open and he pointed his light inside. "Bloody hell."

CHAPTER EIGHT

WHEN JAKE AND RAPHAEL FINALLY LANDED IN ITALY, IT was none too soon. If Jake had had a parachute, he would have jumped out of the plane.

"I don't snore," Raphael said.

"Then you're farting out your mouth."

Raphael looked like he might break Jake in half. Jake figured the guardian could do it too, but he felt so shitty he didn't much care. "You're too big to fly coach."

"I'm not used to traveling on planes. And flying with you isn't fun either," Raphael said. "You talk in your sleep."

Jake didn't like the look on Raphael's face. "Yeah?"

"Yeah."

"What'd I say?"

"I'll tell you later. I'm not sure what to make of it yet."

What the hell did that mean?

They hired a taxi to take them to the castle. Jake fell asleep and woke up shoulder to shoulder with Raphael. Jake jumped, and the guardian jolted awake and sat up straight. He looked as tired as Jake felt. "How do you feel?" Jake asked.

"Like I've been electrocuted."

"That makes two of us."

"We'll need to drink as soon as we arrive."

Or what, Jake wondered. Die a slow agonizing death. Damned Protettori.

The taxi dropped them off at the road leading to the castle. The entrance was gated with a large stone fence surrounding the castle grounds to deter people from trespassing. And if they made it past the fence, the statues would stop them, in a gruesome and lethal manner. The statues had been turned off before Nathan's crew arrived so that no one accidentally got electrocuted.

Jake and Kendall hadn't known about the road or the statues when they'd first found the place. They'd hiked through rugged terrain intended to keep visitors out, not knowing the stone sentinels waited to kill anyone who tried to pass. Lucky for them, the statues had been turned off briefly. If not, he and Kendall would both be toast. It was harsh, but the Protettori didn't like company . . . for good reason.

The castle had lots of company now. Two guards were at the gate, clad in the traditional black uniforms that all Nathan's guards wore. They recognized Jake and Raphael, but still the guards' hands slightly tightened on their weapons. They were nervous around Raphael. Those who hadn't witnessed his inhuman escape from Nathan's mansion had heard stories from the guards who had been there.

One of them politely asked Raphael to enter the code that opened the gate—a surprisingly modern security system considering that ancient statues guarded the rest of the place. "Sorry," the guard said after Jake had stepped through. "Mr. Larraby said we can't be too careful."

"No problem," Jake replied, but Raphael only scowled. Jake lowered his voice so that only the guardian could hear. "They're helping, you know." He didn't blame Raphael for being pissed that the place was crawling with strangers after he and Marco had lived here in solitude for so long. The Protettori didn't like strangers. They passed several guards as they approached the castle. Jake asked a couple of them if they'd heard from Nathan, and got a negative.

After checking in with Hank, the head of security, and getting confirmation that he hadn't heard from Nathan either, Jake brought him up to date. Hank agreed to send a group back to England to check the area again and to stay there in case Kendall and Nathan showed up.

"Have you seen Marco?" Jake asked.

"Not since he and Fergus got back," Hank said. "Check the library. Marco spends a lot of time there."

They hurried toward the library and met Fergus on the way. He was dressed in his butler uniform, a charcoal suit and white shirt, but he looked more like a frightened father. "Any word from Kendall and Nathan?"

Jake shook his head.

"Where can they be? I'm terribly worried for them. Do you think the Reaper is involved?"

"I don't know. But we'll find them," Jake said with far more confidence than he felt.

"Where's Marco?" Raphael asked with a frown.

Fergus's shoulders stiffened with resolve. "Don't be angry at him. Marco put you to sleep for your own good. You needed rest to recover from your injuries, as did Jake."

"Who left the sticky note on my forehead?" Jake asked.

"That would be me. I wanted to make sure you knew where we were right away so you didn't think we were missing as well."

"If you see Marco, tell him to find me," Raphael said.

Fergus nodded and then hurried off, saying there was a problem in the kitchen. The butler seemed to have already taken charge.

Raphael led Jake to the room with the mural on the wall and the round table. Several days ago he, Kendall, and Nathan had found the room. "This is where we keep the water." There were priceless objects all over the space.

"What happened to the treasure under the chapel?" Jake asked. "How did you move it so quickly?"

"That's a secret."

"You have more secrets than Nathan. Sure you're not brothers?"

"Positive." Raphael opened a cabinet and took out two vials. He handed one to Jake. "Drink it slowly. It's very powerful."

Jake knew it was. It had kept him from dying. Twice. He held up his vial. "To health."

Raphael nodded. "To health. And destroying the Reaper."

And finding Kendall and Nathan.

This water tasted different than ordinary water. It had a slight metallic taste, but there was something else. Kendall must be rubbing off on him, because he thought he felt a tingle as the water slid down his throat. He lowered the vial and concentrated on his body. He knew the water had kept him alive before, but now that he wasn't in a life-and-death situation, he wanted to see if he could feel the water working. He didn't understand it. The Fountain of Youth should be a myth, a story to tell to kids, a pipe dream for adventurers, but it was real.

"I think that will do," Raphael said. "How do you feel?"

"Better. How does it work?"

Raphael's eyes were closed and when they opened, the amber color seemed alive. "I don't know."

"Does anyone know anything about how this stuff works?" Jake motioned to the vial and the room where they stood. "Everything's shrouded in mystery."

"True power is difficult to explain."

"You sound like the Dalai Lama."

Raphael closed his eyes again and stood still. He didn't move for so long Jake started to worry. "You're not turning into a statue or something, are you?"

"Prague."

"What?"

"Prague. I think that's where I followed the Reaper."

"You're certain?"

"No."

Someone pounded on the door. Raphael hurried to open it. His movements were quicker than they had been before, so the water must be working. It was one of the guards. "Hank needs you. There's some kind of alarm going off. We don't know what it means."

"The circle room," Raphael said. He left the room at a run. Jake and the guard followed. Jake already felt stronger than he had moments before, and he was surprised that he caught up with Raphael in the corridor.

"You think the Reaper made another portal?"

"Who else could it be?" Raphael said grimly.

Kendall crowded in behind Nathan, gaping at the room. As with the previous space, lighted candelabras had come on when they'd entered, illuminating a large room with marble floors and elaborate enclosed cases and shelves filled with relics and objects from all over the world. She knew they were old from the scents and memories emanating from them. There were ancient scrolls, daggers, swords, Egyptian artifacts . . . They explored for a few minutes, and then started looking for a way out.

Nathan found a door hidden behind a large tapestry. It wasn't locked. A small light flared to life as they stepped through into another room. There they saw a few large objects—tablets with writing, a giant round stone that looked like a disk, and a sar-cophagus with elaborate carvings.

"Look at these hieroglyphs." Kendall touched the cool surface of the coffin and saw quick flashes of a pyramid and chariots. She grabbed Adam's arm—*Nathan's* arm. He was Nathan now, but his expression as he studied the objects was Adam's. "This could have belonged to a pharaoh," Kendall said. "I would love to open it."

"Me too, but I would rather find a way out of here. These relics are a bad sign. Who do we know that loves relics?"

"The Reaper. You think we fell through his portal?"

"We know he had one in the temple. We saw him disappear through it," Nathan said.

"We could be anywhere in the world." Kendall's chest felt hollow. What would he do if he found her? She'd tricked him into drinking from the wrong chalice. Her hand magic might not work this time. And what would he do to Nathan? "If he's here, maybe we can stop him."

"No. We'll sneak out, figure out where we are, and then come back with help."

"But Raphael's injured. We don't know how long it will take him to recover, even if we get the water to him. If the Reaper is injured—"

"You're not fighting him." Nathan's voice was hard.

"You sound like Jake."

"I wish Jake was here. Maybe he could talk some sense into you. We're going to sneak out of here before anyone realizes we're trespassing."

The word chilled Kendall's blood. Trespassing had gotten her and Adam in trouble a long time ago. She looked for the door they had just entered, but it had vanished. There was a wall in its place.

"Bloody hell. It was right here."

"It's probably hidden by another wall," Kendall said. "We must have triggered it to close when we came in. Maybe there's a catch on the floor like there was in the other room."

There was a commotion and voices coming from the wall opposite where they had entered the room. "I think someone's coming. We'd better find someplace to hide," Nathan ordered.

Kendall looked around, quickly trying to find a place. "Where?" The rocks were flush against the wall and too heavy to move.

Nathan grabbed her arm and hurried her toward the sarcophagus.

"We're not." Not that she didn't want to look inside. She did. But she didn't want to hide there. Even if it were empty. The last time she'd hidden inside a sarcophagus hadn't been fun.

"We did it before."

"You remember that?" Their fathers had told them to stay away from the dig, but they had sneaked out and hired a driver to take them there. They'd almost gotten caught and the sarcophagus had been the only place to hide. Like now.

Nathan opened it. "There's a person inside," Kendall said. It was a lovely specimen, thick wrappings darkened with age. She studied the face, the hollows where the eyes had been, the ridges of eyebrows and cheekbones, and what remained of the nose. It was surprising how much a nose shrunk in death. This man had been tall, if it was a man. The size and bone structure looked male. Though bones weren't her expertise, she knew a bit about them. And mummies. She loved mummies and would have enjoyed studying this one, but she didn't want to share the same space.

"It's not really a person," Nathan said. "It's been dead for a long time."

"He," she said. She had touched the chest, unable to keep her hands away. "It's a he." But she tried to block everything else about him. The voices on the other side of the wall were louder now, and she couldn't afford to get sucked into the mummy's life.

"For God's sake." Nathan grabbed the mummy by the arms and lifted him out.

"Be careful. He's fragile."

"So are you," Nathan whispered, gently dragging the mummy behind the sarcophagus. "Get in."

Kendall climbed in first. It was musty with the smell of death. Ancient death. The odor was almost soothing in its familiarity, and made her think of her father, how his face lit with excitement over a new discovery. But it wasn't her father she was hiding from this time.

Nathan climbed in with his back toward her. It was a small space. Her face was crushed against his shoulder, and her breasts pressed into his back. She was glad it was him she was sharing the sarcophagus with and not the mummy. She tried to focus on Nathan's scent to calm her breathing, and as he pulled the cover closed, leaving them in darkness, it was his life that flashed before her eyes, and she had no doubts left about who he really was.

"They've found something," Adam said as they watched the men hurrying toward the tomb her father had discovered, talking in excited but hushed voices. "Do you know what it is?"

He knew about her gift. She told Adam things she didn't tell anyone else. Kendall closed her eyes and concentrated. "No. I don't know. Gold, maybe. I'm not close enough to tell." She wasn't sure she could anyway. Sometimes she knew things she shouldn't know. Sometimes she didn't.

"Let's get closer."

"We're not supposed to be here."

"They'll never know," Adam said.

They'd been told to stay in their rooms in Cairo because a man had been following Adam's father. One of the local men who worked the dig had spotted the watcher. But Kendall and Adam didn't always do what they were told. Having distracted fathers gave them more freedom than most kids. They weren't most kids anyway. Most kids didn't spend the biggest part of their year hunting for relics and bones.

They'd waited a few minutes and then slipped out of the hotel, hiring one of the taxi drivers they knew to take them to the site. He hadn't known they were disobeying orders.

They crept toward the entrance of the tomb. Even the men standing guard had eased inside to see what was happening. Their parents always had guards now that Uncle John was being followed.

Kendall and Adam slipped in behind the men. The tomb hadn't been looted. There were lots of treasures left here. Kendall's blood pounded with excitement as she looked around, trying to see it all. Who needed dolls and toys when she could have all this?

"Look," Adam whispered. "There's a sarcophagus." It was standing against the left wall, well back from where the men were gathered. The door to the sarcophagus was open. "Is there a mummy inside?"

"I don't know."

"Let's get closer. Maybe you can tell."

They had almost reached it when one of the men called out for the guards to get back on duty.

"Quick. We have to hide. They're gonna come this way," Adam said. "Get inside."

"There?" Kendall asked in shock.

But Adam didn't stop. He pushed her inside—there was a mummy inside—and then climbed in behind her, easing the door closed. It didn't shut all the way, but enough to hide them. Kendall's head exploded with memories from the mummy, but she couldn't *escape or they'd get caught and maybe sent home. She closed her eyes and tried to breathe quietly in spite of her panic. She could feel Adam's chest pounding, and then his hand grabbed hers. A strange image passed through her head. A man and a woman, hiding just as Kendall and Adam were now. Then she saw their faces. It was them, but they were grown.*

Shock stunned her for a moment. She'd forgotten about that strange vision she'd had when she was hiding in the sarcophagus with Adam.

The voices were even closer now. A glimpse of swords and ancient clothing flickered through Kendall's head. Nathan's body tensed, distracting her from the vision. He was hot, and a rumbling sound came from his chest. Kendall had never been afraid of Nathan or Adam (though maybe there was a slight tinge of fear when Nathan changed), but she was scared now. Being trapped inside a confined space would probably make him panic and intensify his change, which he still hadn't learned to control. If he accidentally hurt her, he would never forgive himself. The heat was getting uncomfortable. Her hands were trapped at her sides, but she stretched her fingers until she found his. They were too hot.

"Nathan. It's OK." But it wasn't OK.

"Stay here," he whispered. His voice was different. Raspier. Someone started to open the cover. Nathan let out a roar and sprang out, flinging aside the person who'd been trying to get in. He let the cover close behind him, leaving Kendall alone in the dark.

The sounds were terrible. Yells and roars. And then complete silence, which was even more frightening. Had he escaped? Led them away? Or was he dead? Kendall slipped quietly out of the sarcophagus and saw Nathan standing in the middle of the room surrounded by several men. True to her earlier impressions, the men wore ancient clothing and carried swords.

Nathan's eyes were glowing as he watched her, but he didn't move. A sword was pressed against his throat. Kendall had seen him fight, and she didn't question whether he could get rid of the man and his sword. Then she felt the cold blade at her throat and knew why he was holding back. More men had caught sight of her and started speaking quickly in theatrical-sounding voices. Their clothing was strange too, as if they'd stepped off a medieval movie set. A sense of panic struck. Had she and Nathan gone back in time again to Camelot?

Kendall didn't know who the men were, but she was terrified that Nathan would try to rescue her and get himself killed. "Please," she said, giving the men a stiff smile. "Don't hurt us. We don't mean you any harm."

"And who would you be, dressed like a bloody boy?" said the man who had his sword at Nathan's neck. He was big and thick with a mess of red hair. He appeared to be their leader. He didn't look like the men they'd encountered who worked for the Reaper.

"I'm Kendall and this is Nathan."

"What are you doing here?"

She swallowed and felt the blade pinch. "We're lost." She glanced at Nathan. His eyes weren't as fiery now. "What's your name?" Kendall asked, hoping if they had been introduced, he would be less likely to slaughter them.

"Gregor." He looked around the place. "Where are we? Where's the door?"

Kendall glanced at Nathan in surprise. "You don't know?" Nathan asked.

"I wouldn't ask now if I did, would I? I'll ask again, where are we, and how did we get here?" He pressed the sword harder against Nathan's neck. "Have you put a spell on us? Is she a witch?"

"She's not a witch," Nathan said, trying not to move his head.

"Better keep them prisoner until we know for sure," a sharp-faced man said.

"This looks familiar," a short bald man said as he looked around the room. "I believe I know this place."

"Do you know how to get out?" the leader asked.

"There's a bolt-hole in the floor."

"Then you best be finding it before this one turns us into toads."

"She's not a witch," Nathan said. "If you remove your sword, we can help you find a way out."

The man gave a harsh laugh. "You, with your eyes glowing like a dragon. I think not." He maneuvered Kendall next to Nathan and kept both of them under guard while the others searched for the bolt-hole.

Kendall tried to talk to the leader, but she didn't get far.

"Stop talking. I can't understand your words, and I need to think."

A shout finally came from the corner. "I've found it," the short bald man said.

Kendall and Nathan were herded toward the hole in the floor. A big blond who looked like a Viking descended first, followed by two others. "The prisoners next," the leader said.

Nathan was forced to go before Kendall. "Stay close to me," he whispered as he brushed past her. "As soon as I get a chance . . ."

"No talking to the witch," the leader said.

Kendall went next, maneuvering the steps carefully as she climbed into the dark hole. At the bottom there was a tunnel with a dirt floor. Without light, it was impossible to see anything. She could hear the men ahead of her and the ones crowding in from behind and tried to guess which one was Nathan. Then she saw two specks of light. Nathan's eyes. Her captor who was holding the sword couldn't see well either, and his blade eased away. Following the glow of his eyes, Kendall moved closer to Nathan.

The trip through the tunnel didn't last long. Within minutes, Kendall smelled fresh air, and she was shoved through an opening. It was dark, and the only things she could identify were trees. A shout sounded in the distance.

"Someone's coming," the leader said. "Prepare for attack."

In the commotion, someone grabbed her hand. "Stay with me." Nathan pulled her back from the men who had tightened into a group, holding their swords in front of them. With this new threat, they seemed to have forgotten their prisoners.

A cry arose, and Kendall looked back to see something dark rush through the wall of men and scatter them like bowling pins.

The Reaper.

Nathan tightened his grip on her hand and they started to run, but two men appeared in front of them, blocking the way. Nathan growled and lunged at them, but the men had already been flung away. At first she thought Nathan had done it, but she turned and saw another set of glowing eyes beside her. He smelled different than Nathan. He smelled wild.

She tried to lift her hands to fight, but she couldn't move them. She couldn't move any part of her body. Around her, men were dropping to the ground like flies. She heard Nathan growling beside her, but he was also paralyzed.

Raphael opened a door Jake had never seen and then another that led to a set of winding steps. "Hurry!" Raphael yelled. "If it's the Reaper, we can't let him get loose in the castle."

"Don't we need the guards?" Jake asked, trying to keep up. Raphael was hell on wheels, but the more the better.

"We can't let them see inside this room."

"I don't hear the alarm now," Jake said.

"You can't hear it down here. Only upstairs. If someone breaks into the circle room, we don't want the intruder to know we've caught him until it's too late." Raphael reached a door with a large stone disk in the center. He pushed something and the disk began to turn. A door opened quietly, and Jake followed Raphael inside. The room had a high ceiling. Statues lined the walls, tucked into alcoves. There were several of them, although a few of the alcoves were empty.

Jake felt for his cross and remembered it wasn't there. "I don't see anything. Maybe the alarm malfunctioned." Raphael didn't answer. He was standing as still as the statues, his expression so shaken Jake felt a tinge of alarm. He followed Raphael's gaze to the empty spaces on the wall.

"They're gone," Raphael whispered.

"Someone stole some of the statues?"

Raphael walked toward the empty alcoves, muttering to himself. He squatted and examined the space. "Marco. What have you done?"

They heard yelling from outside. Raphael and Jake hurried to the door and found Hank waiting. "Intruders have been spotted behind the castle."

Raphael ran back up the steps, followed by Jake and the guards. When they got outside, Raphael went ahead. Jake was close on his heels, and the guards fell behind. More benefits of the fountain water, Jake thought. He could make a fortune selling this stuff.

They went around behind the castle. Thick trees stood between the castle and the airstrip. One of the trees appeared to be moving, and then Jake saw it was a man. Several of them rising from the ground like demons from hell.

Raphael rushed at them as Jake pulled out his gun and followed. In the chaos and darkness, Jake saw a pair of glowing eyes.

Raphael? But Raphael was on his left. Who was this? Jake's stomach curled into a tight knot. The Reaper?

He was moving fast, a dark blur with those two pinpoints of light. Someone came at Jake with a sword and he ducked to avoid the swing. He knocked the man down and ran onward toward the dark blur. When he got close, he saw a flash of light hair. Blond. Then he recognized her.

Kendall.

CHAPTER NINE

S HE WAS HERE. SAFE. JAKE'S RELIEF WAS SHORT-LIVED. SHE
wasn't safe. Something was moving toward her like a train.
Jake didn't know if it was Raphael or one of the other men. He
was too far away to help her. As he ran toward her, something
rose inside him, filling him, until he felt like he'd been pushed
out of his body and was watching from outside himself. The
men—guards and intruders alike—dropped to the ground. Even
Kendall couldn't seem to move.

Thank goodness for Raphael and his strange abilities, Jake
thought as he reached for Kendall. She looked stunned as he
pulled her to her feet and wrapped his arms around her. The feel
and smell of her seemed more important at the moment than the
men who lay paralyzed on the ground.

Kendall returned his hug, a little desperately, he thought with
relief. "I'm glad to see you. I thought you were . . . hurt."

"Me?" He closed his fingers softly around a handful of her
hair, afraid she was a dream. "You're the one who vanished. God,
I was worried about you."

"How did you get here without the Reaper or his men seeing
you? Did you find the portal?"

"The Reaper?" Jake frowned. "Where do you think we are?"

"Wherever the Reaper is. We fell through his portal."

"If it's the Reaper's, the Protettori is doomed. You're in the castle in Italy."

Her eyes flashed with surprise. "It wasn't the Reaper's portal?"

"Bloody hell," Nathan yelled. "Raphael, let me up." There were several similar requests, and some threats.

Jake loosed his grip on Kendall and turned to see Raphael frowning. "Another gift he hasn't told us about?" Jake said as the men began rising to their feet.

"Don't release them," Kendall warned. "They were kidnapping us."

"They're not a threat," Raphael said.

Nathan jumped up and hurried over to Kendall and Jake. "How did you get here?"

"We flew. Coach. Not something I'd recommend with Raphael."

"We're in the castle in Italy," Kendall told Nathan.

"Italy? How many bloody portals are there?"

"Too many," Jake said. "We thought the Reaper took you. We came to the castle to get water so Raphael could remember where he followed the Reaper. And . . . uh-oh, I think we've got a problem."

The guards and the strange men had risen and were challenging each other to halt, guns and swords ready for a fight.

"Everyone halt," Raphael roared. "No one is a threat. Guards, leave us."

"Nathan?" Hank looked at Nathan for direction.

"Not a threat?" Nathan's voice rose. "They grabbed us in there and tried to kidnap us."

"Inside?" Jake looked closer at the grumbling men who resembled characters from a movie. "Oh hell no . . . they're the—"

From the corner of his eye he saw Raphael raise his hand, and the next thing Jake knew he was waking up on the ground.

"Dammit." He jumped up and stalked toward Raphael, who was off to one side talking to the men while Nathan and Kendall were explaining their sudden appearance to Hank and the guards. "We didn't want to bother anyone while we explored."

Hank didn't seem satisfied with the explanation. Jake had been around him enough to know that he was good at his job, and he took protecting Nathan and his assets very seriously.

Nathan assured Hank that everything was all right, and that they could go back to their posts. "If Raphael vouches for them, it's all right," Nathan said. "They're just some friends of his."

"Strange friends," Hank said, giving Raphael a look that said he was strange himself. "I don't like this."

"Go on," Nathan said. "I'll brief you later."

Reluctantly, the guards walked back toward the castle.

"What the hell did you do that for?" Jake asked Raphael.

Raphael pulled Jake aside. "I had to stop you from revealing something Nathan's guards didn't need to know—" Raphael stopped, jaw dropped, staring over Jake's shoulder at the men. Jake turned to see what had surprised the guardian.

Kendall had gotten a flashlight from somewhere, and was inspecting Nathan's face. For injuries? One of the men, an older man with gray streaks in his dark, cropped hair, was kneeling before Nathan. He said something hushed to the others, and slowly, they all began to kneel until each of them was bowed before Nathan.

"My lord," the older man said. "I beg your mercy. I thought you were dead."

Nathan gave the man a blank look. "Excuse me?"

"Why are they doing that?" Kendall whispered, looking at the first man, who Jake noted was staring at Nathan with a look of adoration on his face. "Who do they think you are?"

Raphael hurried over. "Rise," he said to the men. "We need to get inside. Back the way you came. Quickly."

"We're going through the bolt-hole?" Nathan asked. "What's wrong with the front door?"

"I don't want them to be seen," Raphael said. "Come with me."

The men kept looking at Nathan, but they seemed to know Raphael, and were almost hostile toward him. But they followed, asking him questions that Jake couldn't make out.

The bolt-hole was an opening in the woods behind the castle, leading to an earthen tunnel that ended inside the room Jake and Raphael had gone to earlier when the alarm sounded.

Kendall motioned to the men. "Why are they calling Nathan 'my lord'?"

"They're confused," Raphael said.

"With good reason," Jake said. "Do you want to tell them, or shall I?"

"Tell us what?" Kendall asked.

Raphael's eyes were closed. He looked like he wanted to be someplace else, so Jake explained. "Your kidnappers are statues."

"Statues?" Nathan asked. "Someone tell me what the hell's going on?"

Raphael opened his eyes and sighed. "Until today, they were statues. Marco must have awoken them."

Nathan's eyes widened with surprise. "How can he do that?"

"That's what I want to know." Raphael's shoulders were stiff. "I didn't know he remembered how to get into this room."

"I think Marco is a cunning old man," Jake said.

"Exactly how old are these men?" Kendall asked.

"Different ages when they were put to rest."

"That means turned into statues," Jake said.

Raphael nodded. "Yes," he muttered, obviously displeased to find them no longer stone.

"What are we going to do with them?" Kendall asked.

"We can't let them out in public," Raphael said. "They will have to be acclimated until we can . . ."

"Can what?" Nathan asked.

The men were watching, their expressions suspicious. Raphael lowered his voice. "Attempt to restore the situation."

"Does he mean put them back?" Jake said. "You can reverse the process?"

Apparently the men had excellent hearing even though they had spent the last many centuries as stone. They surrounded Raphael, protesting that they did not want to be restored as sentinels.

Raphael calmed the men down. "Wait here until we make sure the castle is ready to receive you. We have guests who may be shocked at your appearance. Times are different now."

"Most assuredly. You allow whores among you?" a big blond asked.

"A whore?" Jake felt Nathan bristling beside him. "She is not a whore."

The blond frowned. "Honorable women do not dress as such."

The older man stepped forward, his face stiff. "You dare speak to her in that manner? Do you not recognize your queen?"

Jake grabbed Raphael's sleeve. The guardian had changed from his Glastonbury sweats to his usual ninja robes. Raphael must have a closet filled with them, Jake thought. "Your queen? What the hell is he talking about?"

"They have been sleeping for a long time." Raphael's voice dropped to a whisper. "They are confused."

"Bullshit. Who do they think Kendall is?" Jake nodded toward Nathan. "And why are they calling him 'my lord'?"

"Are you ill, my brother?" the older man asked him.

Jake frowned. "Me? No."

"Why would you ask such a thing? You of all men. Have you forgotten your king?"

The hair on Jake's neck rose. "Raphael, you want to explain?"

The guardian looked as if he wanted to vanish through the wall. He pulled Kendall, Nathan, and Jake aside, farther away from the men. "They think he's King Arthur and she's Guinevere."

Kendall let out a crazy laugh that ended on a squeak. "You're kidding?"

"Raphael doesn't kid," Jake said.

"Bloody hell," Nathan said.

"And Jake?" Kendall asked. "Who do they think he is?"

"Lancelot," Raphael said. "They think he's Lancelot."

Jake met Kendall's shocked gaze and knew she was also remembering the couple in the vision. And how she had called Jake Lancelot.

"This is insane," Nathan said. "It's some kind of trick."

"There's something I haven't told you," Jake said. "When I lost my cross in the temple, I opened the tombs to see if one of the corpses had a cross. I figured if King Arthur was buried there, he might have one." He stopped and pulled in a hard breath. "King Arthur wasn't in the tomb. Nathan was in the first tomb, and Kendall and I in the other two."

Nathan shook his head. "You must have been hallucinating. Some mind trick of the Protettori."

"At first I thought it was really Nathan, that the Reaper had come back through the portal and killed him. Then I saw the clothes were different. And you . . ." Jake looked at Kendall. "The woman looked like you, but there were slight differences. I think it was the woman in the vision."

"What vision?" Nathan asked.

"Kendall and I had a vision of a woman . . . and a man. She looked like Kendall."

"I won't ask what you were doing to have a vision together, but what does this have to do with King Arthur and Guinevere?"

"Kendall thought the man was Lancelot."

Nathan's eyes lightened a shade underneath his frown. "Whose tombs are those, Raphael?"

Raphael looked like he was wrestling with himself, and then he shook his head and sighed. "Arthur's, Lancelot's, and Guinevere's."

"So they really existed?" Nathan asked.

"Yes. Part of the legend is true."

"What does this mean?" Kendall asked. "How do they look like us? Or we look like them? Are you saying we're some kind of . . . reincarnation?"

"I don't know," Raphael said. "Not for certain."

"Then tell us what you do know," Jake said.

"It was foretold that King Arthur would return when the world needed him. Many still believe it today."

"You're saying Nathan is King Arthur?" Jake ran a tense hand through his hair. "Well hell."

Raphael shrugged. "You saw the tombs for yourself."

"I was hoping Nathan was right, and it was a mental booby trap designed to drive a person insane."

"I knew Arthur. I knew all three of them," Raphael said.

"And they looked like us?" Kendall asked.

"Very much," Raphael said.

Kendall chewed on her lip, eyes narrowed in thought. "I saw King Arthur in a vision, and he reminded me of Nathan."

Jake had seen King Arthur too. Twice. Each time, he had thought the same thing.

Kendall stopped chewing her lip and looked intrigued. "So King Arthur really was a king?"

Just like her to focus on the historical side of things and not that they were some kind of damned doppelgangers.

"Some recognized him as a king," Raphael said.

Jake scratched his bristly jaw, which needed a shave. "If they think Nathan is King Arthur, it shouldn't be hard to order them to stay here out of sight. Perks of being a doppelganger."

"Doppelganger?" Nathan scowled. "You think we're bloody doppelgangers?"

"Is it really any stranger than reincarnation, or any of the other crazy stuff we've seen?" Jake asked.

"Sounds odd coming from you," Nathan said.

"Will all the men know King Arthur?" Kendall asked.

"No," Raphael said. "But if they didn't know him personally, they knew his name. They're all old. That was part of their problem. They were bored. Living so long sometimes takes a toll."

"If you knew I was Guinevere's . . . double . . . doppelganger . . . whatever, why didn't you say anything?"

"It's been a long time since I've seen her," Raphael said. There was a strange timbre to his voice. "A very long time. I wasn't expecting it."

"We have to do something with them," Nathan said. "They look like they're ready for a mutiny." The men were whispering and scowling. And the big blond was testing his sword.

Raphael nodded. "Ask them to wait here for further orders. Tell them they must rest so they can regain their strength."

"Why don't you tell them?" Nathan asked. "They must have known you."

"They aren't very fond of me," the guardian said. "I'm the one who put them to rest."

"Why is that a problem?" Nathan asked.

"It was against their will."

Raphael tapped his dagger hilt against the wall to get everyone's attention. Nathan stood tall before them and cleared his throat before repeating the message Raphael had given him.

The men nodded, and it was clear from their reactions that those who knew Arthur had loved their king. If he was their king. Jake still wasn't sure who King Arthur really had been. A king? A knight? Just a member of the Protettori? As usual, Raphael hadn't really answered anything.

"Find Marco," Raphael whispered in a gritty voice. "We can't let anyone else see the men or find out what has happened here. Someone has to stay with them. They were put to rest for a reason."

"And that was?" Nathan asked.

"They weren't . . . stable."

"They're crazy?" Kendall asked.

"So you expect us to babysit crazy guardians who were turned into statues?"

"No. I'll stay with them. You find Marco and bring him here so we can figure out how to put them back. Knock on the door five times, and I'll let you in."

"Would there be a bit of food?" the older man asked, and the others rumbled in agreement.

The bald man patted his groin. "And a piss pot."

Raphael's jaw tensed. "Bring food and water, and something for them to . . . relieve themselves in. Damn Marco. Don't let the guards down here. I don't want them finding out who these men really are. And give me my cross."

After Nathan returned Raphael's cross, Nathan, Kendall, and Jake hurried up the winding stairs. "Are you all right?" Nathan asked Kendall.

"I'm wondering if we're all stuck in one of my dreams," she said. "Reincarnation. Doppelgangers. It's crazy. How are we going to keep those men down here?"

"We could let them help us," Nathan said. "The Reaper won't be easy to defeat. I can hire as many guards as money can buy, but these men understand the Protettori."

"But they fight with swords," Kendall said. "I'm not sure they're equipped for a modern battle."

"Some of them looked like they wouldn't even need swords," Nathan said. "There are some big men down there."

Jake snorted. "Big, crazy men. Raphael said they weren't stable."

"And there could be side effects from turning into flesh and blood after being stone," Kendall said.

Nathan nodded. "This is unprecedented. We need to monitor them first. We should run tests. I could get a medical team in here."

"We don't have time for you to play mad scientist right now," Jake said. "We have a lunatic on our hands. Maybe more than one. The blond and the one called Gregor bother me."

"Why don't we just keep an eye on them ourselves," Kendall suggested. "Before we get outsiders involved."

"You sound like a real Protettori keeper," Jake said.

"If I'm going to be a keeper, I need to know what I'm keeping," she said. "As soon as we find Marco, we need to have a long talk. If we're involved with the Protettori, they have some explaining to do."

"They can start with how statues can turn to men," Jake said.

Kendall tilted her head, thinking. "Well, we know that the statues were alive once. We just don't know how."

"You probably know more than anyone besides Raphael and Marco," Nathan said. "You've seen the sentinels when they were alive through your visions."

"I saw men, but I didn't see how they became stone."

"We need a bloody elevator in here," Nathan said when they reached the main level.

"I suppose you'll talk Marco and Raphael into including one during renovations," Jake said.

They arrived at the kitchen and found Fergus making a roast beef sandwich. He hurried over when he saw them, his face alive with emotion. "Nathan, Kendall! Hank said you were back. Where have you been? Marco and I have been dreadfully worried for you both."

"I'm sorry, Fergus." Nathan patted Fergus's shoulder. "We didn't plan any of this. It was an accident."

"They fell through another portal," Jake said.

"Another portal," he whispered.

"This one was in the temple," Nathan said.

"My, but this place does try one's common sense."

"Have you seen Marco?" Nathan asked.

"Not for some time," Fergus said. "He vanished right after we got here. He was acting very odd. This has been a strain on him, and he feels responsible. He keeps saying it's his fault. He was talking out of his head about finding the Reaper before we arrived here. I believe he needs his medication. Is something wrong?" Fergus asked. "You all look rather . . . tense."

"We are tense," Nathan said. "We need to find Marco ASAP. He woke some of the statues."

Fergus's brows moved up his forehead. "Is that possible?"

"There are several ancient-looking men down in the lower level with Raphael," Jake said. "And he's mad as hell."

"Are they dangerous?"

"I think they're crazy," Jake said.

Fergus's eyes widened. "Where are they now?"

"Raphael's keeping them locked up," Nathan said.

"I should be shocked," Fergus said. "But somehow I'm not. What will he do with them? Can he turn them back to stone?"

"He's not sure," Jake said. "Apparently he didn't know they could turn back into men. Is that sandwich for you?"

Fergus pushed half the sandwich toward Jake. "This just gets stranger. Have any of you eaten?"

"Not yet," Kendall said.

"You must eat something. You all look dreadful, and I'm sure you haven't slept properly after all the madness with the Reaper. And if you came through another one of those"—Fergus lowered his voice and looked around to see if anyone was nearby—"things, then you must be tired."

"We are," Nathan said, "but we can't rest yet. We came to get food for Raphael and his . . . friends. He can't stay down there too long. He was seriously injured in that portal. He should be resting."

Fergus tsked. "Get something to eat and then rest. I'll have one of the guards take something down to Raphael."

"No guards. He doesn't want anyone else to know about them," Nathan said.

Fergus stiffened his neck and put on a face worthy of any English butler. "Then I will do it."

Jake offered part of his sandwich to Kendall and Nathan, but they refused. "Oh, and take a really big bowl. One that can be thrown away."

"Why?" Fergus asked.

Jake swallowed the last bite. "So they can piss in it. And anything else they need to do. Better find some toilet paper too. That'll be a pleasant surprise."

Fergus's eyes widened but otherwise his expression didn't change. "I'll take care of it."

"You're a good man, Fergus. If Nathan dies, can I have you?" Jake asked.

Nathan scowled. "I'm not dying. Fergus, are there any rooms available?"

"Most of them are full," Fergus said. "There are quite a lot of people here, between the guards and the staff. There is a room on the third floor that has twin beds. I think it's the only room available."

"Twin beds?" Nathan asked.

"There are at least three, I believe," Fergus said. "I understand some of the maids were staying there, but they heard strange noises and wouldn't go back. They said it was haunted."

"Probably Kendall's father," Jake said.

"That reminds me," Fergus said. "Kendall, your aunt called the mansion and left a message."

"Aunt Edna? Is she all right?"

"I believe so," Fergus said. "She said something about good news. She'd tried to call your cell phone and couldn't reach you."

"Probably because you were in a portal," Jake said.

They gathered some sandwiches and water, as well as Jake's duffel bag that he'd left in the hallway, and went to find their room.

"Where the devil could Marco be?" Nathan asked. "He must know how to revert them back since he's the one who woke them."

"He's probably hiding from Raphael," Jake said.

They found the room Fergus had told them about. It actually had four beds, but he hadn't mentioned how tiny the room was. There were three beds on one side of the room, and a lone bed on the opposite wall.

"Pick a bed," Jake said. "Ladies first."

The room felt even smaller with Nathan and Jake in it. Kendall walked over to the lone bed and sat down. It felt good to sit on something soft after spending all that time lying on stone. Her head was a chaotic whirl of adrenaline and exhaustion from the events of the past few hours, but her body had had enough. If she lay back down, she wouldn't get up.

Jake frowned, as if he didn't approve of her choice of beds. "I think you should sleep closer."

"Are you kidding?" Kendall asked.

"No, I'm not." He tossed his duffel on the bed nearest the door.

Kendall rubbed her arms. She felt grimy. "We're surrounded by guards. What could happen?"

"I remember thinking the same thing just before you entered a maze and wound up in England."

"Smart ass."

Jake scratched his head. "Sorry if I'm being an overprotective ass, but I thought you were dead."

"Eat your sandwich. You always feel better after eating." That sounded like she'd known him for more than a matter of days. It felt like she had known him a lifetime.

Nathan sat down on the bed closest to the wall, leaving an empty one between him and Jake. "Let's eat so we can get some sleep. We all look like hell."

Jake took a drink of his water. "I have an excuse. I nearly got fried by those damned statues after losing my cross."

Kendall pulled a cross from her pocket and carried it over to Jake. "Is this yours?"

"Yeah. How did you get it?"

"It fell out of the ceiling and hit me in the head. I guess it came through the portal."

"That's why I couldn't find it. I guess it did vanish into thin air."

"How did you get out?" Kendall asked.

"I leaped past the statues."

Kendall's heart skipped a beat. "Without a cross?"

Even Nathan looked impressed. "Shouldn't you be dead?"

"Raphael's vial saved me. The Fountain of Youth works, at least for that. I drank the water after I refilled the vial for Raphael."

Nathan looked intrigued. "It worked."

"When I saw the cross I was afraid . . ."

"You thought I was floating around in some other dimension?" He smiled. "I'm flattered. Even with the water, it wasn't fun. But I'm here." And he wasn't going to leave, was the message in his eyes. His hand brushed her cheek.

"Raphael looks worse than he did when we found him. Did he get any water?" Nathan asked.

"A few sips. We needed more. That's why we came here. He had a run-in with the statues too. He woke after I went to look for you two, and he tried to enter the temple to get water for himself. He didn't realize you'd taken his cross."

"Blimey."

"He got a little cooked. Not as bad as me." Jake grinned. "But he looked funny as hell. Like the Hulk with dreads."

"I'm sure you didn't tell him that," Nathan said sarcastically.

"Not a chance," Jake said. He lay back on the bed and groaned.

"You're lucky to be alive," Kendall said.

Nathan nodded. "We're all lucky to be alive after what we've been through."

Kendall took a bite of her sandwich. "I wish we could take a few days to rest before we go rushing off to find this chalice."

"Why don't you take some time off," Nathan said. "I'll send you somewhere safe. Jake and I can get along without you for a few days."

"King Arthur to the rescue," Jake said.

Kendall rolled her eyes at him. "We don't have time. We can't let the Reaper find the chalice first. And unless he's died from his injuries, he probably has a head start."

"We don't even know what the Holy Grail looks like." Jake

set his water bottle down with a hard sigh. "We're going into war blindfolded."

"After Raphael is finished babysitting, he can tell us where we're supposed to start looking," Nathan said. "He should be able to at least give us a good description of the chalice, better than a sketch in a journal."

"The journal," Kendall said. "It's still in England."

"Nope," Jake said, patting his bag. "I brought it."

While he opened the bag and removed the journal, Kendall hurried over to his bed. "I could hug you."

He flashed a grin. "Go ahead." He looked like he wanted to kiss her, but instead he stroked her cheek as he handed her the journal.

Nathan snorted and moved from his bed to the empty one next to Jake's. "Think you can pick up anything else from the journal?" he asked Kendall.

Kendall looked at the worn book and knew it held secrets. "If this belonged to the Reaper, there must be answers hidden in here. I just don't know how to get them out."

"You need to drink water," Jake said.

"What?"

"Raphael said you two need to be drinking water from the fountain to help control your abilities."

"Nice of him to discuss it with you," Nathan said.

"Be glad he told someone," Jake said. "Raphael doesn't like sharing his secrets any more than you do."

"You have your share of secrets too," Kendall said, sitting on the bed next to Jake opposite Nathan, so close her knees almost touched his.

"Mine aren't on purpose," Jake said. "I just can't remember anything."

Kendall looked from one to the other. "There are a lot of similarities between you two. You both have mysterious pasts. You both dreamed of King Arthur."

Nathan sighed. "I need a shower."

"We all do," Jake said.

Kendall gave him a searching look. "Are you saying I smell?"

"You smell heavenly," he said, "but we've all been through hell and back. Nathan, why don't you go first? I want to catch up on things with Kendall."

Nathan gave Jake a hard look. "Catch up?"

"Talk," Jake said. "I want to talk to her."

Nathan looked at Jake's duffel. He seemed tired. "Don't suppose you want to loan me some clothes."

Jake opened the bag and pulled out a pair of underwear, socks, and jeans. He balled them up and tossed them on Nathan's bed.

"Thanks." Nathan took the items and walked to the door.

As soon as he left, Jake turned to Kendall. "Are you sure you're OK?" He searched her face and ran his hands over her arms and legs, as if checking to make sure she was whole.

"Just tired."

"I thought the Reaper had taken you." Jake skimmed his fingers over her cheeks. "Why don't you go someplace for a few days. Let Nathan send you to his mansion. You should be safe there."

Kendall leaned her cheek into his hand. "I'm not leaving you two alone."

"Afraid we'll kill each other?" Jake half grinned.

"No. Maybe. I just don't want either of you hurt."

Gray eyes held hers for a moment, and then he touched her lips with his thumb. "You're supposed to let us take care of you, not the other way around."

She gave him a tired smile. "I have special powers."

"I know you're magic," he whispered, leaning close. "You've done something to me." He touched his mouth to hers. His lips were warm and felt like heaven. She didn't want to start trouble with all three of them in the same room, but she needed to feel and taste him. He stood and pulled her to her feet, holding her tight against him. She slipped her arms around his waist, fingers caressing his back as the kiss grew hungrier and his hands more demanding. His desire combined with hers created an explosion of need. Trust her senses to work when it came to sex. She wanted to push him down on the bed and make love until neither of them could move.

"You taste good," he said against her lips. "Think this door has a lock?"

Kendall slipped back a few inches and slid her hands around to his chest, keeping him back. "Jake, we can't . . ."

"Not with King Arthur here? Feels a little like history repeating itself, eh, Guinevere? Damn. Killed my own mood." Jake sighed, but still held her close.

"Do you really think we're . . . them?"

"I don't know how any of this can be, but if you'd seen those bodies in the tombs." She felt a ripple move through him. "And what about the couple in the woods? They were dressed just like the corpses. We were there, Kendall. I felt it. I felt her. You . . ."

The door opened and Nathan came in, wearing his borrowed clothes. He cleared his throat. "Talk? And to think, just a few days ago you two couldn't stand the sight of each other."

Kendall stepped back and saw Nathan's undisguised look of regret. For introducing her to Jake? Sometimes she felt like she was caught in a tug-of-war. "I'm going to shower."

"Want to borrow my underwear and a shirt?" Jake asked.

"Sure," Kendall said, not because she wanted to cause more tension, but because she felt dirty and grimy, and she would have worn just about anyone's clean shirt and underwear.

Jake pulled out a pair of boxers and a T-shirt and handed them to her. "I'll walk you to the bathroom."

"I think I'll be fine from here to the bathroom."

"Remember the maze," he said in a patronizing voice.

Kendall rolled her eyes but let him walk her to the bathroom. At the door, he kissed her softly. "I could shower with you. I need one too."

"Jake, we can't."

He opened the bathroom door and guided her inside. "Why not? I need to feel you, touch you."

"You want sex."

"Of course I do. Anyone would, but this is different. I'm obsessed with you. I can't get you out of my head."

Kendall's hands were bunched in his shirt, holding him gently back. "Do you want me out of your head?"

He met her eyes, and she saw the flicker of confusion. "Sometimes. I've never felt like this. I'm not sure what to do with it." He stroked her hair. "No. I don't. I need you. I need to feel you inside and out. Your heart, your body, your soul."

That took her breath, in part because she was sure she'd heard Lancelot say the same words to Guinevere in the forest, so Kendall let him kiss her. It was a hot kiss, the kind that made her forget what she should and shouldn't do, and before she realized what was happening, he had her stripped. Jake pulled his lips from hers long enough to remove his shirt. He was fumbling with his zipper, mouth searching for hers again, when she came to her senses.

"Jake, we can't do this."

He reached over and turned the shower on. Contrary to their first opinion of the property—which Raphael must have intended—the castle had been modernized somewhat. "Why not?"

"Nathan's in there waiting."

"Let him wait. He knows we're . . . sleeping together."

"Jake, we need to slow down."

His eyes narrowed. "Slow down. Because he's Adam."

"No . . . yes. I don't know. There's just too much going on."

His mouth tightened, and he nodded. He pulled his shirt back on.

Kendall touched his shoulder. "Jake, it's not that I don't want to. I do. You know that. But the timing isn't right."

Jake's face was tight. "I'll be outside."

She hurried through her shower. When she was finished, Jake was still waiting outside, arms crossed over his chest, as watchful as a sentinel. He escorted her back to the room. Nathan was in bed under the covers, leaning against the headboard, hands propped behind his head. The clothes Jake had lent him were in a pile on the foot of his bed. "Your pants are unbuttoned," he said.

Kendall and Jake both looked down and saw that Jake's top button was undone. Had he left it that way on purpose? He seemed quiet, not in a mood to poke at Nathan. "My turn," Jake said. He grabbed some things from his bag and left the room.

Kendall settled on her bed and started braiding her wet hair. "It's not what you think," she said to Nathan.

"What do I think?" Nathan dropped his arms and crossed them over his chest, which reminded Kendall so much of Jake's. Except for the tattoo. And the cut beside it.

"You're hurt."

Nathan glanced down at his arm. "It's nothing."

Kendall climbed out of bed and walked over to him. She wished she hadn't when she saw how much of his chest and stomach were exposed. "You need a bandage."

"It's not bleeding. It'll heal."

"You always did heal quickly."

"Did I?"

It was the first time he hadn't thrown up a wall when she referred to him as Adam. "Yes. Scrapes, cuts, they always healed right up. You never got sick." Kendall smiled. "I thought you were a superhero. Not really, but you were somewhere above human."

"Did you get hurt a lot?" Nathan's eyes were curious. He scooted over, as if to make room for her, like they'd done time and time again when they were kids. Without thinking about it too much, she sat on the edge of his bed.

"Not much. You were good at keeping me safe. You were downright bossy sometimes. 'Stay away from that rock. It's not stable.' But you were usually right." She told him a couple of stories and felt his mind opening to his memories. Then Jake stepped inside the room, wearing only jeans, his face set. "So you're holding hands the minute I leave the room."

"He has a cut on his arm."

"He's a big boy. He'll heal."

"Leave her alone," Nathan said. "She wasn't doing anything."

"You two are impossible. I should sleep in the tower room," she blurted out, not really meaning it.

"No!" they both said.

"The Reaper is itching to get his hands on you," Jake said. "And if he does, after he gets what he wants—the relics—he's got a little matter of revenge to settle with you. You hurt him. I doubt anyone in centuries has hurt him. No way we're letting you sleep up there alone."

"I'd feel better if you were closer," Nathan said. "I trust my guards, but we're dealing with someone who could be a couple of thousand years old. And if he can open a portal to the Fountain of Youth and bypass the statues, who's to say he can't do it here?"

Kendall hadn't thought about that. If he could open a portal to the castle, he would have access to all the relics kept here.

"You need rest," Nathan said. "We've been to Camelot and back, faced the Reaper, found the Fountain of Youth . . . none of us have really slept since."

"I slept some," Jake said. "Raphael knocked me out."

"I bet you were pissed," Nathan said.

"Yeah, but he got the same thing. Marco knocked him out."

"Marco can do that?" Kendall stifled a yawn. "I shouldn't be surprised that he can wake statues."

"I think Marco can do a lot of things we don't know about," Jake said. "Let's sleep while we can. We need to be alert if we're going to outsmart the Reaper and find the chalice." Jake pointed to the middle bed. Kendall expected him to demand her to sleep there. "Would you please sleep there?" His eyes were intense, and had a look of worry that made her heart feel mushy. "Please. Do it for us."

Nathan's dark eyes had the same worried look. "We would all sleep better. Jake and I need rest too."

Nathan was using the sympathy card, but he was right. Kendall nodded and walked to the middle bed. She turned back the covers and climbed in.

"I'll get the lights," Jake said. He padded over to the light switch and turned it off before returning to his bed. Kendall heard him taking off his jeans. She looked away, glancing at Nathan's bed, and saw him watching her.

Damn. What was she going to do about them?

They were all quiet after that, and she was certain they were deep in thought, like she was. Still, exhaustion took hold and she fell asleep.

She woke sometime later when she heard someone moving in the room. She looked over at Nathan's bed and saw someone standing over him. Her heart pounded in alarm, and then she recognized Jake.

He wasn't murdering Nathan (as she had momentarily feared). He was fixing his sheets. They seemed to be tangled. Nathan had been tossing.

Jake saw her and walked quietly to her bed. "He was dreaming."

"A nightmare?"

"I think so."

Jake cared more about Nathan than he would dare admit. And she fell a little bit more in love with Jake. Kendall stroked his hand. "Thank you."

"For?"

"Being a good man and not the jackass I thought you were at first."

He smiled and bent down. "Do I deserve a kiss?" He seemed in a lighter mood than he had after she refused to shower with him.

She reached for him and brought his face lower. She touched her lips to his, felt the brush of his unshaven jaw. The kiss was soft, almost chaste. When she pulled away, he didn't press for more.

"Get some sleep. I think he's OK now." Jake kissed the top of her head and moved away. But he did let his fingers trail over her breast as he left and returned to his bed. He rolled on his side, facing her.

Kendall lay there wondering if something was wrong with her because, in that moment, she wished they had a king-size bed so all three of them could sleep huddled together for comfort as they had in the tunnel underneath the Tor. She wanted to feel Jake's arms around her, and she wanted to comfort Nathan and keep his nightmares at bay.

Adam walked toward the tent where he and his father were staying. Sometimes they stayed in hotels, but this time, his father didn't want to get too far away from the dig. The men were camped close by. Adam could hear them laughing and talking in their tents. There was always excitement with a new dig, and when it included a burial site, some of the locals were superstitious about curses falling upon the ones who disturbed the tomb.

His legs ached from racing Kendall to the top of the pyramid and back. She could keep up with him now. For a girl, she was bloody fast. He entered the tent, and his father looked up from a table of artifacts and smiled. His father wasn't that tall, but to Adam he seemed larger than other men. His brown hair was rumpled, as it was when he was intently studying his relics. He reminded Adam of Indiana Jones. Of course, Kendall said her father looked more like Indiana Jones. It was a friendly argument between them.

"What are you working on?" Adam asked.

His father put something aside that looked like an urn. Sometimes the Egyptians buried the organs in urns. Adam thought that was morbid, and very cool.

"Just some recent additions. I haven't examined them thoroughly yet." He shared many of his discoveries, but some he protected from everyone. Even his son.

"I need something for Kendall's birthday. It's next month. Can I have something from your collection?"

"You don't want to buy her something nice?"

"Nah. She'd rather have an artifact than something girly."

"Sure, we can find something when we get home."

Nathan was startled awake, disturbed by the dream. He could still see his father's face as plain as if he stood there. His father? Was it his father? Adam's father. His head started to throb just thinking about it. He didn't know why the dream had been so disturbing. What could be troubling about a birthday present? Yet, he was sure there was something else he needed to remember.

He rolled over and looked at Kendall, asleep in the bed next to his. If he hadn't been here, she and Jake would be sharing a bed. The thought made him burn inside. Jake didn't deserve her. But neither did he.

He felt restless and knew he'd never sleep. Lying here staring at Kendall would just make him feel more frustrated. He climbed out of bed, quietly, counting on Jake's exhaustion to keep him from hearing. He pulled on the jeans Jake had loaned him and slipped on his own shirt, which wasn't too smelly.

When he slipped past Jake's bed, Nathan saw it was empty. Opening the door, he checked the hall. He wasn't there, but a toilet flushed from the bathroom a few doors down. Knowing Jake would be back in a second, Nathan kept walking. He didn't feel like talking or answering questions. He curtly nodded to the guard who was at the front door. "Everything OK?"

"All quiet, sir."

"I'm going for a walk. Need some fresh air."

"Shall I get someone to go with you?"

"No, I won't be long."

The guard nodded and stepped aside. All Nathan's employees knew he valued his privacy. They were all paid well to follow orders and not question the boss. If they didn't respect it, they were out. Except Jake. Jake questioned everything and then did whatever he wanted.

Nathan started walking and ended up at the graveyard. He stopped beside the two lone tombstones that lay apart from the others, outside the consecrated ground, wondering if Kendall was right about the graves belonging to her parents. Nathan squatted down by the graves. He was so sick of the shadows in his head, flashes of memories that didn't make sense. He reached out to touch the grave—he couldn't have said why he thought this one may have been William's, but he closed his eyes and said his name. "William.

Uncle William." That's what he'd called him, even though there wasn't any relation. He had been a kind man, intense in his work, but with a ready smile for Kendall or Adam.

Nathan's eyes flew open. He'd remembered something. He looked at his hand touching the gravestone. Or had he picked up a corpse's memories? That was more in line with Kendall's gift. *You bloody fool. Why are you so scared to dig into your memories? What are you afraid of?*

He left his hand on the stone and closed his eyes again. He took the scrap of memory and this time didn't run from it. He let it settle, let it breathe and take form. In the space of a heartbeat, he was no longer in the graveyard, but on an airplane headed for hell.

"Where are we going?" Adam asked.

"Away from here. I have some business to take care of," his father replied.

He was worried, Adam thought. He had that line in his forehead. He was probably upset over the trouble at the castle. What trouble? He couldn't remember, but for a second he'd remembered getting into trouble with Kendall. They got into trouble a lot. Why couldn't he remember? "Are Kendall and Uncle William coming?" Adam asked.

"Not this time."

Adam didn't have time to reply. An explosion rocked the plane, throwing him from his seat. He felt flames hot on his face and smelled smoke, but everything was black. He crawled to his knees, but he couldn't see. "Dad!" he screamed.

Kendall woke up again, and this time she was alone. What a crock, she thought, after all that fussing about them protecting her. She stepped outside the door in time to see Nathan vanish down the hall. Where was he going? Curious, she followed him. He and Jake had better not be having some midnight meeting, plotting to send her away for her own safety.

She saw Nathan speak to the guard at the front door, but she didn't see Jake. She didn't know this guard's name, but she'd seen him around. "Which way did Nathan go?" she asked.

The guard pointed. "That way. He's taking a walk. Should you be out here?"

"I'm going to walk with him."

The guard's lips quirked. Kendall could imagine what he must be thinking, with them taking a walk in the dead of night. "I'll take you to him."

"That's not necessary. I'll catch him."

"Hurry then. He'll have my hide if you're out here alone for two seconds."

"I will."

She lost sight of him once, and was afraid he'd changed and was using his speed skills. She'd never catch him then. The moon was almost full, giving ghostly shadows to the castle and the trees. She smiled to herself, thinking how he was sort of like a werewolf. Not in terms of the hair, fangs, or four legs, but with the ability to change to something else.

She caught sight of him near the graveyard. Why would he come here unless he was meeting Jake?

He squatted down beside the graves and reached out to touch one. There was a set to his shoulders that made her heart ache for him. Sadness and confusion rose off him so clearly that if she were a normal person, she'd have thought she was seeing a ghost.

She waited in the trees out of sight and watched, not wanting to pry, but too concerned to leave. She saw it happen. One second he was touching the grave, and the next he was lying on the ground. Kendall ran toward him and knelt down. "Nathan. Can you hear me?"

His voice was hoarse as he cried out for his father. Kendall shook him gently. "Wake up, Nathan. It's just a dream."

He let out an agonized cry, and lurched to his feet.

She knew it was dangerous, considering his abilities, but she rose and touched his cheek, wet with tears, and her head felt like a bomb had gone off behind her eyes.

Flames were everywhere, stinging his eyes and burning his throat. He couldn't see, but he could feel the heat. "Dad!"

Someone grabbed his arm and pulled him. He stumbled trying to keep up. "Father?"

"No, it's William."

"Where's my father?"

"Hurry, Adam. We have to hurry."

"We can't leave him."

"We must or we'll both die." William pulled him away from the crackle and heat of the flames. "Come with me. I'll take you somewhere safe."

"What about my father?"

"I'll go back for him."

But he heard the truth in William's voice. There was no chance for his father.

He couldn't fight his uncle, he couldn't even see. Caught in his shock, he allowed himself to be pulled away. When he woke again, he had no idea where he was or who he was. There was a man with him, urging him to hurry. He was breathing strange, rasping, and kept saying he was sorry. So sorry. "Tell her I love her." And then he wasn't breathing anymore.

Kendall opened her eyes, overwhelmed at what she'd seen. Her father's death through Adam's eyes, and the crash that killed Uncle John.

Nathan was watching her, his eyes amber, but she wasn't afraid. "It was just a dream." She wiped his damp cheek and knew she was crying too. For him, for her. For his father and hers, who had died to save Adam.

Nathan held her hand there, his eyes filled with pain. She could feel the residue of memories crashing through his brain like waves battering a ship. He touched her face softly and then pulled her into his arms. He held her there, his chest pounding against hers, her tears soaking his shirt.

CHAPTER TEN

J AKE RETURNED FROM THE BATHROOM AND WENT DEAD-STILL
at the sight of the empty beds. His stomach dropped and he
yanked open the door, calling Kendall's name. She didn't answer,
so he started downstairs. He'd just gone to take a piss. She
couldn't have gone far. The guard was still at the front door. He
frowned when he saw Jake running.

"Is everything OK?"

"Have you seen Kendall?" Jake asked.

"She went for a walk."

"You let her go out in the middle of the night!" What the hell
was she thinking? What was the guard thinking?

The guard looked defensive. "She's not alone," he said stiffly.
"Mr. Larraby is with her."

Nathan was with her? Jake didn't care that Nathan had superpowers. He had no business wandering around with Kendall after
they'd just been lost. "Where did they go?"

The guard looked as if he was unsure whether to tell him.

"Tell me now."

The guard frowned and pointed.

Jake hurried in the direction, wondering what the hell Nathan was thinking. A better question might be, what was he thinking with? He had worked himself into a frenzy by the time he saw them. And when he did, he felt like he'd been hit with a sledge hammer.

They were hugging. More than hugging. They looked like vines that were intertwined.

"So you sneaked out so you could be alone?" Jake ground out.

They jumped apart, both looking guilty. "Jake? We were . . ."

"I can see what you were doing. Couldn't you have found an empty room instead of out here in the open where anyone could attack you?"

"We didn't . . ." Nathan rubbed his chin, and Jake saw a damp trail on his face. Tears?

"It's not like that," Kendall said. "I followed him. I thought you two were meeting behind my back, plotting to send me somewhere that the Reaper couldn't find me."

"That led to this?" Jake was hurt and pissed, and he wanted to kick something. Starting with Nathan.

Nathan's eyes narrowed. "It was just a hug."

"Don't do that," Kendall said, turning on Nathan. "It wasn't your fault. It wasn't anyone's fault. It was just a . . . moment." She glared at Jake. "He was having a nightmare and I touched him. I got pulled into it."

"He was having a nightmare in the graveyard?"

"He touched my father's grave, and he remembered the fire. He remembered his father dying. And mine."

Well hell. He looked at the tears on Nathan's cheeks.

He must have noticed because he wiped them away with his hand. "She was just comforting me."

"Looked like you were ready to throw her down right here." He hadn't intended to say that last part out loud, but hell, they could have comforted each other with a pat on the back or a few kind words, instead of with their bodies pressed together like moss on a rock.

"Jake!" Kendall's eyes flashed green fire.

"Show a little respect," Nathan said, his voice hard.

"I'm going back to the room," Kendall said, and stalked away. Nathan and Jake lagged behind.

"Don't be mad at her," Nathan said, his body stiff with tension.

"I'm not. I'm mad at you. You know how I feel about her."

Nathan's face tightened, and they walked on in silence. The guard looked at them as they approached. "Everyone OK, sir?"

"Fine."

When they got to the room, Kendall was coming out. "Where are you going?" Jake asked.

"To sleep someplace else."

"No, you're not."

"I am, and you're not going to stop me. Neither are you," she said, looking at Nathan. "You can post a damned guard outside my door." She stomped off toward the tower room.

"I guess we can take turns watching the door," Jake said.

"I think we'd better get some guards," Nathan said. "She needs some distance from us."

"Trouble in paradise?"

Jake turned and saw Raphael standing behind them. "Paradise? More like hell."

"What's wrong with Kendall?" Raphael asked.

"She's pissed," Jake said.

"I can tell."

"I'll post two guards outside her door," Nathan said.

"What about that damned secret entrance?" Jake asked. "Do we want to tell them about it?"

"No," Raphael said. "I'll guard the secret doorway. The guards already know too many of our secrets."

They posted guards and Raphael went off to sit near the secret doorway, leaving Nathan and Jake free for a whole lot of awkwardness. They settled into their beds, with Kendall's empty one lying between them like the Grand Canyon.

"You weren't supposed to fall for her," Nathan said after a while.

"I didn't mean to," Jake said. "She got under my skin."

"She does that." Nathan was quiet for a moment. "Just remember your first priority is to protect her, not . . . anything else."

"I'd die to protect her," Jake said.

"So would I." Nathan's voice was low, almost menacing. "And I'd probably kill anyone who broke her heart."

Jake met his gaze and quietly nodded. "Me too."

It took him a long while to go to sleep, and he still hadn't cleared his head of the image of Kendall and Nathan wrapped in each other's arms like lovers.

It was happening, he thought, his chest aching. He was losing her.

Raphael stood over the bed, wondering if he had the courage to kill her. It would be a high price, but it might be the only way. There would be hell to pay from Nathan and Jake. That was an understatement. Both of them were in love with her. It wasn't a surprise. She was nearly as beautiful now as she had been then. There were some differences, her clothing and her manner. He hadn't recognized her at first. But he hadn't been expecting her. He sighed, still holding his dagger over her chest, watching it rise and fall with mesmerizing rhythm. He lowered the tip of the blade until it almost touched her breast. A perfect target. It would just take one strike.

The mind-numbing comfort of exhaustion had finally stilled Nathan's thoughts with sleep when he woke with the realization that something was wrong. He sat up and saw Kendall's bed empty. The first rush of panic faded when he remembered she was in the tower room with the guards and Raphael keeping watch.

Jake wasn't in bed either. Where was he? Nathan hadn't even bothered to undress before getting in bed, so he shoved his feet into boots and hurried from the room. The sense of danger was growing stronger as he climbed to the tower. He saw someone at the top of the stairs. Not one of the guards. His eyes started to burn and he was about to lunge when the figure turned. It was Jake.

"What the devil are you doing?" Nathan whispered.

"The same thing you are. Checking up on her."

"Can't you keep away from her for two seconds?"

"I couldn't sleep, so I sent the guards away. Might as well stand guard myself and let them go somewhere more useful. I've got a bad feeling—" As if on cue, a scream came from inside. Jake wrenched open the door in time for them to see Raphael standing over Kendall's bed with a dagger.

Nathan's body fired up like dry timber soaked in gasoline. He shoved Jake aside and lunged across the room toward Raphael, who was frowning at the dagger that had fallen from his hand. Just before Nathan crashed into him, Raphael looked up and grabbed Nathan's arms, holding him back. Nathan's head felt like it would explode. He was too hot. Burning up. Images flashed in his head. Kendall when she was a girl. Falling in the tomb, trying to hide her damp eyes after she'd had an intense vision. Staring at the dead snake that had almost struck her. Her shame as his father ruined her birthday. Pain seared his head like a poker had been driven into his eye. He felt himself melting like hot metal.

Kendall jumped out of bed and rushed to Nathan. "What did you do to him?"

Raphael started to kneel, but Jake grabbed the dagger that had fallen and pointed it at him. "Don't move." He knew it was foolish. Raphael could turn him into hamburger, but he was operating on adrenaline. It was pounding through his system, making him tingle all over.

Raphael's eyes narrowed, but he didn't fight. "I didn't hurt him."

"Doesn't look that way to me," Kendall said, bending over him.

Jake's hand tightened on the dagger. "What were you doing with this?"

"Thinking about whether or not to kill Kendall."

Jake's mouth dropped open. He pointed the dagger at Raphael's throat. "Kill her!"

Raphael looked unmoved. "I decided not to."

Kendall raised her head and stared at Raphael. "Why would you want to kill me?"

"To keep Luke . . . the Reaper from finding the chalice."

Kendall and Jake fell silent. Nathan stirred and Kendall leaned closer. "Nathan, are you OK?"

He groaned and climbed to his feet. "Keep Raphael away from her."

"I am," Jake said.

Nathan rubbed his head. "What the hell was he doing?"

"Deciding not to kill her," Jake said.

Nathan's eyes flared and a rumbling noise sounded in his throat.

"Calm down, Nathan." Kendall touched his face. "He was trying to protect the chalice."

"By killing you?"

Kendall held on to Nathan's arm. "To keep the Reaper from using me to find it. It's extreme, but I see what he was thinking."

"You can put my dagger down," Raphael said to Jake. "I'm not going to kill anyone."

Jake didn't budge.

"If I wanted to kill her," Raphael said, "I would have already done it. If I wanted to kill her badly enough, I would have gone through you and Nathan to do it. I don't want to kill her."

"I don't trust you," Jake said.

"I can understand that. I wouldn't either in your situation. I merely considered killing her as the means to an end. The Reaper will try to use Kendall to find the Holy Grail. If she's dead, he can't." Raphael's voice sounded thick with emotion. "Don't judge me. I know you've all been faced with tough calls, weighed the odds."

Jake had many times, but this was Kendall. And it was his fault she had slept alone in the tower room. If he hadn't reacted with jealousy when he saw Kendall and Nathan hugging, she wouldn't have felt the need to get away. "How can we be sure you won't try again?"

"In part, because I need her to find the chalice too. And if I kill her, the Reaper will probably find some other way to locate the chalice."

"Geez, thanks," Kendall said, lips tight.

Raphael looked at her, his eyes steady. "I swear to you, I will not kill you. I will protect your life with my own."

Kendall stared at the guardian, and Jake was certain she was reading his thoughts. She didn't usually *pry*, but this would warrant it. Her eyes widened slightly and her lips parted as if she'd seen something startling. Raphael looked fierce, protective, but then his expression went blank. "I believe him," Kendall said. "Now, do you know what's wrong with Nathan?" She tried to help him toward the bed, but his legs weren't steady. He was a lot more solid than he looked. Jake took his arm and helped him.

"Damned curse," Nathan muttered.

"It's not a curse," Raphael said. "You just don't know how to use your powers yet."

"Whose fault is that?" Nathan asked. "You're the one who knows how all this works, and you haven't told us anything. If we're going to be part of the Protettori, we need to know what we're doing."

"Taking a vow you didn't understand when you were children doesn't make you part of the brotherhood," Raphael said.

"You don't know." Jake smiled, his lips hard. "The person you decided not to kill is the Protettori's next keeper, according to Marco."

Raphael looked disturbed. "He said this?"

"He did, and he said Nathan is a guardian. Looks like you're not alone anymore."

"But how can he be a guardian? He's . . ."

"I'm what?" Nathan asked.

Raphael didn't answer.

"King Arthur?" Kendall asked. "You think he can't be a guardian because he was King Arthur?" Kendall frowned. "That doesn't sound ridiculous at all."

"He isn't ready," Raphael said.

That wasn't what he was going to say. Jake wished he had Kendall's gift to read minds. He looked at her to see if he could pick anything up secondhand, but Kendall wasn't paying attention to her would-be murderer now. She was trying to get Nathan to lie down.

"I'm fine," Nathan said. But he was leaning on Kendall, who had sat beside him wearing Jake's boxers and T-shirt. Now her soul mate, returned from the dead, was injured. Another mark in Nathan's favor.

"If he was once King Arthur—" Jake stopped. Kendall was right, it did sound ridiculous. "Then he's already been one of the Protettori."

Raphael pulled out a vial and handed it to Nathan. "Drink this. It's not poison," he said when Nathan stared at it, his eyes narrowed in suspicion.

"Isn't drinking the water dangerous?" Kendall asked.

"Not if taken correctly. It will become your lifeblood. It gives you strength and helps you control your abilities."

Nathan rubbed his head. "What if I don't want them? When you were holding me in the temple you said there was a way to get rid of my . . . abilities."

Raphael's eyes were so still he looked like a corpse. "It would require a great sacrifice."

"What?"

"That's something we can discuss later. Now isn't the time."

"Drink the water," Jake said to Nathan. "It kept me from dying when I passed those statues."

"He could have switched it with something else," Nathan said.

"If he poisons you, I promise I'll kill him," Jake said.

And he would.

Raphael shook his head. His hair didn't look as wild now. Was the water responsible for that? Jake touched his hair. It didn't feel as dry and stiff, and he realized he didn't feel as cooked inside.

Still eyeing Raphael suspiciously, Nathan opened the vial and drank.

"It'll take effect quickly," Raphael said.

A knock sounded at the door. Everyone turned to look.

"Are you going to get that," Nathan asked Jake, "or just stand there playing with your hair?"

Jake dropped his hand and walked to the door. It was Hank and three guards.

"Everything OK?" Hank asked. "We heard a scream."

"Kendall saw a mouse," Jake said.

Hank frowned.

Jake knew it was a bad excuse. Kendall wasn't the kind of girl to be scared of a mouse.

"What are you doing here?" Hank asked. "I thought your room was on the third floor."

"We were . . . having a meeting," Nathan said, trying to look alert.

Hank didn't seem convinced. Neither did the other guards.

"Everything's fine," Nathan said. "We won't be much longer."

Still frowning, Hank motioned the other guards away.

After they left, Kendall convinced Nathan to lie down for a few minutes. "I think all these memories on top of falling through a portal was too much."

"It probably didn't help," Raphael said. "Where did you enter the gateway?"

"Near the wheel that opens the fountain. *I was going to fill your vial*," she said, reminding her would-be assassin that she had been trying to save his life. "But when I touched the wheel I had a vision or something, and I think my sixth sense blasted me. I fell backward. Nathan reached for me, and we ended up here."

"It worked?" Raphael looked surprised and alarmed. The alarmed look worried Jake.

"What do you mean?" he asked.

"My new gateway. I hadn't tested it."

"You mean we fell through a portal that wasn't ready while we were trying to help you?" Nathan asked.

"What the hell. You just leave unfinished portals lying around waiting for someone to fall in?" Jake didn't want to think what might have happened.

"Nathan was injured. He could have died!" Kendall looked like a mother bear defending her cub. Except Nathan wasn't her cub. He was her lost soul mate returned from the dead. Jake knew he had to give her and Nathan some space to rekindle their friendship or he would end up pushing her away.

"I appreciate the help, but no one besides me was supposed to be in the temple." Raphael's look of remorse turned to a glare aimed at Jake. "No, I don't leave unfinished *portals* lying around for someone to fall in."

"What if the portal hadn't worked?" Kendall asked, voicing Jake's real concern.

A tattoo moved under Raphael's eye. "I think it's best we didn't find out."

"Bloody hell," Nathan said, holding his head. "You mean we could have ended up with parts of our bodies all over the place? Maybe that's what's wrong with me. Part of my brain is somewhere else."

Raphael walked over to the bed. This time no one stopped him. He tilted his head as he studied Nathan. "What happened before you passed out?"

"When I saw you standing over Kendall's bed with that dagger, all these flashes went through my mind. Memories. I don't know. That's all I remember."

"You're remembering parts of your past and it's interfering with your abilities," Raphael said.

"Shorting him out," Jake said.

"Is it dangerous?" Kendall asked.

"It could be," Raphael said. "This isn't something I've encountered. We need to watch him."

Kendall was already worrying over him like a mama bear . . . or a girlfriend. But Jake was more alarmed than he wanted to admit. He and Nathan argued, and Jake was jealous as hell of his relationship with Kendall, but he trusted Nathan to help keep Kendall safe. His abilities, while troubling, had come in handy. If Nathan was going to faint in the middle of a fight, Jake couldn't trust him to protect Kendall. Or himself. Jake would have to keep a closer eye on them both.

Raphael stood back, arms folded over his chest. "He needs to get his memories back or let them go. They're messing with his head."

"Are you a therapist too . . . along with your ability to do magic tricks?" Jake asked.

"I've studied humans for a *long* time," Raphael said quietly.

"We need to go back to where he was raised." Kendall's expression was soft as she looked at Nathan.

We? As in her and him or all of them? "I thought that was all over the world," Jake said, checking to see if Kendall's bare legs were touching Nathan's.

"We traveled a lot," Kendall said. "But if he went back to his home when he was a kid, saw his old room, it might jog his memories."

"No." Nathan's jaw was set.

"Why not?" Kendall asked.

Jake knew Nathan was terrified that he wasn't Adam. Jake was terrified that he was. But after that little scene at the grave-yard—if they were telling the truth about what prompted it—Nathan should be convinced.

"We don't have time," Nathan said, his voice firm, as if trying to convince himself. "We have to find the chalice and stop the Reaper. I'll travel down memory lane later. I'll try to block the memories for now."

"I'm not sure that's good," Kendall said.

"He has a point," Jake said. And it wasn't just because he didn't want Kendall and Nathan off exploring their childhood memories. "If Raphael's right and the Reaper is going to try to use you to find the chalice, you have to limit your activities to what's absolutely necessary. And even then, you're not to be alone at any time." He felt like a hypocrite for not remaining by Kendall's side.

"They're right," Raphael said. "I could have killed you if I had wanted to. Luke is very smart. And he's desperate."

Nathan looked at Raphael. "If we're going to find the Holy Grail before the Reaper does, I think it's time for an unveiling. You need to tell us everything we should know."

An expression crossed Raphael's face, so potent and loaded with secrets that Jake felt them like a physical thing. For a moment, he could understand how Kendall felt when she read someone. She had noticed the expression on Raphael's face too and was frowning. Jake wondered what she'd seen. He was certain of one thing—whatever Raphael told them, it wouldn't be everything.

Raphael seemed to come to a conclusion. "You want to know about the Protettori?"

"Yes," Nathan said.

"Do you feel well enough to walk?" Raphael asked Nathan.

"Yes."

"I'll help him," Kendall said.

"Then come with me."

"What about the men, the statues?" Nathan asked.

"Fergus is with them."

"Is he safe?" Nathan asked.

"They won't kill him. They know they'll have to answer to me."

"Kill him? How crazy are they?" Nathan asked.

"Fergus will be fine."

Nathan followed Raphael, with Kendall close beside him.

Jake stayed back, not sure the invitation had been extended to him. He wasn't a new keeper or guardian.

Kendall stopped and looked back. "Come on."

"I'm not part of the Protettori." Which pissed him off. Kendall and Nathan already shared a connection. Now this?

"You've done as much for the Protettori as any guardian," Kendall said, her jaw set.

Raphael nodded. "Come."

There were four levels to the castle, three aboveground and one underneath. The main level consisted of a living space, common areas, the library, the kitchen, meeting rooms, storage, and a few bedrooms. Most of the top two levels consisted of bedrooms to accommodate the large number of Protettori who had once lived here, and also the room with the mural on the wall, where the water from the Fountain of Youth was kept.

The towers on either end of the castle were identical, Raphael had said. The underground level was where most of the secrets were, and this is where Raphael took them. "Isn't this near the room where the men are?" Kendall asked.

"Close," Raphael said. He took them down a wide corridor to a large metal door that looked like it could withstand a bomb blast.

He took out his cross and used it to open a lock, which in turn activated another lock, and another. Five times he used the cross. When he was finished, he put the cross back around his neck and opened the metal door.

Jake caught Kendall's arm. "What if this is a trap?"

Raphael looked at him as he might a dimwitted child. "What?"

"You're showing us stuff you don't want to. Maybe the Protettori secrets are more important than a few lives. After all, you were considering killing Kendall to protect the chalice."

Raphael gave Jake a withering look. "We need to stop the Reaper, and as you so wisely pointed out, we don't have anyone else. We need Kendall to find the chalice."

"No pressure," Kendall muttered.

Raphael led the way. Nathan and Kendall were behind him, and Jake brought up the rear.

Jake was stunned when he stepped inside. "Looks like someone dropped the Smithsonian inside here." He saw rows of shelves and glass cases holding hundreds of objects. Swords, books, figurines . . . a jeweled crown?

"This isn't the room Nathan and I were in," Kendall said. "I didn't realize the Protettori protected so many relics."

"We have collected many artifacts and treasures over the centuries. Some of the most powerful religious relics are here. But not all the relics are religious, and many are from different cultures."

"How do you find and keep track of them?" she asked.

"There used to be a catalog, but it disappeared."

"I guess it's easy to track the relics when you can just think about a place and appear there," Jake said. "He doesn't need portals like the rest of us mortals."

"You can just travel anywhere . . . without traveling?" Kendall asked.

"It isn't that easy, but in a manner, yes."

"That's how he makes it look like he walks through walls," Jake said. "He transports himself out of the room when he reaches the wall."

"Exactly how does it work?" Nathan asked.

"It's difficult to explain."

"Try," Jake said. "We're putting our lives in danger to help you. The least you could do is share a little knowledge."

"I think about where I want to go. And I go."

They waited, but he didn't say anything else. "That's all," Jake said. "You can't do any better than that?"

"It's difficult to explain to someone who doesn't share the ability. I have to be in good health, have taken water. I think about the place in my mind, or an object I'm following, like the Reaper. I focus on it and I'm there."

"Is that something that can be taught?" Kendall asked.

"No. It's a gift."

"Is that what Kendall was doing when we appeared in Camelot?" Nathan asked.

"Perhaps," Raphael said. "Are you ready to see more?"

The next room was the one where the awoken statues had been. "Where are the men?"

"I moved them to a more secure location."

"Are you sure Fergus is all right with them?" Nathan asked.

"I put a sedative in their water," Raphael said.

"Couldn't you just put them to sleep?" Kendall asked.

"I tried. It didn't work."

"Your gift is flawed?" Jake asked.

Raphael gave Jake an irritated look. "My gift works on humans. I don't think they've been flesh and blood long enough."

Jake had moved on, his attention caught by something else. "Is that a sarcophagus?"

"Complete with a mummy," Kendall said. "Or it was before Nathan removed it."

Raphael's expression was one of horror. "You moved him?"

"We had to hide," Nathan said. "There wasn't room for all of us."

"You hid inside a sarcophagus?" Jake asked, trying to imagine them crammed inside, bodies pressed together.

"It was a close fit," Nathan said, holding Jake's gaze.

"Where is he now?" Raphael's voice was tight.

"I put the body behind the sarcophagus," Nathan said.

"He didn't damage it," Kendall said. "Why do you look so disturbed? I assure you Nathan has been around mummies before."

Damned comforting, Jake thought. More of their history together.

Raphael looked more than disturbed. "It was someone . . . important."

"A pharaoh?" Kendall asked.

"More important than a pharaoh," Raphael said.

"Who?" Kendall's green eyes twinkled like emeralds.

Raphael's jaw looked as if it had been set in concrete. "Moses."

Kendall gaped at him. "Moses in the Bible?"

"Yes," Raphael said.

"His body was never found," Nathan said. "Supposedly God buried it in Moab."

"We found it."

Kendall covered her mouth. "Nathan, that was Moses you shoved behind the sarcophagus. How is Moses a mummy?"

"The body was well preserved when we found it. We needed a place to keep it safe, somewhere it wouldn't be found. We had an empty sarcophagus already, and Moses was the adopted son of Pharaoh's daughter. It seemed a good fit."

"Appropriate. If I didn't know better, I'd think you had a sense of humor," Jake said.

"I don't," Raphael said.

"Do you want us to help you put him back?" Kendall asked.

"No." Raphael gave a frustrated sigh. "I will do it later. Shall we continue?" He led them from the room, down a narrow hall to a stone door covered in writing.

"What is this?" Nathan asked.

"Nothing that need concern you now," Raphael replied.

"Why am I not surprised?" Jake said.

The door had an unusual lock in the center, a round circle resembling a small shield. "What's with the Protettori and circles?" Jake asked.

"Circles represent completion, unity." He pushed the center of the stone and it moved back, exposing a smaller stone. This one had a hole. He removed his cross, inserted it into the hole, and the door opened. He turned to them, his face sober. "Proceed carefully. This is our most sacred area."

"More sacred than the room with Moses and the temple with the Fountain of Youth?"

"Yes." He stepped inside and they followed. This room was smaller, not as elaborate, but there was a feeling of reverence, as if they'd stepped into a cathedral. Wooden cases stood along the walls, but it wasn't apparent what they held.

They walked closer and looked in the first case. "What are those?" Kendall asked.

"Nails," Raphael said.

"What—" Kendall's question died as she touched the glass. She pulled in a breath. "*The* nails." She turned to Raphael with wide eyes.

"The nails," he said, his face growing more somber than usual.

"You mean the nails used for the crucifixion?" Nathan had moved beside Kendall and was standing quietly. "How did you get them?"

Another cryptic look on Raphael's face. "It's an old story." One he didn't seem inclined to tell.

He led them to more objects, things Jake hadn't even known still existed. Raphael paused by a case containing a crown, not jeweled as the one he'd seen in the other room. This one was made of thorns. Wicked, long thorns. They all stood before it in silence. Jake cringed at the thought of it being forced onto Christ's head, piercing his scalp, ripping flesh until it met his skull. The thorns looked darker than the rest of the crown. Blood? A tear rolled down Kendall's cheek. As disturbing as Jake's thoughts were, he couldn't imagine what she must be feeling. He wanted to touch her, but he didn't want to intrude, and if he were honest, he was leery about what he might see. More than once he'd sensed some of what she felt and saw while touching her. It was intense, and that was an understatement.

While he was wondering if he was a coward or just giving her space, she turned to Raphael, her expression confused. Raphael's eyes widened a bit, and then his face went blank. Quickly, he moved to another case. This one held part of a beam. It was rugged and stained with dark splotches.

"The cross," Kendall said. Her hands were shaking, and she clasped them in front of her.

"The cross." Raphael's voice was tight, his expression grave. "There are other pieces here and there, but this is the largest."

Emotions rolled over Kendall's face, and finally, with trembling lips, she turned away. "How did you get it?" She watched him as if the question were a test.

Raphael seemed uncomfortable, which meant he was sullen. "It would take a while to explain. We should finish the tour so I can check on the men."

"Fergus is probably going nuts," Nathan said.

Kendall looked tired. The relics were taking a toll on her. Jake had been touching her the first time she saw the crucifixion. He'd felt a bit of what she felt, but nothing compared to seeing it, experiencing it. He was starting to feel like he'd abandoned her by purposely trying not to imagine the horror, while Kendall couldn't help seeing it all.

Nathan had noticed the effect it was having on her as well and stayed close to Kendall. Jake took her hand in his. Her palm was cold and sweaty. She would need to rest after this.

"What's this?" Nathan asked, pointing to a cloth.

"The burial cloth." Raphael made the announcement without fanfare, as if it were just an old sheet.

"The Shroud of Turin?" Kendall asked.

"That shroud is a fake. This one is real." He showed them more objects, worn sandals, a bloody loincloth, and a whip that made Jake feel sick even though he couldn't experience what Kendall saw. Jake stood on one side of her and Nathan on the other as she silently wept. She had pulled her hand free of Jake's, and he didn't know whether it was to protect him or if she wanted to be alone.

She sniffed softly and they continued on, looking at holy relics most people would never view. Jake loved the search for treasure, and he enjoyed a good legend as much as anyone, but after his trip through the Protettori's relic rooms, he understood the passion and devotion that drove Kendall and Nathan.

"I've never seen so many holy relics," Jake said.

"We've spent centuries collecting and protecting them," Raphael said. "There are many who would misuse them. And as we know, some of them are extremely powerful." He moved on and pointed out several holy artifacts that had been kept in the abbey. "We had many relics there, but King Henry the Eighth wanted them for himself, so we had to hide them."

"Could he have taken the chalice?" Kendall asked. "You said you didn't actually see the Reaper take it."

"No, we still had it then. It must have been Luke. He's the only one who knew I had it. We were very close, traveling the world in search of relics and objects of power. One night I was injured on a journey, and as I slept, I revealed the secret of the chalice and the Fountain of Youth, that drinking the fountain's water from the chalice would give eternal life. Luke asked me about it when I awoke, and I had to lie to him. I told him I must have been rambling in my dreams. I trusted my brothers, but not with the knowledge of the fountain. I couldn't move the fountain, but it was too dangerous to keep the chalice nearby, so I moved it to a new hiding place, separating the two pieces. Not long after, Luke told me he was leaving the brotherhood. He'd fallen in love with a woman." Raphael's eyes clouded. "I knew he'd been acting strange. Luke confronted me about the chalice and the fountain. He knew I had lied. As I said, we were very close. He said he wanted to see them before he left. I refused and he got angry. He cursed me and the brotherhood. I took his cross and told him he didn't deserve to wear it." Raphael's stony face twitched with emotion. "I moved the chalice again, and he must have seen me bury it. After he left, I went to check on it and the chalice was gone. He must have taken it and then lost it sometime later."

"But if he knew what the real Holy Grail looked like, then why did he think the Blue Chalice could be the real thing?" Kendall asked.

"Maybe he forgot exactly what it looked like," Jake said. "He could have lost it a long time ago."

"Luke never came back?" Nathan asked.

"No. We took precautions and moved all the relics to new locations and increased our guards. We put sentinels in place, here and everywhere we had sacred relics, which allowed no one to pass without the Protettori's cross. I searched for Luke and the chalice over the centuries, but I never found him. We didn't see or hear from him until his men attacked us several years ago."

"How did they get inside?" Jake asked.

"Someone disarmed the statues. He must have been working with someone inside," Raphael said. "We never learned who it was, since almost everyone died in the attack."

"Leaving just you and Marco," Kendall said.

"And the Reaper," Raphael added. "Marco and I weren't here at the time. We had gone to move some of the relics to another location."

Nathan frowned. "How could the brotherhood not know about the fountain if they were drinking the water to stay strong?"

"They didn't know where the water came from. They knew it was holy water, given to them by me. I think some of them suspected it came from the Fountain of Youth, but they had no idea if it was a place or an object. They questioned me at times, and when necessary, I lied. Only one person besides Marco and I knew the location." Raphael's smile was sad. "But he died."

"King Arthur," Kendall said.

"Yes. King Arthur. He and I protected the fountain and the chalice."

"You knew him well?" Nathan asked.

Raphael studied Nathan for a moment. "Very well."

There were so many things Jake wanted to ask about King Arthur. He had been obsessed when he was a kid, but knowing that Nathan was connected to the legend made it awkward now.

"So the fountain was right there under the brotherhood's noses and no one knew about it but you, Marco, and King Arthur?" Jake asked, glancing at Nathan.

"And Luke," Raphael added. "But he didn't know where it was. If he finds the chalice before we do, we're all in trouble."

"If he does, and he drinks from the fountain and becomes eternal, would that really be the end of the world?" Jake asked.

"He turned his back on his vow to protect the relics, which in turn protects humanity. And he's looking for other powerful relics. I believe eternal youth is only one piece of his plan."

"Eternal youth and power," Jake said.

Raphael looked grim. "And more."

"More?" Jake asked.

"It's too soon to speak of that."

"You expect us to help you, but you're still holding out. This is like going on a mission without a sitrep," Jake said.

"This isn't the military, and you're not Protettori," Raphael said. "You'll get a situation report as you need it. For now we need to focus on the chalice."

Jake's fists clenched. He didn't like being kept in the dark, but what could he do? He couldn't force Raphael to talk, and though he might not be part of the Protettori like Kendall was, he was her protector, and by God he couldn't walk away and leave her here. It wasn't just a sense of duty. His jackass attempts to put her off and keep her at arm's length had backfired, and now he was in love.

"How many of the brotherhood were there before?" Nathan asked.

"At one time, there were dozens of us."

"That must have made it difficult to do your job," Nathan said. "Couldn't you have made some of the dead into sentinels, at least?"

"No. Guardians must be alive to become sentinels."

"That seems strange," Jake said. "They have to be alive to become stone."

"Where did you bury the ones who died?" Kendall asked.

"Some were put in the catacombs, some in the graveyard."

"Why have both?" Kendall asked.

"Originally the keepers were buried in the catacombs, and the guardians who chose to die were buried in the graveyard."

"My father and mother were buried outside the graveyard," Kendall said.

"Yes," Raphael said. "Your father was no longer part of the Protettori. It was out of respect that we buried them here at all. I know that must be hard to understand."

"Why did you bury my mother here?"

"Your father requested it, and out of respect for him, we allowed it. I think he wanted her here, where the Reaper couldn't touch her, even in death."

"In the vision I saw, she said she had betrayed my father. She was sent by the Reaper to seduce him."

"And she fell in love with your father," Raphael said. "That's part of the reason we agreed to bury her here. She did love him, even though she was sent by the Reaper. But you can see how we couldn't bury her, or later on him, in our consecrated ground."

"You mentioned the Reaper's child before," Kendall said. "So he does have a child? If he and my mother were that close . . ."

"It isn't you," Raphael said. "He had a son."

CHAPTER ELEVEN

Jake saw the relief in Kendall's eyes, and he was glad. Her fear that the Reaper was somehow her father had worried her more than she admitted. "Had? He's dead?" As old as the Reaper was, he could have generations of descendants running around.

"I don't know."

"Do you know who he was?" Jake asked. "You knew him better than anyone."

Raphael looked tired. "Obviously not. The man I thought I knew wouldn't have stolen our relics. He wouldn't have had his brothers slaughtered. I wonder if I ever knew him."

"If he attacked the castle, he must have thought you had the chalice?"

"We didn't."

"He killed his brothers to reclaim a chalice that you didn't have," Nathan said.

Raphael's eyes were sad. "Yes."

"Does he still believe you have it?" Kendall asked.

"I don't think so," Raphael said, "or he would have tried again. So now we have to find out who does."

"How do we even know that what we're searching for is the real Holy Grail?" Jake asked.

"I saw the chalice being used to catch Christ's blood," Kendall said.

"I know. I was there," Jake said. He hadn't seen everything she had, but he'd seen and felt enough to know it was real. "But that doesn't mean the artifact we're supposed to find—assuming this entire story is true—is the real Holy Grail." He needed to know they were on the right trail before he let Kendall risk her life on this bizarre quest.

"The legend is partially true," Raphael said. "The cup that Christ drank from at the Last Supper was priceless, even if it hadn't been used to catch Christ's blood. His enemies and his followers alike wanted it, so it had to be hidden. I assure you the chalice was buried there, and it was the Holy Grail."

"How can you be certain," Jake asked, "unless you saw it buried?"

Kendall's eyes flared. "It was you. You buried the chalice."

Everyone was silent for a brief, tense moment.

"Yes, I buried the chalice," Raphael said. "That's how I know it was the Holy Grail."

Nathan wasn't looking at the relics now. He was focused on Raphael. "You're Joseph?"

Raphael looked irritated. "No, I'm not Joseph. I told you, not all of the story is true."

"He's not Joseph," Kendall said quietly. "He was a Roman soldier. I saw him in my vision."

"You were a Roman soldier . . . at the crucifixion?" Jake had been with Kendall the first time she'd had a vision of the crucifixion. He'd experienced some strange things, but he hadn't seen Raphael. He hadn't seen any faces.

"I saw you when I looked at the nails," Kendall said. "You looked different then. You didn't have the tattoos and long hair."

Raphael looked as stony as the statues outside the castle, and then his tattoos twitched. "I wasn't a soldier. I was a centurion."

Kendall's and Nathan's jaws dropped as if they'd met a rock star. "A centurion," Kendall said. "You're Longinus."

"Who's Longinus?" Jake asked, though he thought he'd heard the name before.

Nathan's face was almost glowing. "He was *the* centurion, the one who presided over the crucifixion of Christ."

"You crucified Jesus?" Jake knew the story in the Bible. After witnessing all the horrors that had been inflicted on Jesus, the centurion had seen nothing but love and forgiveness. In the final moments, when Jesus cried out in despair and died, and lightning flashed from heaven and ripped the veil in the temple from top to bottom, something not humanly possible, the centurion had realized his error, that this poor insurgent he'd crucified, the man they mocked as King of the Jews, was in fact the Son of God, not some local troublemaker that Rome needed to silence.

Raphael's expression was dark. "I didn't know who he was. Not until it was too late."

"And you've been trying to make it right ever since," Kendall said. "You started the brotherhood. You were the one who first gathered the relics."

Raphael's gaze focused on the piece of the cross. "I didn't intend to. I took the spear as a reminder of what I had done. The other relics came over the years. I had helped Joseph take . . . the body down and bury it, and I protected him. His support of Jesus had been a secret until then, and he was in danger for publicly helping. Joseph and I became friends. Even though I had taken part in the crucifixion, Joseph knew I had done so in ignorance. Those were troubled times. The disciples were afraid for their lives. They were confused. After the body disappeared, there were those who would have destroyed anything connected to Christ, and then others who wanted anything that could be used as a reminder of faith. Joseph was afraid someone would steal the chalice and destroy it . . . or use it. It was still stained with Christ's blood, and he believed it was blessed. I didn't believe him—not then—but I was his friend, so I agreed. He asked me to return it to the place where he had traveled with Jesus when he was a boy. They had found a cave there. Joseph was thirsty, but they had no water. Jesus touched the wall, and a spring started to flow from the rock."

Kendall's face was glowing with excitement. "Jesus made the Fountain of Youth when he was a boy?"

Raphael nodded. "So Joseph said, and I believe him. I made a vow to him that I would return the chalice and hide it there." Raphael frowned. "It took a long while to keep my promise to Joseph. Along the journey I noticed that there were unusual things about the relics."

"Like?" Kendall asked.

"I could feel their power. I was becoming stronger. Joseph was right. The chalice was blessed. So were the other relics. If anyone had found out the power the objects held, it could have caused untold trouble. I had to keep them hidden. That became my mission. I found the entrance to the cave just as Joseph had said and the fountain of water flowing from the wall. I hid the chalice there, and I carved a bowl of stone to catch the water. Later, I made the cave into a temple, a place where I could go and reflect on my life, on the gravity of my sins." Raphael paused. "I discovered that the water was even more powerful than I had thought. I wasn't aging. I knew it was crucial that I keep it hidden."

Jake shook his head, still trying to process that Raphael was the centurion in the Bible who had presided over the crucifixion of Christ.

"Did you drink from the chalice?"

Raphael paused. "Yes."

"Then you're . . ." Kendall's green eyes sparked, but she didn't finish the thought either.

"Going to live a very long time," Raphael said.

"You're bloody eternal," Nathan said.

"Eternal is a complicated word," Raphael said. "No one knows if such a thing exists for humans."

Jake laughed, but without humor. "You're over two thousand years old, and you look like you're twenty-five. You died here at the castle. Kendall and I both saw you, and now you're alive. I'd say that's a pretty good indication."

"Not everything is as it seems."

"That could be the Protettori mantra," Jake said.

"So the Chalice Well and White Springs didn't come from the chalice being buried as legend says?" Kendall asked.

"The legends are only partially true. The Chalice Well and the White Springs come from the same spring as the Fountain of Youth, and they have some mild healing properties, but not like the actual fountain."

"You built the temple alone?" Nathan asked. "You said no one else knew about it. Don't tell me you killed everyone who knew about it . . . Bloody hell. You did."

"I did what I had to do to protect the objects."

It was harsh, but Jake understood. Sometimes in the course of things, hard choices had to be made.

"My experience with the relics convinced me that I had to keep them hidden, and there were many more relics that needed to be found. I couldn't do it alone, so I found men who were worthy, and I established the brotherhood."

"What about women?" Kendall asked, frowning.

"Things were different then," Raphael said. "But there have been a few women who helped me along the way." His eyes clouded again. "Strong women." He took a breath as if separating himself from that thought. "Eventually, the brotherhood flourished in secret. Many were monks, and we helped build the abbey and hid among them. Now, I have only you to help me. Marco is old, his memory fading."

"We will help you," Kendall said, her face fierce as a warrior. "We will find the Holy Grail."

"We need to start quickly," Raphael said. "We have lost a lot of time."

They left the room, and Jake looked back at the relics, hidden and protected for so long. "I can't believe you're the centurion."

"That was a long time ago. Now I'm Raphael."

No wonder he'd looked so mad when Jake had called him Attila the Hun. Romans hated Attila.

"There's a statue of you at St. Peter's Basilica," Nathan said.

Raphael made a sound of derision. "I've seen it. It's not a good likeness."

"The legends say you died a martyr," Kendall said.

"The legends were wrong. I'm going to check on the men."

"I'll go too," Jake said. "I would pay to see Fergus with them."

"Gentlemen!" Fergus raised his voice, but the men weren't listening. They were all asking questions, most of which he didn't understand. They wanted more food. More drink. They wanted out of this room. They were confused. And rude. All the things he'd done for Nathan—protecting him, sheltering him, keeping him healthy and sane—had been a walk in the park compared to this. He was going to suggest a long vacation after they got rid of this abominable Reaper.

"What are you then?" the big blond man asked, touching the lapel of Fergus's suit.

Fergus discreetly pulled back. "A butler."

"What's that?"

"I take care of things."

"For the king, eh?"

"The king?"

"King Arthur?"

He'd forgotten about that. Raphael had mentioned something about the men thinking Nathan was King Arthur. "Yes, the king." Perhaps if they believed that, they would leave him alone.

But they didn't. They crowded around him, eating, burping, and asking questions. His head pounded, and he took one of his headache pills and washed it down with a large swallow of water, wishing it was something stronger.

"Where does one piss in this place?" the bald man asked.

Fergus walked to the wall and pointed to a large mixing bowl he'd borrowed from the kitchen. He hoped the cook had another because this one was out of service permanently. "We've brought a chamber pot." He tried—unsuccessfully, he feared—not to grimace. "You can place it around the corner until other arrangements are made." Dear God, where was Raphael?

Finally the din died down and the men sat down or lay on the floor. They seemed tired. Perhaps eating after hundreds of years of stillness had a tiring effect on the body. Slowly, the room filled with the sounds of sleep, snoring and worse. Fergus sat on a stone bench of some sort—he hoped it wasn't an altar—and closed his eyes.

Raphael led Kendall, Nathan, and Jake back to the room where the men were being held. He opened the lock and they stepped inside. The room was empty. Fergus was lying stiff as a board on a stone surface, fast asleep.

"Fergus!" Raphael roared.

Fergus shot up off the bench, every hair in place, not a wrinkle in his suit. "Yes." He looked around the room and blinked. "What happened? Where are they?"

"You tell me," Raphael said.

"I don't know. I fell asleep." He looked frantic.

"Did you drink the water?" Raphael shouted.

"Yes," Fergus said.

"It contained a strong sedative."

Fergus's mouth dropped open. "And you didn't think to warn me?"

"I didn't expect you to share drink with them."

"I had a headache." Fergus's voice rose above his normal, controlled tone. "I needed water to take my pill."

Raphael rubbed his forehead, his brows tense. "We must find them."

"Is it such a problem?" Fergus asked. "They're odd, and irritating, but they're just men."

"They are rogues. I put them to sleep because I couldn't kill them."

Fergus's eyes bugged out. "And you left me here, defenseless, with those monsters?" he yelled.

Raphael looked surprised. Fergus didn't often get rattled. "That's why I sedated them."

Fergus's face was so red it looked like it might explode. "I'm going to my bed. You can find these bloody rogues yourself."

"What is that smell?" Kendall asked.

"That's the mixing bowl," Fergus said, his shoulders stiff as he marched from the room.

"What do you mean, you put them to sleep because you couldn't kill them?" Nathan asked. "I knew they were unstable but . . ."

"They went rogue. They were out of control," Raphael said.

"You have rogue sentinels?" Jake asked.

"Rogue guardians. They were never intended to be sentinels to continue their work in statue form. I merely turned them to stone to keep them out of trouble. Sometimes living so long can have a negative effect. It can become tiresome just existing for so many centuries. Some guardians turned to drink or lost sight of their mission. If one of them got out of control, they had to be put to rest."

"How do you keep the rogues from becoming sentinels?" Nathan asked. "For that matter, what makes the guardians turn into sentinels?"

"A guardian who chooses to become a sentinel takes a vow . . . and other things take place. A ceremony."

"What kind of ceremony?" Kendall asked.

"That doesn't matter now. We have to find these rogues."

"They couldn't have vanished," Jake said. "Unless they found your unfinished portal." That caused a few moments of chaos, until they found a clue—a sandwich crust near a far wall.

"The bolt-hole," Raphael said. "They found the bolt-hole. I forgot about it."

"Do all the rooms have bolt-holes?" Nathan asked.

"No. But this one hasn't been used in centuries. It's not stable." He gritted his teeth. "I hope it collapsed on them." He pulled out his dagger and dug at a stone near the sandwich crust. There was a clicking sound and two stones slid back, leaving an opening in the floor similar to the one in the temple that led to the fountain.

"Where does it lead?" Jake asked.

"To the railroad. Damn Marco. Why did he wake them?" Raphael looked like he wanted to take someone's head off. "I'll check out the bolt-hole. You find Marco. Have the guards search the castle and grounds."

Raphael grimaced and started down into the hole. There appeared to be steps.

"Don't you need a flashlight?" Jake asked.

"No."

"You can see in the dark?" Nathan asked.

Raphael's eyes lightened until they were so pale they glowed. "So can you," he said as he disappeared.

"That's nice," Jake said, his voice flat. "You can see in the dark too."

Kendall threw him a warning glance.

Nathan found Hank and had the guard and his men start searching for Marco. "Let's check his room again. Maybe he's in bed now."

"I'm getting worried that no one's seen him in hours," Kendall said.

"He reminds me of my grandmother," Jake said. "She had Alzheimer's there at the end. Her memory came and went. Half the time she didn't know who she was. She talked crazy shit, sometimes wandered around the neighborhood."

They found Marco's room unlocked. He wasn't there, and his bed—a four-poster that looked like something from the dark ages—showed no signs of being used.

"Look at this place," Kendall said. "This furniture is old, really old. I can't begin to date it." In addition to her expertise with relics, Kendall knew a lot about antiques.

"Like Marco," Jake said. "Where could he be?"

They moved around the room, looking at the heavy pieces of furniture, hoping for some clue. Kendall turned with a worried frown. "I don't think he's been here for a while."

"Is that your sixth sense talking?" Jake asked.

"Maybe. I just can't feel him here. Not that my sixth sense has been on track lately. I hope he's not wandering around outside. His memory comes and goes. He could be lost."

"The guards haven't seen him," Nathan said.

"Marco probably has ways in and out of this place that we don't know about," Jake said, feeling Kendall's sense of alarm. "Look for his suitcase."

"I'll check the closet," Kendall said. "No suitcase, but he has a lot of robes, and one pair of jeans."

"Marco in jeans?" Jake lifted a brow. "That's hard to picture." Even harder was the tighty-whities he found in a dresser. He didn't show the others. It felt too irreverent.

Nathan was checking the top of the closet, where Kendall was too short to reach. "He'd probably be as young as Raphael if he hadn't stopped drinking the water."

"Was he old when you and Nathan were here as kids?" Jake asked.

Kendall tucked a robe back into place. "He was younger, but not a lot. He must have stopped drinking the water before then. But I glimpsed him as a much younger man in a vision the first time I met him, when Jake and I were locked up in your hotel."

Nathan frowned at the memory. "I'd like to know why he stopped drinking. It must be some sort of punishment."

"Self-imposed?" Jake asked. "What could he have done to deserve that? Maybe Marco's the Reaper's son."

"I seriously doubt it." Kendall bent and looked under the bed.

Jake saw Nathan glance at her ass. He cleared his throat and when Nathan looked up, Jake lifted a brow.

Nathan's jaw tightened. "I don't see a suitcase."

"It's not here either," Kendall said.

"I don't think he's at the castle any longer," Jake said, voicing what he felt in his gut.

"This doesn't feel right," Nathan said.

"Look at this." Kendall held up a map that was lying on a heavy antique desk. "Looks like he was planning on going somewhere."

Jake and Nathan crowded close, staring at the map. Jake cursed.

"What?" Kendall asked.

"It's a map of Prague. That's where the Reaper's portal led."

CHAPTER TWELVE

P RAGUE." RAPHAEL STOOD IN THE DOORWAY. HIS TATTOOS contrasted with his pale face like ink on a newspaper.

Jake pointed to the map. "Marco's suitcase is missing and he has a map of Prague."

Raphael walked inside, his face bleak. "Marco's going after the Reaper. We have to stop him before he gets killed."

"We can take the jet," Nathan said. "I'll check with the guards again to make sure no one's seen him before we go rushing off after him."

"No." Raphael shook his head. "I'll go to Prague and look for the Reaper while you start searching for the chalice."

"You're still injured," Kendall said. "You shouldn't be alone."

"It's more important that you are protected," Raphael said. "The Reaper needs you to find the chalice."

"We'll protect her," Nathan said, sharing a look with Jake that said at least on this they agreed. Each of them would die for Kendall.

"I suggest you start searching for the chalice immediately," Raphael said. "Let Nathan's guards look for the rogues, wherever they are."

"No sign of them?" Jake asked.

Raphael shook his head. "I don't want them exposed to the public, but we can't waste time looking for them. I'm afraid for Marco."

It was obvious to Jake that Raphael cared for the old man. "Nathan's guards are good. They'll find them."

Nathan looked a little surprised at the admission from Jake. "Should I tell the guards who the men really are?"

"No," Raphael said. "I'd rather they continue to think the men are my friends."

"Your old, crazy friends who don't even speak like modern men," Jake added. "They'll probably buy it. You're not exactly normal."

"We don't even know where to start looking for the chalice," Kendall said.

"You'll find it," Raphael said.

"You sound sure," Jake said. "Do you know something we don't?"

Raphael studied Kendall, his expression soft. "I trust her."

Jake didn't like the way he said it. It wasn't the words, it was the possessive way he'd said them. He hoped Raphael wasn't falling for her too. Jake already had enough competition in Nathan . . . King Arthur. What the hell . . .

"You were considering killing her just a couple of hours ago."

"I explained that already," Raphael said, walking to the door. "I must depart."

"Are you strong enough to travel?" Kendall asked.

"I have to be."

"Don't you need more water before you go?" Jake asked.

"We all do," Raphael said. "This is going to be dangerous." They followed him to the room where the water was kept.

"This is where I saw the vials," Kendall said as she passed the round table. "I don't suppose this table was used by King Arthur?"

"It was," Raphael said. "This was a scaled down version of the original." He found the vials Kendall had discovered and handed one to each of them. "Later, we'll have a ceremony, but for now, carry this with you."

"What kind of ceremony?" Nathan asked.

"A confirmation." Raphael opened his vial and took a drink of water.

"What do we do with the water?" Kendall asked. "Drink if we're injured?"

"Drink some now," Raphael said. "Save the rest for if you need it."

"It's a Protettori first-aid kit," Jake said. He turned up the vial and took a drink. The water left a strange sensation as it rolled over his tongue and down his throat. He felt . . . more. More alive. More alert.

"Wow," Kendall said. She looked like she'd jumped off a cliff and landed on her feet.

Her senses probably heightened the sensations of taking her first drink of water. "Intense?"

She looked at the vial. "I feel like I could fly."

"Don't take too much," Raphael said. "It can be dangerous."

"Raphael, I know you have confidence in my abilities, but do you have any ideas about where we should start in our search?" Kendall said.

"Start with Luke's journal. He's been searching for the Holy Grail for a long time. I'm sure he will have notes, probably in code, on what he's discovered. That may eliminate some false leads. Trust your instincts." Raphael took another drink of water. "Happy hunting," he said and disappeared through the mural on the wall.

Kendall laid the journal on the round table, thinking how incredible it was that King Arthur had used it. She wondered which seat he had used, and briefly considered trying to find out. Then Nathan sat next to her. She looked at him and felt light-headed, thinking that he could have some part of King Arthur in him. She didn't understand reincarnation, had never believed in it, and wasn't sure she did now, but there had to be some explanation for all this. If Nathan was King Arthur, she and Jake had betrayed him. While she had been married to Arthur, she'd fallen in love with Lancelot. And had an affair with him, if her visions were correct. Poor Nathan.

"Do I have dirt on my face?" he asked.

She shook her head, feeling guilty and sad. "No. Just thinking."

"Want to share?" Jake sat next to her.

Kendall looked from him to Nathan, her thoughts whirling. She couldn't explain *that* part of her thoughts, but she could discuss the rest. "What if it's true?" She didn't need to explain her question. They knew what she meant. "Here we are sitting where they probably sat." Although that may not have been true for Guinevere. Women were treated so poorly in those days, being looked at as property, and worse. But *they* hadn't treated her that way. Kendall froze. Holy crap. Were those her thoughts? Or Guinevere's?

"Can anyone else join that conversation going on in your head?" Jake asked.

Nathan grinned. "She's always been like this."

That made Jake frown, and then Nathan too, as he realized what he'd said.

"Sorry, I was just . . ."

"I know," Jake said. "It's a lot to believe. King Arthur and the Holy Grail, the Fountain of Youth, Christ's crucifixion. I feel like I'm stuck in one of my screwed-up dreams." He put his elbows on the table, and Kendall wondered if Lancelot had ever sat that way. He grinned. "Hell, maybe you guys aren't even here."

Nathan reached around Kendall and knocked Jake's arm out from under him. "That answer your question?"

Kendall was afraid he'd hit Nathan back, but instead he snorted. "Thanks, Arthur. I guess if it's a dream, we're all in it."

Nathan leaned back in his chair, his brow in a puzzled frown. "I still don't see the whole King Arthur thing. And Guinevere and Lancelot. It's too far-fetched."

Jake and Kendall shared a quick, knowing glance. They had both seen King Arthur in Kendall's vision, and each had commented on his resemblance to Nathan. Jake ran a finger along a scar on the table. He almost seemed to follow it without looking. *Had he made it?* Kendall wondered.

"Like statues that used to be alive and a guardian who's two thousand years old," Jake said.

Kendall ignored the intoxicating male scents wafting from either side of her and focused on the smell of old leather. She knew some things about the journal. It had belonged to a man, but that was no surprise. It was high-quality leather, handmade. She knew the shop where it had been purchased. Not where, but she could see the interior of the shop. She could even glimpse handwriting at times and smell the ink. But those things didn't tell her who the Reaper was or where the chalice was hidden.

Jake and Nathan watched her, their faces anxious, waiting for her to find some clue. She'd just drunk the water. Raphael said that would help her sixth sense, but it hadn't revealed the journal's secrets so far. Maybe she needed more water. Turning to the sketches, she studied them again. There were four drawings, four relics. The first one was the Spear of Destiny. The second one was the bowl from the Fountain of Youth. The third one was also a bowl or a cup, but smaller. This was the chalice, the Holy Grail that she'd seen cradled in Christ's hand at the Last Supper, and later, clutched in Joseph's as he knelt at the foot of the cross, catching drops of Jesus's blood. Like the bowl in the Fountain of Youth, the chalice wasn't fancy. Just an old wooden cup.

The fourth sketch was faded, hard to make out. One thing at a time. Kendall looked at the third picture again. She put her fingertip on it and tried to concentrate, to pick up a hint of anything that might help. She flinched.

"Did you get something?" Nathan asked.

"I saw you."

Nathan's brows rose. "Me?"

"Adam." Just a quick flash of him as a boy. "Maybe you're supposed to figure it out." She handed him the journal. "You were good with languages. Part of this is written in Latin, some Italian, some very old English, and some in code."

Nathan didn't deny that he was Adam. After his memory at the grave, maybe he was beginning to believe it. Nathan took the book. He had nice fingers, and Kendall found herself trying to picture Adam's hands. They had usually been dusty.

Nathan sniffed the journal.

"What are you doing?" Jake asked.

Nathan shrugged, and a hint of smile touched his lips. "I'm not sure." He flipped through the pages of writing and sketches. "I think the answers are in here if we could figure them out. The Reaper must have found clues about who stole the chalice from him."

"I can't imagine anyone powerful enough to steal from the Reaper," Kendall said.

"It doesn't take power," Jake said. "The Reaper couldn't have kept it with him all the time, and half the world is searching for it. What do you know about the chalice, Nathan? You must have looked for it. Every other collector has."

Nathan turned another page. "I checked out the common legends, explored a couple of them, but never found anything that seemed legitimate." He frowned at the page. "There's an indention here." It was on one of the pages near the sketches. He tilted it to the light. "I can't make it out. Anyone got a pencil and paper?"

Kendall found a pencil and scrap of paper. Nathan laid it over the page and softly began to make a rubbing. Shapes started to emerge. "Those are letters," Kendall said.

When he was finished, he held it up, and they all studied it. "It's a name," Nathan said. "Maryanne."

"Who's Maryanne?" Kendall asked. She touched the rubbing, trying to pick up something. She didn't see anything, but she felt an overwhelming sense of dread.

"Get anything?" Nathan asked.

"No, but I felt something. Fear. What do you think that means?" She looked at Jake and saw him staring as if in a trance. "What do you think?"

"I don't know." He shook his head. "I think we need to get out of this room. Feels like it's closing in."

"Why don't you go down and get some drinks," Nathan said. "We'll keep working."

Jake nodded, which surprised her after the scene at the graveyard. He seemed to be watching her closer than usual.

He left the room, and Kendall and Nathan bent back over the journal. There were references to the Fountain of Life, which they assumed was the Fountain of Youth. What they needed was some reference to the Holy Grail.

Jake came back with refreshments a few minutes later. "Any luck?"

"No." Nathan blew out a sigh and rubbed his shoulders.

"Too bad we can't just blink and go where we want like Raphael. We're stuck with flying or using outdated portals—" Jake stopped, and a half grin touched his lips. "Hell, I can't believe I said that."

They all chuckled, and she and Nathan continued poring over the journal. Jake started exploring the room. He was examining a particularly valuable parchment, which was making Kendall nervous. "Don't touch that. You might accidentally destroy something."

"Want me to go blow something up while you two play with the journal?" His sarcasm was a cover for frustration. He didn't have the same appreciation for rare objects that she and Adam—Nathan—had. Jake was a great treasure hunter, she had no doubts, but he didn't have the patience for the small details.

"No, we need you here." She smiled and let her eyes tell him that *she* needed him here.

His face relaxed, and he continued to wander the room as she and Nathan studied the journal.

"What do you make of this?" Kendall asked. It was a word. The first letter was faded. The last three were *u-l-a.*

Nathan studied the word. "Maybe an *a. A-u-l-a.* That's Latin for *palace.*"

"Palace?" As in the palace of a prince. Kendall looked at Jake, who was studying a crown that she seriously hoped he wasn't considering trying on.

"Palace." Jake frowned and put the crown back. His face looked stiff. "The one in Iraq, I would assume."

Kendall tapped the pencil on her jaw. "We know the Reaper was in Iraq looking for relics, and Thomas told Brandi the Reaper was really searching for the Holy Grail. So he must have had reason to believe the prince had the chalice."

"Didn't the Iraqis accuse you of stealing the relics?" Nathan asked, eyeing Jake with a suspicious gleam.

Jake sat down next to Kendall again. "What now? You think I've had the Holy Grail all this time. You remember I was in prison."

"Of course he doesn't have the Holy Grail," Kendall said, daring Nathan to say differently. "But if the Reaper didn't find the chalice, either the prince didn't have it or someone else took it."

"Who?" Nathan asked.

"Thomas?" Jake said.

Nathan rubbed his chin, which Kendall noted that, like Jake's, needed a shave. "Wouldn't he have told his sister that he had the Holy Grail if that's what he and Brandi spent so many years searching for?"

"Maybe Thomas didn't know what he had," Kendall said. "Was there anyone else who could have stolen it?"

"As far as I know, the Reaper and Thomas were the only ones who came out alive," Jake said.

"And you," Nathan added.

"Well, I don't have the chalice, and the Reaper doesn't seem to either. That leaves Thomas."

"We need to find Brandi," Kendall said.

"I have her number," Nathan said.

"How'd you get her number?" Kendall asked.

"I had my research team retrieve it."

"Is that legal?" Kendall asked.

"Legalities aren't on my radar right now," Nathan said.

Jake nodded. "This is about—"

"Survival," Kendall finished with him. "Well, let's call Brandi and tell her that her brother may have been hiding something from her."

"You'd better call," Nathan said. "She freaks out around me."

"I'll call," Kendall said.

"Let me." Jake pulled out his phone. "I think Kendall freaks her out too, after that episode in the temple. I can put the fear of God into her, but in a more human way." Jake called Brandi's number and told her that they needed to meet. "You won't believe where she is," he said after he hung up. "The inn."

Kendall looked surprised. "Our inn?" she said, and then caught Nathan's frown. "The inn where we stayed?"

"The very one," Jake said.

"You think she's been following us?" Kendall asked.

"I'd bet my stock in Microsoft that she has," Nathan said.

Brandi didn't wait at the inn as she'd been told to do. She waltzed right up to the castle's railroad tunnel and demanded to see Nathan. Six armed guards escorted her at gunpoint to the library and waited until Nathan, Kendall, and Jake arrived. Unfortunately, Raphael got there first. He was looming over Brandi, who was backed up to the wall. She was wearing a pair of jeans that looked like she'd slept in them, and the sleeve of her purple shirt was torn. The guards looked undecided about who they should protect.

"What the hell?" Nathan said to the frightened redhead. "My guards could have shot you."

"Raphael could have squashed you like a bug," Jake added.

"What is she doing here?" Raphael demanded. "She refuses to speak to me."

"We called her," Kendall said quickly. "She has information we need."

"This is unacceptable," Raphael said. "This castle isn't a Holiday Inn."

"Why didn't you stay at the inn?" Jake asked.

"I had to get away," Brandi said. "Someone's been following me."

"It's usually the other way around," Nathan said.

Jake scratched his head. "So what, you led them to us?"

"No. I lost them."

"Who were they?" Nathan asked.

"There were two men. But one of them looked familiar." Brandi hesitated, as if she couldn't believe what she was about to say. "I think it was Thomas."

CHAPTER THIRTEEN

T HOMAS IS DEAD," KENDALL SAID.

"I know. I buried him, but I swear it was him. Can that be possible?" Brandi looked both frightened and hopeful.

Kendall thought about the rogues who had been stone for centuries and were now breathing, flesh and blood . . . and wandering around God knew where.

"Things don't always stay dead," Jake said, as if he'd read her thoughts.

"What are you saying, that he's some kind of zombie?" Brandi looked horrified.

"He could have faked his death."

"Oh no, he wouldn't do that to me after what happened to our parents," she said.

"Maybe he had no choice," Jake said. "You said his cover was blown. The Reaper knew who he was. Maybe he wanted the Reaper to think he was dead. Dead men can't be killed."

"No." Brandi shook her head, but she looked unsure.

"Where were the two men?" Nathan asked.

"At the inn. I saw them watching the place. They weren't being obvious, but I've learned a few things about tracking someone."

"You've gotten a lot of practice following us," Nathan said.

Brandi scowled at him. "I'm in this just as much as you are."

"But with different goals," Nathan said.

"Don't you two start fighting over the relics," Kendall said. "Let's find them first. Then we can figure out whether to save them or destroy them."

Jake scratched his head. "You two should be a little more sympathetic. The Reaper probably killed both your fathers."

Brandi gave Nathan a surprised glance. "He killed your father?"

"I suspect he did," Nathan said. "My father's collection was one of the best in the world. I'm sure the Reaper knew about it."

"Your fathers must have known each other," Jake said. "They probably fought over relics." He gave a short laugh. "Guess you're carrying on in their stead."

"Did Thomas say anything more about the Holy Grail?" Kendall asked Brandi. "He must have heard the Reaper mention something."

"The last time I spoke to him, he was frightened. He said this thing with the Reaper went deeper than he had thought. He must have discovered something else."

"Like the Holy Grail," Jake said. "Maybe the reason the Reaper couldn't find it was that Thomas had already taken it."

"No. He would have told me if he'd gotten hold of something that important."

"I don't think he told you a lot of things," Jake said.

"He may not have known what he had," Kendall said.

"He didn't have it on him when he died," Nathan said. "He had the journal in his bag, but nothing else."

"The Spear of Destiny had already been stolen from his bag," Jake said. "Who's to say he didn't have the Holy Grail too?"

"We're still at square one," Kendall said.

"We need to go back to the source," Nathan said.

"Please tell me we're not going to Iraq," Kendall said.

"We may not need to," Nathan said. "Do you have Thomas's bag?" he asked Brandi.

"Not with me, but I still have it. Why?"

"For Kendall."

"Ah, she's going to play bloodhound," Jake said, catching on to Nathan's train of thought. "It's about time your sixth sense astounded us."

"There's a problem," Brandi said. "The bag's in Washington, DC."

"No problem," Jake said. "Billionaire boy has a jet."

"So this is how the other half travels?" Brandi said, touching the plush leather of the seat.

"You think his jet is nice, you should see his mansion," Jake said, dropping into a seat next to Kendall's.

Nathan frowned and sat opposite them. Brandi gave him a wary look. "I don't bite," he said.

"But don't startle him," Jake said.

Kendall reprimanded him with a playful slap on his hand, and then let her hand rest next to his. He could feel the warmth from her fingers and couldn't stop his from slipping over hers. She didn't pull away. Ignoring Nathan's solid stare, he started forming a battle plan.

They would go to DC and search Thomas's house. No one was certain that Thomas had the chalice, but he had stolen the Reaper's journal, and he had taken the Spear of Destiny from the Reaper's thieves in Italy. It was as good a place to start as any. Better than most, considering they had squat to go on. Kendall and Brandi fell asleep on the way. Better to rest now, Jake thought. Sleep could be a rare thing until they found the chalice.

Nathan left to talk to the pilot. Jake could hear him talking to his security guards and tech team. They were trying to identify where in Prague the Reaper may be living since Raphael still couldn't remember much about his trip through the portal with his former comrade. The guardian had been ready to collapse and had used all his mental focus to get back to the fountain.

Jake called Clint, his military buddy who was house-sitting for him after a recent break-in. No one had come back, but Clint said he felt like someone was watching him.

Jake turned to Nathan, who had returned to his seat while Jake was on the phone. "Did you bug my damned house?"

"No."

"Nothing inside at all?" Jake asked.

"Nothing." Nathan closed his eyes.

"It's not bugged," Clint said. "I checked that. Couldn't find anything, but this place makes my hair stand. I'd rather be back in Afghanistan fighting the Taliban."

"Maybe the house doesn't like you." Jake laughed, but Clint didn't.

"Damn place is messing with my head. Either you've got a carbon monoxide leak—didn't think to check that—I'm losing my mind, or you've got a ghost."

A ghost? Who the hell would be haunting him? Unless his grandmother was still there. But he wasn't going to admit that to Clint. He told him to leave. If the Reaper was watching his house, he didn't want Clint anywhere around. If the house was vandalized or destroyed, so be it. With everything else going on, his house didn't seem so important. Jake put his phone away and looked at Kendall, who was still sleeping. He needed a few hours' rest himself, so he could be up to this task. Taking on a two-thousand-year-old man wasn't going to be a walk in the park.

CHAPTER FOURTEEN

T HE DRIVE FROM THE AIRPORT INTO WASHINGTON, DC, passed quickly, and the stately buildings lining the streets faded behind them as they headed into a residential area of town houses.

"Turn here." Brandi pointed out a small one-way street. "Thomas's town house is at the end. I have a spare key. I used to visit him sometimes when he wasn't traveling."

"We'd better park down the street," Jake said. "The Reaper could be watching the house."

"I don't think he knows about it. It's not in Thomas's name. He was paranoid about that stuff. He used a fake name, no lease, paid cash. The landlord was probably some kind of drug lord, but Thomas needed somewhere private and safe. Damned relics."

"Have you always hated them?" Kendall asked.

"I loved them when I was a kid. The ones my father would let me see. Thomas did too. His dream was to follow in his footsteps. But afterward . . . we couldn't even bear to mention relics and antiquities. You don't know what it's like seeing your family murdered."

"You saw it?" Kendall asked.

Brandi nodded. "We found the bodies."

"I'm so sorry." Kendall put her hand over Brandi's.

At least she remembered them. Jake had nothing, just some mixed-up dreams about a grave. The same damned grave he'd dreamed about all his life. "Was your father's entire collection stolen?"

"All of it."

"I remember it," Nathan said. "I was interested in buying it just before he died."

"When was this?" Jake asked.

"I don't know, maybe seven years ago."

"You were collecting relics back then?" Jake asked.

"I've always loved relics, even when I was a kid."

So had Kendall. And Adam. Nathan was remembering his life before. Jake wished he could remember his. He and Nathan had more in common than just their feelings for Kendall. They both had blank spots in their pasts.

"Did your father buy from the black market?" Kendall asked.

Brandi shrugged. "I wouldn't know. He may have bought some things illegally, but I know his collection was the envy of the relic community. He had a lot of rivals. There was always a race to find the rarest object, and then a battle to see who could win the bid. He was really excited in the weeks before he died. He'd found something important and was worried about two other bidders. I believe one of them must have been the Reaper."

Jake scratched his jaw. "Wonder what the object was?"

"You mean you wonder if it was the Holy Grail?" Nathan asked.

Jake lifted a shoulder. "Obviously the Reaper lost it at some point. Someone had it. The prince got it somewhere. Maybe he was the second bidder."

"I remember my father telling my mother that he would need enough money to beat royalty. I thought he was joking. If the Reaper killed my parents to get the Holy Grail, maybe the prince stole it from the Reaper. Then the Reaper hired you to get him into the prince's palace to steal it back."

"Sounds like a chess game," Jake said.

The town house was in a middle-class section of town. The yards were small, the buildings old. Thomas's looked blank. No personality.

"I assume he didn't spend much time here," Nathan said as they approached the front door.

"More than you would think. But he wasn't really living." Brandi pulled out a key and opened the front door.

It looked more like an office than a home. There was an old couch, a chair, a desk, a computer, and maps everywhere. Europe. Asia.

"I told you he was obsessed," Brandi said.

"Knowing his sister, I'm not surprised," Nathan said.

"Like you're not obsessed about anything," Brandi said, glancing at Kendall.

Nathan scowled at her. "Where do we start?"

"Here." She walked over to a bookshelf that held magazines— *National Geographic* and travel guides among them—as well as an old set of encyclopedias that looked like they'd never been used. She pushed a section of books, and the shelf started to turn, revealing a door. "This is where he kept most of his research." She stepped into the room, and the others followed. Brandi walked over to a desk and turned on a green banker's lamp.

The room was small, with dark walls covered in more maps. A long table was pushed against the wall. It was littered with papers and a few candy bar wrappers. Brandi sighed. "He loved junk food." She cleared her throat. "Any files should be here in the desk. He kept pretty good notes."

"What about the computer?" Nathan asked. "Or a laptop."

"He didn't trust computers. He kept that one but rarely used it."

"How did the Reaper contact him?" Jake asked.

"He didn't say. By phone, I would guess."

They found a notebook that contained a page of names. "These must have been his Reaper suspects," Jake said.

"He started looking for the Reaper a few years ago. He researched the biggest collectors, even from a few decades ago. He didn't know how old the Reaper was. If someone was interested in relics, he went on Thomas's list."

"Your name's probably here," Jake said to Nathan.

Nathan tilted his head and examined the book. "Blimey. It is."

"Are you the Reaper?" Brandi asked with a tilt of her lips. "Maybe that explains those eyes."

Nathan frowned and continued scanning the list. His finger stopped underneath a name, and his frown deepened.

"John Whitmore," Jake said, following Nathan's index finger.

"That's Uncle John," Kendall said. "And my dad's here too. William Morgan."

"Was he a collector?" Jake asked.

"Somewhat, but he was more involved in the archaeological side of things. He handled the digging. Uncle John handled the finds."

"Thomas made notes of their activities," Brandi said. "I've never seen this book, but he told me about it. He put together dates and places where different collectors had traveled. He wasn't sure about the Reaper's identity until recently."

"Is there a name?" Kendall asked. "We still don't know the name the Reaper's using now."

"Could be more than one name," Jake said. "He may have several identities."

"We need to search the rest of the house. I want to see Thomas's bag," Nathan said.

"I left the bag in his bedroom," Brandi said.

"Kendall can stay with me," Nathan said. "We'll keep searching this room."

"Or she can stay with me," Jake said. "You both have habits of falling through portals."

Brandi grabbed Jake's arm. "It's my brother's house. I choose you. Your eyes don't glow."

He didn't argue. He'd wanted an opportunity to talk to Brandi. She probably knew more about what happened in Iraq than anyone besides Thomas and the Reaper.

She led him upstairs to the bedroom, sparsely furnished with a bed, a chair, and one chest of drawers. A few items of clothing were thrown about the room. Brandi picked up a flannel shirt. "I didn't have a chance to do anything with his things."

"I'm sorry he died," Jake said. "I didn't really know him. Just the brief contact when he hired me, but I guess it turns out we were on the same side. I wish I'd known. We could have combined our resources."

"He didn't trust you. Not then. I think he did later, after the girls."

Jake's jaw tensed. The girls. He hadn't wanted to talk about them.

"Thomas didn't know the prince was involved with human trafficking. He said the Reaper didn't either. Thomas admired you for saving them."

He hadn't saved them all.

"Thomas was coming to help you get the girls when he saw someone beyond you getting ready to take a shot. He thought the man was aiming at your back, so Thomas shot at him. Turned out the guy was actually getting ready to shoot at Thomas. He'd found out what Thomas was up to."

"I thought your brother was shooting at me. I never saw the other guy. Who blew up the helicopter carrying my team?"

"Thomas didn't know if it was the Reaper or if it was the prince protecting his collection of relics."

"Did Thomas kill the prince?"

"I think he did. He was very upset over the whole thing."

"If it was him, he did the world a favor," Jake said. "It took a lot of balls to double-cross the Reaper."

Brandi picked a leather bag off a chair. "This is it. His bag." She ran her hand over the leather, and her face tightened. "I hope Kendall can find something from this. I want this bastard dead."

"That bastard is old and powerful. You'd be better off if you got out now. I know he killed your family, but he's dangerous. Let us get rid of him. That'll be your revenge."

"I can't back off until I see those relics destroyed myself. The Reaper isn't the only one who would misuse them. Half the population would probably kill to get their hands on items like that."

She had a point, but it wasn't his call. "It's not up to you or me. The Protettori is in charge."

"Nathan is the one who has the Spear of Destiny." Her eyes narrowed with speculation. "Tell me where he hid it, and I'll tell you a secret."

"About what?"

"The Reaper. Do you ever wonder why he hired you?"

Jake had spent dozens of hours wondering about the mission in Iraq. He'd never met the client, just the man who made the arrangements. That hadn't bothered him. These rich guys usually had someone to do everything for them but wipe their ass. "Maybe."

Brandi's eyes narrowed further. "I think I know."

The way she said it implied she knew something he didn't, but he didn't have the info she needed, and he didn't have time for her games. But still . . . it couldn't hurt to ask. "Why did he hire me?"

"First tell me where Nathan hid the Spear of Destiny."

"Nathan's keeping that a secret."

"Then I'll keep mine."

A tingle crawled up his spine like a spider climbing an icy web, but he'd had so many warning tingles lately, he was becoming immune. That was a dangerous thing. Kendall might have her sixth sense, but his gut feelings had saved his ass many times.

"Just keep in mind that Raphael wants those relics protected even more than Nathan does. And he's a bad dude."

Brandi looked a little apprehensive. "I believe it after what happened in the temple. But I'm in this to the end."

Jake sighed. "Let's get this bag to Kendall."

"You don't like leaving her with Nathan. Does she know how bad you've got it for her?"

"Mind your own business."

She smiled. "I don't blame you. He's obviously crazy about her, and he's like the catch of the century, if you don't count that freaky thing with his eyes. Don't look so annoyed. You've got a lot going for you in the hot department too."

"I'm touched."

"Smart-ass." She handed the bag to Jake and something fell out.

"What's that?"

"Looks like a photo," Brandi said, bending to pick it up. "It's a woman."

"Did Thomas have a girlfriend?"

"Are you kidding? He didn't even take the time to eat properly. He didn't have time for a girlfriend. I don't know who she is."

Jake looked over at the picture and felt the blood drain from his face.

He approached the grave slowly, feeling sicker the closer he got. Blond hair lay against the dirt. Finally he stood over the grave and looked at the woman's face.

"Jake?" Brandi's voice came from far away. "You look like you've seen a ghost."

He had. He had seen the woman in a grave. How the hell could that be?

"The photo looks old. Look at her clothes. Late eighties maybe. Let's put it with the notebook," Brandi said. "Maybe it's one of the Reaper's contacts."

Jake's head was spinning as he followed Brandi downstairs. Kendall and Nathan were still in the room, standing close together, looking at a map. They looked so damned right together. They had the same interests. Nathan treated her with respect. He hadn't hit on her like a moron in the beginning to keep her at a safe distance from his heart. Damned lot of good it'd done. She was firmly lodged there now.

Kendall turned and her smile pierced his heart. Then she frowned—her and her senses, not that they'd been up to par lately. He looked away because he didn't want her to know his thoughts.

"We found a map," Nathan said. "Prague. Same as the map in Marco's room. The Reaper must be there."

"If only the chalice was."

"Maybe Kendall will pick up something from Thomas's bag," Nathan said.

"Oh, we found this in the bag. A picture of a woman." Brandi showed them the image. "I know Thomas didn't have a girlfriend. She must be connected to the Reaper. That's all Thomas ever thought about."

Kendall took the picture from Brandi. "I've seen her before."

"This woman?" Brandi asked. "Where?"

"In Jake's house."

Nathan's eyes narrowed. "Jake's house?"

"That's impossible," Jake said. "She's dead."

"How do you know?" Nathan asked. "Did you kill her?"

"No, but I saw her in a grave."

"Was she one of the girls in Iraq?" Kendall asked.

"No. I saw her long before that. Not really saw her. It was more like a dream."

"You've dreamed of her?"

"I've dreamed of her most of my life."

"What was she doing in your house?" Nathan still looked suspicious. "She must be connected to the Reaper."

Kendall turned the picture over. Her face went still. "There's a name on the back." She looked up at Jake. "Maryanne."

"The name in the journal." Nathan gave Jake an angry glare. "Who is she?"

"I don't know who the hell she is," Jake said. He looked confused.

"You saw her name in a journal?" Brandi asked.

"It wasn't written in ink, but we saw the impression." Kendall chewed on her lip. "The Reaper must have known her."

"You think she was working with him?" Brandi asked.

"If you say she's dead—" Kendall stopped. "That explains it. That's why she never spoke to me. She just seemed to appear. And why Jake didn't see her. Why her gown and hands were dirty. She hadn't been in a garden. She was in a grave. She was a ghost."

"A ghost," Jake said, his frown getting deeper.

"I don't care if she's a woman or a ghost. I want to know what she was doing in his house," Nathan said.

Brandi made a small surprised sound. "Maybe Thomas was right the first time."

"Right about what?" Jake asked.

"That you're the Reaper's son."

CHAPTER FIFTEEN

THAT'S CRAZY," KENDALL SAID. "WHAT MAKES YOU THINK Jake could be the Reaper's son?"

Brandi eyed Kendall warily. "When Thomas found out that the Reaper had a child, he thought it might be Jake. The Reaper insisted that Thomas hire Jake."

"That doesn't mean anything," Kendall said, feeling a knot growing in her stomach. "Jake's good at what he does."

Nathan stepped closer to Kendall, his eyes starting to pale. He addressed Brandi, but his watchful gaze was on Jake. "And you're just now telling us?"

The redhead gave her lips a nervous lick. "Thomas wasn't sure, and then later he changed his mind. After Jake rescued the girls, Thomas didn't think it was likely that he could be the Reaper's son. And Jake seemed to have no idea who the Reaper was."

Kendall's hands tightened on the photo. "Just because he recognizes the picture doesn't mean he's the Reaper's son. It could be anyone. He could have been Todd for all we know," she said, speaking of the one-time neighbor who had been working for the Reaper. "And as old as the Reaper is, his son could be ancient."

"Just because you slept with him doesn't mean you should be blind to the truth," Nathan said, finally turning to look at Kendall. His dark eyes were swirling with amber, and they were filled with anger and hurt. "What else could it mean? The Reaper says he has a child and insists Jake work for him. We find a name in the Reaper's journal and a picture of a woman with the same name as the one Jake's seen in dreams. I knew there was another reason he was working for the Reaper. Even Jake believes it's true. Look at him."

Jake looked like he was going to throw up. He had sat down on the edge of the desk. Kendall shook her head. "We don't have any idea what the truth is. We can't jump to conclusions."

"I need to get out of here," Jake said.

"Don't go." Kendall touched his arm. "We'll figure this out."

She turned to Nathan. "Don't forget what you told me when I thought I may be the Reaper's child. You said it wouldn't make any difference. Remember that?"

Nathan scowled. "You're not Jake."

"Jake's been working for you as long as I have. No more talk about the Reaper's son. Not until we have something to go on besides speculation." Kendall's gaze was hard. They couldn't allow this to divide them. "What we do know is that the Reaper wants the chalice, and maybe me. Forget his son, whoever the hell he is. Got it? Now where's Thomas's bag? Let me see if I can sense anything."

Brandi smiled at Kendall's outburst and took the bag from Jake, handing it to Kendall. The leather was soft with use. Kendall closed her eyes and tried to sense the bag's secrets. She heard a loud noise and opened her eyes. Everyone looked shocked.

"Did you hear that too?" she asked.

"That wasn't you," Nathan said.

"It came from the front." Jake pulled his gun and hurried to the door. The room was filling with smoke. A window had been broken, and a canister lay on the floor. "It's tear gas," Jake said. "We've got to get out of here. Is there another way out of this room?"

Brandi shook her head. "No, I don't think so."

Jake pulled his shirt up over his mouth and nose. "Cover your faces and follow me."

Kendall covered her face, but before she could follow Jake, Nathan scooped her up and streaked past the others. In the time it took her to blink, he was putting her down in the hallway. Jake and Brandi joined them.

Brandi's eyes were wide above her shirt. "We can go out the back."

"Whoever threw that canister will be waiting," Jake said.

"But we can't stay here," Nathan said.

They moved into a back room farther away from the tear gas. "What's back there?" Jake asked.

"A small yard and another row of town houses behind this one," Brandi said.

Jake used a window and made a quick scan of the back. "Two guys with guns, one on each corner. Probably the same in the front. We can put the women in a room away from the gas, and we can take them out."

"I don't like splitting up," Nathan said. "I'm sure they're after Kendall."

"You don't want her to be alone with me, but I'm not working with the Reaper," Jake said. "You're going to have to trust me."

Nathan's jaw was hard. "What's your plan?"

"We can do two things. First option, you can get her past the guys in the back. If you move like you did a minute ago, you'll be two blocks away before they see you streak past—"

"That leaves you to fight them alone," Kendall said to Jake.

"They want you, Kendall. We have to keep you safe. Second

option is you and Brandi stay in here, far away from the gas. Nathan and I will disable the men outside."

"You're not fighting them alone," Kendall said. "Nathan can help you. Brandi and I will stay here."

"Go upstairs into the bathroom and close the door," Jake said. "Don't come out until one of us comes to get you." He squeezed Kendall's hand and moved to the back door.

Nathan looked at her, an eerie sight with his lower face covered and his eyes in flames. Kendall shivered. He lowered his shirt. "Don't come out for anyone except me." He glanced at Jake. "Please."

Kendall knew he was shaken by the revelation that Jake could be the Reaper's son. Rather than argue now, she nodded, and she and Brandi started up the stairs. The gas cloud was moving closer, and her eyes were stinging. She remembered the vial of water but didn't want to use it for something as trivial as stinging eyes. And she didn't want Brandi to see the vial.

Brandi showed her the bathroom, and they hurried inside and closed the door. Brandi threw a towel against the crack under the door. "I don't know much about tear gas, but just in case."

They hadn't turned on the light, and the bathroom was dark. A window looked out over the backyard. Kendall eased the curtain aside and peeked out.

"Should you do that?" Brandi asked.

"It's dark in here. No one can see me. There they go." Brandi hurried over beside her and looked. Both women held their breath as Nathan moved like a dark blur across the yard. One of the men flew backward as if he'd been hit by a wrecking ball. The other man watched, his attention diverted. Jake came up from behind, hit the man across the back of the neck, and he went down like a rock.

"They're handy in a fight," Brandi said.

Jake turned and looked at the window as if he sensed exactly where she stood. Nathan emerged from the bushes, his eyes still burning.

"And kind of terrifying too," Brandi added.

Both men split and went around the side of the house. "I can't see them," Kendall said.

"We can't leave. They'll kill us both."

They sat for a few minutes that felt like it stretched to an hour. "This is driving me crazy," Kendall said.

Brandi froze. "That sounded like Thomas."

"I didn't hear anything," Kendall said.

"It sounded like Thomas's voice. What if Jake's right and he faked his death? He would do anything to destroy the Reaper."

"I'll come with you," Kendall said, looking out the window for some sign of activity. She saw Nathan and Jake coming back. Two men were creeping up behind them holding guns, but Nathan and Jake hadn't spotted them. Kendall threw open the window. "Behind you!" She was already throwing up her hands, not considering whether her powers would work from this distance, when Nathan and Jake whirled.

The men didn't fly backward as had happened when she did this before. They fell to the ground, guns dropping from their unmoving hands. Paralyzed like the rogues had been. How had she done that without even fully lifting her hands?

She turned around and Brandi was gone. A feeling of unease settled along the back of Kendall's neck. She went to the bathroom door and looked outside. "Brandi?"

"Here." Brandi appeared at the bedroom door.

"Who was it?" It couldn't have been Thomas, unless he was back as a ghost or really had faked his death. Neither was entirely out of the question.

"No one. Just my imagination, I guess. Probably because it's his house."

"We should go back to the bathroom and wait."

"I think it's safe now."

"I just saw Nathan and Jake outside with two more men. I think I paralyzed them." Kendall looked at Brandi and felt a chill. Brandi's face seemed to shift. Kendall felt as if she were being sucked into a vacuum. Was it the gas? As she fell, she thought she heard a voice. But not Brandi's.

"It's OK, Kendall. Sleep now."

Jake bent over the fallen man. "Where is the Reaper?"

"I can't tell."

"If you don't, I'll kill you."

The man's eyes flickered. "Prague."

"Damn," Nathan said.

"Where in Prague?" Jake pushed the barrel of his gun harder against the man's forehead. But he slumped. He was going to pass out. "Where is he?" Jake asked, one last time.

"Here. He's here."

The bottom dropped out of Jake's stomach. "Kendall." He jumped up and ran toward the house. Nathan did his speed thing and got there first. He was up the steps before Jake climbed the first one.

"She's gone," Nathan said, eyes on fire. "They're both gone."

"Dammit. How did he get past us?"

They heard a car start, and both men raced outside and down the street. A black Porsche pulled away from the curb. Jake caught a glimpse of light hair. "Get the car!" He started to move toward their rental, which was parked in front of the town house, but his feet wouldn't move. His entire body was stuck in place.

Beside him, Nathan was in full change, growling and straining like a wild beast against his invisible chains. They watched helplessly as Kendall and Brandi were taken away.

Jake cursed as the car's taillights vanished around a curve. "This isn't working." They were stuck. Nathan's eyes looked like they were on fire, and his face was red with exertion. "Stop struggling before you explode. Strength isn't working. We have to use our heads to get out of this. The water. Damn, I can't reach it."

Nathan stopped moving, and his eyes started to dim. "We have to get free."

"Don't you have some other secret ability that can get us out of here?" Jake asked.

"You're the one who could be the Reaper's son. You must have inherited something from him."

"Don't start with that now. You're the one with the superpowers."

"Superpowers that I don't know how to control or use," Nathan said. "Raphael still hasn't explained it."

"I wish he was here," Jake said, and just like that, the guardian appeared. "What the hell are you, a damned genie?"

Raphael did something with his hands and Jake and Nathan fell free. "I'm not a genie," he said, as though insulted.

"Follow them," Jake said. He was going to see her safe or die trying. "Do your vanishing trick. Can't you appear in his car?"

"No. I'm not strong enough. I transported here."

Jake reached into his pocket and pulled out his vial of water. "Here, drink this. Nathan, give him yours."

"You might need it," Raphael said, looking at the vials hesitantly.

"We need to get Kendall back," Jake said. "Now."

Raphael drank both vials.

"Well?" Nathan asked.

Raphael closed his eyes, then opened them. "It's not working yet."

"Dammit," Jake said. "Then get in the vehicle." He ran toward the car. "I'll drive."

"I will," Nathan said.

"Why you?" They had to hurry. There wasn't any time to lose.

"Do you own a race team?" Nathan asked.

"No."

"I do. I'm driving."

"Someone drive the car," Raphael yelled.

Jake climbed into the backseat because he doubted Raphael would fit. "Hurry, or we'll never catch up." The Reaper was in a Porsche and they were in a Honda. It'd be a miracle if they caught up.

Nathan knew how to drive, Jake would give him that. And for someone who could fly without an airplane, Raphael was paranoid about riding in an automobile. He cursed and gripped the seat as Nathan darted around cars and made illegal turns.

"No sign of them," Nathan said. "Where would he take her? Back to Prague?"

"It has to be Prague," Jake said. "The Reaper's man said he lived there."

Nathan gripped the wheel as the car screeched around a turn. "He could be taking her somewhere else. He seems to get around easily."

"He probably has as many homes and hotels as you do. They headed west," Jake said. "They could be going to Reagan National Airport or Washington Dulles."

"I'll call Hank and have him check flights."

"Find out if Marco took a flight," Raphael said.

After a minute, Nathan hung up. "There's a private jet from Prague scheduled for a return flight at Reagan National."

"I'm surprised he's taking her there if he just wants information," Jake said. "Unless he believes the chalice is in Prague."

"At one time, we had many relics in Prague," Raphael said. "What about Marco?"

"Yes, he flew to Prague earlier."

"That fool," Raphael said. "He'll get killed." But his voice was filled with worry.

"Pedal to the floor," Jake said. "We can't let him get her on that plane."

"I have a contact at TSA. A guard who used to work for me. He can get someone out there."

"He doesn't know what the Reaper looks like. Hell, nobody really knows what he looks like."

"He knows Kendall." Nathan shifted in his seat. "He was . . . close to her. That's why I let him go."

"Another man with the hots for her?" Damn. "Is he going to intercept them?" Jake asked. "That could be dangerous."

"Don't try to stop him," Raphael said. "We need to know where Luke is taking her."

"Call him the Reaper," Jake said. "The man you knew isn't the same. I don't care where he's taking her. I plan on stopping him."

"I'm not sure that's the best thing to do," Raphael said.

"I'm sure," Jake said. "We can't let him get away with her."

"Stop thinking with your hearts," Raphael said. "We have to play this smart. We have a chance to find out where he's been hiding. We don't know where he is going in Prague. If we follow at a discreet distance, we can find out exactly what he's doing and kill him there."

"Why wait to kill him there?" Jake said.

"You're not telling us something," Nathan said.

Raphael was silent. "He has something I need. Something that belongs to the Protettori."

"What?"

"A relic. I believe it's the fourth relic sketched in the Reaper's journal."

"The fourth relic is missing?"

"Yes. I believe Luke—the Reaper—has it."

"What is it?" Nathan asked.

"The Tree of Knowledge."

Nathan turned to look at Raphael, and the car drifted toward the guardrail. He jerked it back. "From the Garden of Eden?"

"Yes."

"That makes sense," Jake said. "The Spear of Destiny gives him power. The Fountain of Youth and the Holy Grail give him eternal life, and the Tree of Knowledge gives him wisdom."

"He has the whole tree?" Nathan asked.

His expression of awe disturbed Jake. Who cared what part of the tree he had. They had to destroy it or destroy the Reaper. God, now he was thinking like Brandi.

"Not the whole tree," Raphael said. "A piece. We've had it for many, many centuries. It was one of our most valuable relics. We only recently realized it was missing. We discovered that the box our portion was kept in was empty. We don't know who took it or when it went missing, but I believe the Reaper is somehow connected to its disappearance."

"So you can't kill him until he tells you where he's hidden it," Jake said. "I wondered what the fourth sketch in the journal was."

"The Tree of Knowledge," Nathan said. "Imagine that. I can't wait to tell Kendall. She won't believe it."

They had to find Kendall first. Jake pushed aside the grip of fear. "I'm surprised he was alone. Seems he usually has his minions do his dirty work."

"He's desperate," Raphael said. "He can move faster if he works alone."

Jake pushed aside the fear gnawing at his guts. "You should have killed him anyway. He wouldn't have Kendall now. Forget about the tree."

"It's not that simple."

"I don't see why not. You're powerful, older than him, and you've been drinking from the Fountain of Youth. If anyone can kill him, it should be you."

"I can't kill him. Members of the brotherhood can't kill each other."

"Can't?" Jake asked.

Raphael brushed a knuckle across his cheek. "I've never seen it happen, so I can't say it's impossible, but if it weren't, it would be very difficult and carry great consequences."

Nathan scowled. "That's bloody insane. Didn't the Reaper kill most of the Protettori?"

"He had others do it for him," Raphael said.

"So you can mastermind the destruction, but can't personally carry it out," Nathan said. "Here I was thinking you were the one who would finish him off."

"It won't be me."

"I guess we can draw straws," Jake said to Nathan.

"I'll kill him," Nathan said. "I'm not officially Protettori yet."

He'd have to get to him first. No one was going to threaten Kendall and live.

Nathan navigated a turn, taking them off I-95 near the Pentagon. He accelerated at an alarming speed.

"There's the car," Jake said. The black Porsche was parked on the side of the road that led to the airport. Nathan slammed to a stop behind the car. His eyes were alight before he opened the door and got out. "Careful."

Raphael got out just as quickly, and they sped toward the

car. Jake followed, holding his gun. The car was empty. "They've ditched it," Jake said.

"He could have taken them anywhere," Nathan said. "Can he fly around like you can?"

"Once he had similar abilities, but I thought he had lost some. It appears he's regaining those powers in spite of being injured in the temple. I found him at the Abbey House in Glastonbury."

"What were you doing there?" Nathan asked. "I thought you went to Prague."

"I went to get more water from the fountain first. Since I was already there, I decided to check in the Abbey House. That's where he thought Kendall was staying. He was watching for her. I waited and followed him to Washington, DC."

"You can't track him now?" Jake asked.

"No. But if he's injured, and he's already gone from England to DC, he must be getting too tired to teleport," Raphael said. "He's probably had someone pick them up."

Nathan called Fergus and had him make arrangements for a flight. There weren't any private jets available, so they would have to fly commercial. Again.

Nathan hung up, frowning. "They found one of the rogues."

"Where?" Raphael asked.

"He was in jail for urinating in public. Fergus just got back from bailing him out. The others are still missing. Hank thinks some of them may be hiding in the catacombs. They seem to think we're sorcerers. They don't understand the change in time. What was Marco thinking?"

"He didn't know they were the ones who had gone rogue," Raphael said. "I'm the one who put them there. I believe he thought we needed more help to fight the Reaper."

Jake shook his head. "And now Marco's on the way to Prague to find the Reaper."

Marco didn't particularly like flying, but he didn't like using the gateways either. They were hard on an aging body. He settled back in his seat and watched the people around him. Times had changed so much in the centuries that he'd been alive. He remembered traveling on horseback or taking a carriage. It was a simpler time. Things were complicated now. So much technology and new ideas, but humans were much the same.

He knew that what he was undertaking was a dangerous thing, but what else could he do? He had tried to wake the sentinels so the Protettori would have more help, but when he left the room, they were still stone. After that failure, it was up to him to stop Luke. The Reaper. Marco closed his eyes, feeling every year of his great age. He was aware that he might lose his life, but if he could keep Kendall, Nathan, and Jake from danger, it would be well worth it. And he still had a few tricks up his sleeve.

Raphael wasn't happy about leaving his dagger in the car. Jake supposed he was used to traveling by portal, but Nathan promised him he'd replace it if something happened to the weapon.

"It can't be replaced," he said.

"Don't tell me it's as old as you," Jake said.

"Close," Raphael said.

"Jesus," Jake said.

Raphael's hand flew out and slammed into Jake's chest. "Don't say his name in vain," the guardian said with a growl.

Jake couldn't say anything for a few minutes. He was trying to catch his breath. He didn't retaliate, since Raphael had good reason to feel that way after presiding over the crucifixion of Christ, watching him die. Jake rubbed his chest and considered that he may need to clean up his language. He didn't want to antagonize the guardian. They needed to be unified if they were going to take on the Reaper and rescue Kendall and Brandi.

This trip was longer than the one he'd taken with Raphael, but it should have been more comfortable thanks to Nathan's money, which allowed them to travel first class. They had more leg room, which they all needed, particularly Raphael, but the attention he drew made discussing their plans to find the Reaper impossible. Even dressed in jeans, Raphael looked frightening with his tattooed face and frustrated frown. Nathan wasn't helping matters. He was trying to hide his face so he wouldn't be recognized, which drew even more attention. One flight attendant dared approach him with a smile, but she made herself scarce after she got a glimpse of his scowl.

When things settled down, Raphael quietly told them what he remembered of his "landing" in Prague when he'd followed the Reaper through the gateway, but there was very little to go on. "I saw him walk inside a tall building. A church, maybe."

"Bloody hell. That's all you remember?" Nathan asked. "There are hundreds of churches in Prague."

"I was lying on a street corner, near death. I could hardly see straight," Raphael hissed, his face dark. A small child who'd been staring at him curiously quickly vanished below the back of his seat.

"I thought you could extract memories," Nathan said. "I'm sure you did it to me. Can't you do it to yourself?"

"No."

"Don't suppose that's also one of Nathan's newfound talents that you could give him a quick lesson in? Let him read you?"

"I don't yet know what he's capable of," Raphael said. "If we get the Reaper out of the way, we might have time to find out."

"We can't do that if we can't find him," Nathan said, his tone harsh.

"And you blame me?" Raphael said. "If it weren't for me, you'd still be back there stuck in the Reaper's invisible chains like flies in a spiderweb."

"So we're just going to get a car to drive us around to look at churches until we find one that looks familiar?" Nathan barked out a laugh. "That's a rotten plan. Why didn't you have someone else kill him when you had the chance? Then we wouldn't have to worry about his abilities."

"It's not time."

"Not time? What are you waiting for?" Nathan said. "He's already found the Fountain of Youth, and now he has Kendall. What more do you want?"

Raphael looked suspiciously secretive. "He has something I need."

"He has something I need too!" Nathan yelled. "Kendall!"

After they convinced the flight attendant that Nathan and Raphael weren't fighting, Jake leaned close and growled in Nathan's ear. "If you don't calm down," Jake whispered, "your eyes are going to start glowing and people are going to start screaming. Then you can forget finding Kendall. They'll lock you up in a lab and study you like a rat. Chill. Your team will keep us informed where the Reaper's jet lands."

"I can't let anything happen to her."

"*We* won't," Jake said. "I've got as much to lose as you. Maybe more."

Nathan frowned. "You'd better not be playing with her heart. I'll rip yours out and feed it to you."

"I'm not playing at anything. And the same goes for you. She believes you're Adam. If you're not, you'd damned well better let her know now. I don't want her hurt over him more than she already has been."

"Can you two shut up so I can rest?" Raphael said.

"Try not to snore," Jake muttered.

"I don't snore."

"You don't think the Reaper would hurt her . . . ?" Nathan asked.

Jake pushed away the dark thoughts pressing in on him. "No. He needs her healthy." *For now.*

Nathan looked out the window, his face tense. "Hank's sending some of my hotel security guards to the airport in Prague to see if they can spot them."

Raphael cracked one eye. "You have a hotel there?"

"He has hotels all over the world," Jake said.

"Hmmm . . ." Raphael closed his eyes again, and in minutes he was softly snoring.

"We don't have anything to go on," Nathan said, and then pointed to the dozing guardian. "He must have seen something he can identify?"

Jake could feel his frustration. "Raphael's our only chance," he said in a whisper, "unless your hotel security guard catches sight of Kendall. So don't piss him off. We don't want him vanishing from the plane."

"I hadn't thought of that."

"I hope he hasn't either."

Ten minutes later, Raphael gave a loud snore and bolted upright. "I know where it is," he said loud enough to startle everyone near him, as well as a few of the sharper hearing passengers in coach. He lowered his voice. "It wasn't a church. It was a town hall."

"A town hall? That's where the Reaper went?" Jake asked.

"I'm almost sure it was. I heard a clock chime. It had a distinctive sound. The place is a historical landmark. The clock in the tower has the twelve apostles on it."

Jake shoved at Raphael's arm, which was digging into Jake's elbow. "I've heard of cuckoos in a clock, but never apostles. Where is it?"

"It's near the Old Town Square."

"I know that area," Nathan said. "I could see the Reaper having a place there. It's old and full of history."

"Just like him," Jake said. "What would he do inside a town hall? I expected a castle or something grand."

"The tower is old," Raphael said. "Maybe there's some significance."

"I can't see him taking Kendall to a town hall. He must have a place there. He'll have to convince her to help him." Jake's stomach turned just saying the words.

When they landed in Prague, it was evening. Nathan touched base with his team and learned that the private jet they believed Kendall was on had already landed, but the guard hadn't seen any sign of the woman.

"We have a starting point anyway," Nathan said. "Assuming you're right about the clock."

They hired a car to take them to the tower. This wasn't the first time Jake had been to Prague, and the other trip hadn't been fun either. It had involved chasing a jewel thief. The owner had paid Jake well to find it. Jake hadn't told the man that it was his mistress who'd taken it. She was a pretty thing with way too much charm, and she'd made him feel sorry for her. But he'd given his word to recover the jewel, so he returned it without exposing the mistress's secret, for which she had been very appreciative. Foolish of him. If the jewel's owner had found out, Jake would probably be missing some important parts of his anatomy. The man was very powerful and had a violent temper.

He supposed he'd have to tell Kendall about that one day. He had a lot of past sins to confess. If he was around long enough. The hug he'd witnessed at the graveyard crept into his head again. Nathan had a bond with Kendall that would never break. Not even death had stopped it before. Now that Adam was alive, nothing would separate them. And now there was a possibility that Jake could be the Reaper's son. What chance did he have with her?

He felt the nausea coming and put the thought out of his head, focusing on the ancient city with its beautiful buildings and grand churches. But the sights just reminded him that this wasn't a vacation. It was a rescue mission. He could only pray that the Reaper wouldn't hurt her until he got what he wanted. The chalice. Thank God she didn't know where it was.

He looked at the woman lying in the bed, *her* bed, and he felt the loss as fresh as he had that terrible day. After all this time he still loved Maryanne. No matter how many centuries he would live, even until the end of time, he would always love her. Some souls were meant for each other. They had been, until she found out about him. He had many regrets, so many things he wished he had done differently. Perhaps if he had explained, she would have understood. Perhaps not.

He touched his cheek, feeling the rough texture of skin that had aged the instant he had used the wrong chalice to drink from the Fountain of Youth. Kendall had known it was the wrong chalice. She had lied to him. He should be angry with her for tricking him. He should kill her, but he needed her to find the real chalice, and in spite of her deception, he admired her spirit.

He limped to the bed, his bones aching. And the aging wasn't limited to the outside. He had grown older inside, his organs and tissues and bones. His mind and his abilities weren't as sharp.

For the first time in his life, he felt like an old man. He needed the chalice quickly, before more damage was done. He placed his hands on Kendall's head, softly so as not to wake her. He closed his eyes and sank into her mind.

He didn't find out where the chalice was. She didn't know yet, but he was confident it would come. Her gifts were extraordinary.

"Time to wake up, Kendall."

CHAPTER SIXTEEN

*K*ENDALL WAS IN A ROOM FILLED WITH CHALICES. *BIG ONES, little ones, gold, silver, wood. Each was beautiful in its own way. As she explored, she heard someone call her name, and she looked around for Adam.*

It must be Adam. She wouldn't be exploring a room like this without him.

Then she felt darkness closing in around her, and she was afraid. "Adam!"

Kendall awoke to find she was in a large room. Not the chalice room. The bed she lay in was quilted, an odd design, kind of retro. Her thoughts were foggy as she tried to remember how she'd gotten here. The last thing she remembered was being at Thomas's town house and going to look for Brandi. Kendall sat up, alarmed. Brandi had told her everything was all right, and then her face had changed. Had Brandi done this? No. She hated the Reaper.

"You are awake, finally."

Kendall spun around and saw him sitting in a chair on the other side of the bed. His face looked different than it had in the temple, but she knew he was the Reaper. He was dressed elegantly, his hair short, his eyes kind. But those weren't his real eyes. Nothing about him was real. "Where am I?"

He sat back, casually, as if they were just visiting. "You're in my home."

"Where?"

"I can't tell you that. Unless you help me." He spread his hands, which were wrinkled. "Then I'll not only tell you where you are, I'll share my home with you. I'll share everything with you, Kendall. Power . . . knowledge . . . the world."

Her head felt thick. She needed the vial of water Raphael had given her, but she could feel her pocket was empty. The Reaper must have taken it. "What if I don't want it?"

He laughed, a soft rolling sound like water in a stream. "You may be surprised to find what you like. I wasn't always like this." His face changed slightly, then he shrugged and sat forward with a look of calculation behind his brown eyes. Brown? Or were they blue? "What do you want, Kendall?"

"I want to go home."

"Would you rather have your friends?"

"Where are they? Did you take them too?"

"Perhaps. But what if I offer you their lives in exchange for your help? You find the relics for me, I spare your friends."

He said it in such a calm way, it made her fear worse. This man was old, probably more than a thousand years old. How could she fight him? She twitched her fingers, wondering if she could do her trick again. She'd done it twice. Once she'd knocked the Reaper down, the other time, Raphael.

The Reaper looked at her fingers. "That won't work again. You caught me unprepared last time. So, do you want to hear me out?"

What else could she do? "Tell me what you want."

"I want the spear and the chalice, for now."

"I don't know where the spear is."

"I daresay you could find out. You have a lot of power where Nathan Larraby is concerned." Nathan's name sounded strange rolling off the Reaper's tongue.

"He won't tell me," she said, and then immediately worried that she had focused the Reaper's attention on Nathan.

"Then let's start with the chalice. We'll deal with the spear later."

"And if I won't?"

He leaned closer. Kendall didn't know what color his eyes were this time, but they weren't kind. "Your friends will suffer."

Kendall licked her lips and wiggled her fingers.

Before she could attempt to blast the man, the Reaper moved his hands, and she felt herself falling asleep. "No—"

She stood at the window looking over the estate. Her stomach was a knot of nerves as it had been ever since she'd discovered his secret. How had she not known what evil lay hidden beneath that beloved exterior? And now, now there was so much at stake. She closed her eyes. So very much at stake. She had to get away before it was too late. There was no way around the agonizing decision. This is what must be done.

Kendall woke up in the same bedroom as before, but this time she was alone . . . except for the woman who had been in her head. The frightened woman. She had been a prisoner here too. Not locked up, but something had held her here. Who was she? Maryanne?

There was a tap at the door, and someone called Kendall's name. A man stepped in. He was young and muscular. He wore a suit and a gun holstered at his waist. "I am Aaron. I have brought your food." He carried a tray to the bed and set it down.

Kendall reached for the tray and deliberately touched his hand. "Can you tell me where I am?" she asked.

He pulled his hand back and looked toward her, but didn't meet her eyes. "No."

He'd been warned about her gifts. So much for reading him. She raised her hands a few inches off her lap, but her fingers felt numb. Had the Reaper done something to them? "I just want to know where I am," she said, trying to sound nonthreatening. "Are we in Prague?"

His eyes flickered. "I can't tell you."

But he already had. She was in Prague, in the bedroom of a woman who had been terrified of the Reaper. Were Jake and Nathan here too? Brandi? Had he hurt them? They must be alive if the Reaper was using their lives as a bargaining tool. But for how long?

"Can you tell me if a woman stayed in this room before?" Kendall asked Aaron.

"I think his . . ." He stopped. "I don't know. But I would make a suggestion. Do what he says. Tell him what he wants to know. You should eat something. He'll be here soon to talk to you again." He closed the door.

Kendall didn't plan to be here when he arrived. She had nothing. No weapons, mental or otherwise, but she had one thing that could help her. She was certain the woman who'd been here before had known a way out. If Kendall could connect with her, she could find it. She got up and started moving around the room. She grabbed handfuls of the rich, feminine covers, touched the retro furnishings, walked barefoot on the shag carpeting, and tried to connect with the woman. If she ever needed a vision, it was now.

She got brief glimpses of the woman from the items in the room. She was probably in her thirties, very intelligent. Kendall needed more than that. She tried the first of two interior doors and found a bathroom, which she quickly made use of since she didn't know when she'd have the chance again. The second door was locked. She sensed the woman's presence stronger near that door. Working with the butter knife from the tray, Kendall fiddled with the lock until she heard a click.

She'd hoped she would find a way out, a back entrance, but it was a closet. A huge, walk-in closet filled with clothes, gowns, shoes, and handbags as if the woman still lived there. Kendall saw a pair of wooden clogs. Everything was old, not today's style, from twenty years ago or more. As Kendall touched the items, she felt the woman's presence so vividly she almost glimpsed a face. The woman had loved someone, fiercely, and she was terrified. Not for herself, but for someone else. That was why she needed to leave. Kendall strained for more, but she couldn't see her face or get a name. She knew that the woman was dead. Had the Reaper killed her?

Kendall dug through a dressing table looking for something else to touch. Jackpot. She found brushes and combs lying as if they had just been placed there minutes before. Had he kept it this way to honor her memory? She had just found a small photo when the door to the room opened.

Without looking closely at the image, Kendall shoved the photo into her pocket. She needed a weapon, but there wasn't time to search for scissors or something sharp. Her eyes swept over the handbags and shoes, and she grabbed the wooden clogs. They might put a dent in someone's head, unless it was the Reaper. One in each hand, she quickly moved behind the closet door, heart thudding so loud she knew the visitor must hear it.

It wasn't the Reaper. Aaron stepped inside, and Kendall hit him on the head with all of her strength. The wooden clog made a solid thunk, and Aaron dropped with a groan. Kendall rolled him over until she could reach his gun. She removed it and looked for something to tie the guard up. She had to settle for stockings. Not the best, but Adam had shown her lots of things about knots. After securing the guard's hands, she gagged him with a silk blouse. His eyes were still closed, so she checked his wallet and saw his ID. Czech Republic.

Gripping the gun, she closed the door, wedged a chair under the knob, and slipped from the room. It probably wouldn't stop Aaron for long, but it might give her a few extra minutes to get away. Get away? To where? She didn't even have money to make a phone call. She should have kept Aaron's wallet. And what if the Reaper had taken Nathan and Jake? And Brandi? Kendall knew Brandi wasn't behind her kidnapping. She hated the Reaper as much as anyone. How had he made himself look like her?

With no clear idea where to go, Kendall sneaked past several rooms, all lavish, with elaborate furniture and objects she would have loved to examine if she weren't trying to escape. The older items whispered to her, but she blocked them out. She didn't want to hear from inanimate objects. She wanted to hear Nathan and Jake.

She crept along, listening and then opening doors, but she didn't see them. In fact, she hadn't run into anyone. A place this opulent must require a lot of care. From the appearance of the interior, it would seem the property was a castle or a palace. The Reaper probably didn't want many people around to discover his secrets.

She'd grown so accustomed to the silence, the crash startled her. It sounded as if something heavy had fallen. She ducked into the nearest room and quietly closed the door. Holding her breath, she waited. There were other noises, thumps, and thuds.

It was quiet after that, and she decided to slip out and see if it was clear. Her hand was on the knob when she heard soft footsteps outside the door, stealthy, like someone hunting for her. Aaron must have freed himself. Anyone who worked for the Reaper must be trained well enough to escape a pair of dated stockings.

Tightening her grip on the gun, she eased back against the wall. Her free hand flexed, and she rubbed her fingers together, priming them. The knob turned, and the door began to open. As soon as she saw the top of the man's head, she slammed the gun over his skull.

"It's a bloody tourist attraction," Nathan said. They had found the town hall Raphael remembered seeing before, and although it was evening, there were several tourists about. "What would the Reaper be doing with a gateway here?"

"It may be that he discovered a natural gateway," Raphael said.

"Like the maze," Jake said.

"What makes them?" Nathan asked.

"I don't know. They're just there, like the mountains and the sky. There are mysteries humans can't explain."

"Is there a way to destroy them?" Nathan asked.

"I'll have to find a way," Raphael said. "The maze is protected, but I can't allow an unsecured gateway to the fountain."

"If the Reaper can teleport, why did he need a portal to get to the Fountain of Youth? Couldn't he just teleport himself directly there and to the castle, avoiding the sentinels?"

"He can't teleport past the statues," Raphael said. "That takes mental ability, and the sentinels would block him, but a natural portal, or a created one, that doesn't require the same power."

It wasn't easy searching for a portal in a tourist hotspot, especially with Raphael there. He either inspired fear or lust. Several women flirted with him. Whether or not they spoke English, it was obvious what they wanted. Jake and Nathan got more than a few smiles too.

"Now I see why you have to transport yourself," Jake said. Nathan wasn't much better. His eyes kept changing. "Might as well be traveling with Santa."

Both men gave him a quelling stare from their amber-colored eyes.

After they had examined every section of the town hall, frightening off some tourists, Jake knew they'd hit a dead end. "This is getting us nowhere. We need to ask someone where we can find Cedric Alexander." According to Nathan's people, that's who owned the private jet. Cedric may or may not be the Reaper's alias, but the lead was the only one they had for now. "Stay here and try not to scare anybody while I ask." Jake found a man who conducted tours. He spoke English, and when Jake asked about Cedric Alexander, he told Jake about a château not far away.

"Few kilometers that way," he said, pointing. He gave them directions. "It's hard to find. He's a private person, from what I hear. Doesn't like company. Not sure I'd pop in on him. I've heard strange stories about people who disappear. But if you're deter- mined, look for a statue of a knight at the gate. The road's there."

Statue? A souvenir from his past?

The man was right. It was hard to find, but they located the statue. It was not like the Protettori statues. This one was smaller, but the figure had a sword like a knight. A tall stone fence adjoined a heavy gate. Jake estimated it at about ten feet high. "Doesn't look very welcoming," he said as the three men studied the place from their hired car, which was parked a safe distance down the street. "We need to do some surveillance first, find out what we're up against."

"How do we plan to get inside?" Nathan asked. "There are cam- eras at the gate. I'm sure he'll have a top-notch security system."

"With your superpowers, I'm sure you could leap the fence," Jake said. "Raphael could just walk through it. I'll have to use my muscles and my training."

"Want me to give you a piggyback ride?" Nathan asked.

"Hell no."

"I can get in and check out the place," Raphael said.

"Are you up to *traveling*?" Nathan asked.

"Yes. The rest helped."

Nathan drummed his fingers on his thigh. "We don't even have equipment or weapons. Not that you two need them."

"We'll make do with what we have. You two stay out of sight," Raphael said. "I'm sure the Reaper's men know exactly what you look like. We don't want to alert them."

Jake nodded. "The only thing to our advantage is that he won't know that we've figured out where he is."

They pulled the car farther down the street, and Raphael slipped out. "Keep an eye on the statue," he said. "I'll come down there when it's clear."

"Can you believe he's a Roman centurion?" Nathan asked as they watched Raphael slip up the street. He walked behind a parked car and never came out.

"There he goes," Jake said. "Walking through walls. Must be nice."

Nathan crossed his arms and stared out the window. "The Reaper won't hurt her as long as he needs answers," Nathan said, as much for himself as Jake. "The most important thing to him is finding the chalice. And we know she doesn't know where it is."

"If he believes her. She lied to him once about the other chalice. He won't forget that."

"No, but he knows she's the only one with the ability to find the real one. If he could have found it himself, he would have already done it. He needs Kendall safe."

Nathan sat up straighter. "There's Raphael."

Sure enough the guardian was standing by the statue of the knight, motioning to them. "Here goes." They put on baseball caps to help hide their faces and walked casually to the gate. Raphael opened it just enough for them to squeeze in.

"What did you find?" Jake asked.

"Several guards. They're unconscious for now. Let's hurry before they wake up."

Easy as that, they walked up to the Reaper's château past his unconscious security. The home was four stories tall and sat on several acres of well-tended grounds. The Reaper might not have the chalice, but he had money. There were lots of windows. That might come in handy. But no balconies.

Two guards were unconscious near the door.

"I found four more around back," Raphael said. "I think it'll be easiest to go in here."

"What about alarms?" Nathan asked.

"We're about to find out." Raphael did something with his hand and woke one of the guards.

"I wish I knew how he did that," Jake said.

Raphael had already disarmed the man, and now he had his hand clamped over his mouth while holding the guard's weapon against his crotch. The guard was tough, but Raphael was tougher. The frightened man admitted that Mr. Alexander had brought a woman here. She was blond, and he had put her in one of the second-floor rooms. The alarm was off because Mr. Alexander was expecting company.

Raphael put him back to sleep and let him fall. "Company? We'd better hurry. I'll go first. If anyone's inside, I'll knock them out. If they get past me, you two will have to handle them."

The plan worked. As they encountered another guard, Raphael put him to sleep. No yelling, no gunfire, no fighting. "I wish I could have had you with me on my missions," Jake whispered.

Things got trickier when they rounded a corner and saw four guards carrying a crate. The men looked up and dropped the big container. It crashed to the ground, and the guards pulled guns. Before they could fire, Raphael put the men in front to sleep. Two in the back didn't fall. Nathan growled and started running. He slammed into them, and the guards slid down the corridor like hockey pucks. Nathan turned, his eyes fiery, and looked back at Jake. One of the guards raised his gun and aimed at Nathan.

Jake's body spiked with adrenaline, but he couldn't get there in time to help.

He didn't have to. The guard fell back, and the gun dropped from his hand.

Nathan turned back to look at the fallen guard, and then met Jake's eyes. "What was that?"

"Raphael and his magic."

"What?" Raphael asked. He was bending over the first two guards, removing their weapons.

"Thanks," Nathan said. "I owe you for that one."

Raphael frowned. "Grab those weapons and let's go."

Jake had already collected the weapons and stuck them in various parts of his clothing.

Further armed, they hurried up the stairs to the second floor. Another man approached. Before he could call out, Raphael flung out his hands and the man dropped like a teddy bear.

"How do you do that?" Jake asked.

"I don't know."

"Can all Protettori members do things with their hands?" Jake asked.

"Not all. The gifts vary."

"When we get back, you're giving me a crash course in mine," Nathan said. "I'm tired of being a slave to this . . . whatever it is."

"It's you," Raphael said. "Most people, even normal ones, have untapped potential. You've tapped into yours."

"Whether you want it or not, I guess," Jake added.

Raphael pointed to his ears and then to the room ahead of them. He'd heard someone inside. The man was a walking weapon, but he was looking a little weary. Jake motioned that he'd go first. He raised his gun and stepped inside. Before he could survey the entire room, something crashed down on his skull. He recognized her smell as stars circled behind his eyes.

"Jake, I'm sorry." Kendall patted his cheeks as Raphael and Nathan pulled him up. "I didn't know it was you. Where's your water?"

"I gave it to Raphael." Jake winced and rubbed his head. "And I thought you missed me."

She threw her arms around him. "I did. I didn't know if the Reaper had kidnapped everyone. He wouldn't tell me." Her voice was muffled against his chest. His arms were tight around her. She could feel his relief in his embrace.

"No. We tried to stop him in DC, but he got away."

Kendall released Jake and hugged Nathan. "I'm so glad to see you." She leaned back and looked at Raphael. He had one brow cocked. "Oh hell. I'm even glad to see you." She grabbed Raphael and hugged him. He looked surprised, and Kendall had a fleeting impression of sadness. Odd. She stepped back. "How did you find me?"

Jake searched her face, as if trying to make sure she was really all right. "Nathan's people found out there was a private jet flying to Prague right after the Reaper took you. We figured it must be him."

"Good thing you came. I wasn't sure what I was going to do when I got out. I don't have any money."

Nathan was also looking at her like a collector checking his prized relic for damage. "You saw the Reaper?" he asked.

Kendall shivered. "He offered to spare your lives if I agreed to help him."

"He's not in a position to bargain." Jake's jaw tightened. "Did he hurt you?"

"No. He was . . . almost a gentleman. But I think he took my vial of water."

"Then he will have started to heal," Raphael said, his voice heavy with dread. "You didn't see Marco?"

"No. Do you think he's here?"

"He must be," Nathan said. "He took a flight here. What about Brandi?"

"He took her too?" Kendall asked.

"We thought he had," Nathan said. "We didn't find her."

"I haven't seen her," Kendall said. "The last time was at Thomas's town house. She thought she heard Thomas. She left the bathroom. When I found her, she was . . . different. Her face, I don't know, it changed."

Nathan frowned. "Changed?"

"She didn't look like Brandi."

"What did she look like?" Jake asked.

"I don't remember. I blacked out."

"Maybe it was the tear gas," Jake said.

"I didn't think about that," Kendall said. "The gas probably messed with my head. What if the Reaper killed her before he kidnapped me?"

Nathan touched her shoulder. "I'll call Hank and have him check the town house."

"We need to hurry before those guards wake up," Nathan said.

Kendall tucked her hair behind her ears. "There's one tied up in the closet where I was held. I expect he'll be waking up soon."

"You tied him up?" Jake asked.

"Yeah, with stockings. That's all I had." She smiled at Nathan. "You would have been proud of the knot." He smiled in return, and she saw Jake's mouth tighten.

"Did you see anyone else?" Jake asked.

"Not alive."

That drew curious frowns. "I felt a woman in the room where I was held, but I think she's dead. Everything in the room looks like a throwback. Everything was still there . . . clothes, brushes, shoes."

"You think he killed her?" Nathan asked.

"I don't know, but she was afraid of him."

"Let's get moving," Raphael said.

"How are we going to find Marco?" Nathan asked. "We don't know if he's roaming around here, a prisoner, or lost in the middle of Prague."

"With his memory loss, I'd be surprised if he found this place," Jake said. "I think we should get Kendall out first, then come back for Marco."

Nathan nodded. "She's the main target. It's not safe to keep her here."

"I can't leave without checking to see if he's here." She owed her life to Marco.

"Raphael can look for him. He can move a lot faster than you and I can," Jake said. "What do you think, Raphael?"

Raphael wasn't listening. He was studying a small painting on the wall.

"We don't have time to appreciate the Reaper's art," Jake said.

"This is it," Raphael said.

The object of the painting was a cup, a plain wooden cup sitting on a table. "It's what?" Kendall asked.

"This is the chalice."

"The chalice?" Kendall asked. "The Holy Grail?"

"Yes."

"Not very impressive," Jake said.

Nathan stared intently at the painting. "I think I've seen it before."

"You've seen the Holy Grail?" Jake asked.

Nathan looked confused. "I don't know how I could have."

"We don't have time to figure it out now," Jake said. "We have to get Kendall out of here before the guards wake up."

"I don't want to leave without Marco," Kendall said.

"Raphael can find Marco." Jake cupped Kendall's cheek. "I'll carry you out of here if I have to."

"Get Kendall to safety. I'll make sure the guards are still knocked out," Raphael said. "You're the key to this now, and there's more at stake than just us."

She nodded. Raphael went first. Nathan and Jake put Kendall next and they followed close behind her. She felt like she was royalty being sheltered.

They passed one room, and Jake suddenly stopped.

"What's wrong?" Nathan asked.

Jake stepped inside the room, and she and Nathan followed while Raphael stood at the door. Like the rooms she'd examined, this one was beautifully decorated. There were antiques on every surface and art on the walls. Jake crossed the room to another door. He stood there as if in a daze.

Kendall glanced at Nathan. He frowned and shrugged. Kendall touched Jake's arm. "You OK?" An image appeared. A little boy standing in the same place where Jake was.

No, you must not go in there.

The woman's voice was clear. The episode only lasted a few seconds. Jake recognized a door, Nathan recognized the Holy Grail, and she kept seeing some woman who may have been a prisoner here.

"What are you doing?" Nathan asked.

Jake rubbed his forehead. He looked confused. "Déjà vu." He tried the handle. "Locked. I wonder what's in there?"

"Can you pick it?" Nathan asked.

"This is an unusual lock," Jake said. "You might have to do your thing and knock it down."

"Is it that important to get inside?" Nathan asked.

Raphael pushed them all aside. "Stand back." He walked up to the door, took a breath, and vanished.

"He doesn't need keys," Nathan said.

"I wish I could do that," Jake said.

A moment later, the door opened. "Welcome," Raphael said, his tone sarcastic.

They stepped inside. "I think we've found your chalice room," Nathan said.

The room was glorious. Rare objects filled every space, and one entire wall was covered in shelves that held chalices, cups, and vases. "I saw this room in a dream," Kendall said. Some of the chalices were ornate, and some were simple. She quickly searched for the one from the painting, even though she knew it wasn't there. If the Reaper had it, he wouldn't be after her. He would be at the fountain trying to drink.

"I recognize this," Nathan said.

He held a small obsidian knife. A ceremonial knife the Aztecs used for sacrifices. She remembered when Uncle John found it. "It was your father's," she said. "This must be his lost collection."

His eyes bore a spark of regret, followed by hatred. "I guess the Reaper did kill him."

Kendall touched his hand. "I'm sorry, Nathan. But at least you know why he died."

He nodded and stuck the knife in his pocket. "I'll kill him," Nathan said calmly.

Kendall squeezed his fingers lightly. "I know." As Raphael hurried them along, Kendall recognized several objects that had belonged to Uncle John. "I'm sure there are lots of collections here."

Jake's lips thinned. "Too bad we can't take everything." He looked at Raphael. "You can't move all this like you moved the treasure under the chapel can you?"

"I didn't move it."

"You said you did."

"I didn't really move it," Raphael said.

"It's some kind of mind trick?" Nathan asked.

He smiled. "I'll show you when we get back."

"I've seen enough treasures," Jake said. "We need to get out of here. After the Reaper is dead, we can come back and explore the place from top to bottom."

Raphael walked them out. One of the guards was mumbling and trying to move. Raphael waved his hand, and the guard fell back to the ground. "Go on. Get Kendall out of here. I'll look for Marco."

"Do you want one of us to stay with you?" Jake asked.

"I'm fine. I can move faster without you." Raphael looked worried. "I'll meet you somewhere."

"We'll be at my hotel," Nathan said, and he told Raphael the address.

"I'll be there as soon as I find him," Raphael said.

Kendall, Nathan, and Jake hurried past the sleeping guards and out the gate to the car. "That was too easy," she said when she got inside.

"Don't question it," Nathan said. "We've been through a lot of strange things in the past week."

The drive to the hotel should have been amazing. The lights of the city twinkled like jewels in the night, and old churches and cathedrals sparkled like diamonds. But architecture that normally would have engrossed Kendall for hours paled and became nondescript buildings. History that would have whispered to her, luring her with its tales of romance and grief, whizzed by in a blur.

Nathan and Jake questioned her about the Reaper. Kendall told them everything she remembered. "I only saw him for a few minutes when I was awake. It's frightening how he changes his appearance."

"Has to be mind control," Jake said. "No way he can actually change his appearance from minute to minute."

"We've witnessed a lot of impossible things," Nathan said.

"He looked older," Kendall said. "Drinking from the wrong chalice wounded him."

"I wish it had killed him," Jake said.

"I'm surprised he wasn't angrier," Nathan said. "You did trick him."

"I'm sure he would have been if he didn't need me," Kendall said.

"He'll be angry now," Jake said. "You realize this is serious. You can't go anywhere without us. He'll be looking for you."

"Is the hotel a good idea?" she asked. "I'm sure he knows about it. He probably knows everything about you."

"We won't be registered," Nathan said. "We'll sneak in."

"You gonna break in to your own hotel?" Jake asked.

"No. You are."

"Still doing your dirty work."

"You're good at it. I could get the manager to let us in, but I'd prefer no one know we're there."

"Won't they figure it out?" Kendall asked.

"I have a suite that's always available," Nathan said. "I just don't have the key. We'll have to steal it or break in."

"Let me check the lock. What about cameras?" Jake asked.

"No cameras," Nathan said. "I don't want everyone to know my business."

"You don't want your staff to see you sneaking women in," Jake said.

Nathan frowned. "I think you're confusing me with yourself."

The room was on the top floor. After inspecting the lock, Jake declared it was a decent one, but it was probably easier to break in than slip down and take the key. Kendall and Nathan kept watch to make sure no one came up to the floor.

"Being rich does have it perks," Jake said, when they'd gotten inside.

It was a suite of rooms, not terribly fancy but very comfortable. There were two bedrooms, a kitchen, and a bath.

"Let me guess," Jake said. "I'm sharing a bed with Nathan."

Nathan almost smiled. "Unless you want the floor."

"I'd rather—" He stopped at Kendall's warning glance.

"I call the bath," she said. "I'm filthy, and my whole body aches."

She took a hot bath, not as long as she would have liked since Nathan and Jake would need to take a turn. She tried not to think about how they would look soaped up and naked, but in spite of her attempts, a few images made it through. She finished and redressed in her old clothes and pulled her hair back in a tie. When she left the bathroom, Jake and Nathan were smiling.

"I don't think I've ever seen you both smile at the same time. What's so amusing?"

"We were talking about Fergus and the rogues," Nathan said.

Kendall couldn't help a smile herself. "He did look out of his element."

"You dropped something." Jake reached down and picked up the photo Kendall had put in her pocket. When he looked at it, his face went pale.

The woman hadn't known the camera was focused on her. The expression on her face was fear. And then Jake remembered who she was.

He was afraid. She pulled at his hand, urging him to run faster. "Hurry, Jake. You have to hide."

"But why?"

"I can't explain now. There, behind those trees." She helped him into the bushes and made him sit. "Don't come out until he's gone. Promise me." Her hands were like ice on Jake's face, but her touch was soft.

He nodded.

She bent and kissed his forehead, and then squeezed him tight. "I love you."

"I love you too, Mama."

The voices were closer now. Jake's mother looked over her shoulder and then looked at Jake again. Her eyes were glistening like they did when she cried. She didn't like him to see her cry, but she cried a lot. Sometimes she cried when she watched him. Like her heart was broken. He knew she wasn't mad at him. She loved him more than anybody in the world. But even though Jake was only four, he knew his mama had dark secrets.

"Jake?" Kendall's brows were drawn as her hand touched his. "What's wrong?"

"I remember her now." Jake's voice was a stunned whisper. "She's my mother."

"Your mother?" Kendall hadn't had a chance to look at the picture, but now she recognized the woman she'd seen in Jake's house.

The same woman in the picture they'd found at Thomas's town house. Maryanne. "I thought you didn't remember your parents."

"I didn't. I only remembered her grave."

"You remember her funeral?"

"No. Her murder. I was hiding. She made me hide. He was coming, and she said I couldn't come out until he left. She made me promise. When I finally came out, she was dead." Jake swallowed, his face pale. "When I saw her picture at Thomas's town house, I knew she looked familiar, but I didn't know who she was. I . . . I don't think I wanted to."

"That explains why she was in your house. She's been watching over you."

Nathan had walked up behind them. He wore a frown. "I guess this eliminates any doubt that you're the Reaper's son."

CHAPTER SEVENTEEN

W HAT ARE YOU THINKING?" KENDALL WAS SITTING ON THE
sofa in the hotel suite, watching Jake worry.

"You don't know?" he asked. His tone was a little harsh.

The lines of his forehead were deep. She wanted to hold him
and make him understand that he was all right, no matter who
his father was, no matter who his mother was. "I don't pry, you
know that."

"Maybe you should." He looked weary. "Do you think you
could tell . . ."

"If you're the Reaper's son? I didn't sense it before when we
were touching." She gave Nathan an awkward glance and saw his
face was tight. If Jake were the Reaper's son, wouldn't she have
picked something up? They had been as close physically as two
people can be, more than once. The only thing she'd sensed was
the couple in the woods who may or may not have been Guinevere
and Lancelot. "He may have just been obsessed with your mother.
The room I was in looked like a memorial. And she was afraid. I
could feel it."

"I remember her fear." Jake rubbed a hand over his eyes.
"She tried to hide it, but I remember the fear in her eyes. And the

sadness. She was so sad. She would hug me and whisper, *what have I done?* . . . Don't look at me like that," he said to Nathan who was sitting on a plush chair, his dark eyes fixed on Jake. "You know I'm not working with him. If he's my father, I want no part of him. He killed my mother."

"But I think he loved her," Kendall said. "I sensed something in him when he had me in her room. He cared for her."

"Lots of murderers care for their victims in a sick way," Jake said.

"We can sort that out later," she said. "Now we have to get the chalice."

"Maybe you and I should go to your Aunt Edna's alone," Nathan said.

Jake turned on Nathan. "You're gonna use this as a wedge between us. You just want her away from me."

"Damn you both. Stop it!" Kendall yelled. "Nathan, you know Jake's on our side."

He looked slightly ashamed. "I don't know anything right now. I'll be watching you," he said to Jake.

"Like you haven't been already. I'll be watching you too."

"Damned pissing contest," Kendall muttered. "Sometimes I think having a penis is detrimental to one's mental health."

Nathan's phone rang. "It's Hank." Frustration crossed his face as he listened. "They can't find Brandi."

Brandi woke in a closet. After a moment, she realized it was Thomas's closet, and when she remembered how she'd gotten there, she ran to the bathroom where she and Kendall had hidden. She wasn't there. Brandi checked the entire town house and even the yard. She was alone. Had the Reaper taken the others? She was certain he was the one who'd knocked her out . . . with his mind. His dark eyes had locked on hers and sucked her mind dry, like a spider consuming a fly. She reached for her phone, throat tight. It wasn't in her pocket. She ran back and checked the closet to see if it had fallen out, and then retraced her steps to the bathroom where she and Kendall had hidden, but the phone wasn't anywhere. The Reaper must have taken it. She thought about his dark eyes, locking on hers, sucking the life from her soul, and for a moment she wanted to leave and forget about the Reaper and relics and all this craziness, forget she'd killed a man—even though he was evil and she'd only been protecting herself.

She was tired of the violence and danger, not knowing where she would sleep because she was so busy chasing clues, following Nathan, Jake, and Kendall, searching for these damned relics. She had become as obsessed with the Reaper as Thomas. Then she thought about her parents, their senseless deaths, the pain and loss she and Thomas had suffered, and how Thomas had died fighting this battle. She couldn't run away and forsake him. She was going to see the Reaper dead and the relics destroyed if it killed her. But she couldn't do it alone. The landline in the town house had been disconnected after Thomas had died, so there wasn't a way to call the castle to warn them or get help. She ran to the nearest busy street and hailed a taxi.

"This is like being a prisoner," Jake said, pacing the suite. "We can't leave or even order food."

"We can sleep," Nathan said.

"You have all that adrenaline for fuel, but some of us need food."

"I don't think it's a good idea to leave the room," Nathan said. "The Reaper must know by now that we broke into his château. I'm sure he knows everything about me, including that I own this hotel. He'll look for us here."

"I'm not going to sit here and starve to death while we wait for Raphael."

"Don't go, Jake." Kendall put her hand on his chest. "It's too dangerous."

Jake pulled her close. "I do like it when you worry about me." He smiled and kissed her hair.

It would have felt good if Nathan hadn't been watching. She stepped away and Jake sighed. "He knows," he whispered.

"I just don't feel comfortable."

His gray eyes were troubled. "Is that why?" His jaw set with determination. "I'm going to get food. I've gotten behind enemy lines more than once. Surely I can sneak into a snack shop."

Jake left, and Kendall turned to Nathan. He was studying the picture with a frown. "Don't tell me you recognize her too?"

"No, but I recognize the cup behind her." Nathan handed Kendall the picture.

They had been so focused on the woman that they hadn't noticed the objects in the photo. "It's the chalice in the painting. I wonder if she knew it was the Holy Grail?"

"So much power in something so plain." Nathan grimaced and rubbed the back of his neck.

"Headache?" She was surprised he hadn't had another episode.

"Yeah. These bloody memories are splitting my head apart."

Kendall put the picture down and moved behind Nathan. She started massaging his shoulders. They were tight. "Maybe you should stop trying to remember."

"I can't. I need to know."

"But I don't want you . . . hurt. I would rather have you not remember the past." *Not remember us.* "If that's what it takes to make you well."

Nathan turned, his eyes warm as he brushed back Kendall's hair. "I need to remember you. Everything about you, not just the pieces." He smiled, a soft smile that tugged at her soul. "He's a lucky man."

Jake walked in as if he'd heard them talking. He paused, eyes narrowed as he saw them standing close. He was holding three bottles of water, and his pockets were full. "We won't starve."

"Did you see anyone suspicious?" Nathan asked.

"No." Jake put the food down. "If we're lucky, he won't figure out we're here."

They ate their stash from the vending machine and went to bed. As soon as Raphael arrived with Marco, they would have to leave. It wasn't safe to stay any longer than necessary.

Jake ended up sleeping on the couch. Kendall heard him moving around after Nathan had gone to bed. She knew he wanted to come to her bed, but it didn't feel right with Nathan there. They needed sleep anyway, and she and Jake in bed together would probably end up in sex.

Today was her birthday. Adam held his gift carefully, smiling as he imagined Kendall opening it. Bea, the housekeeper, was the one who'd wrapped the present. She was the only person on the staff who he felt comfortable with. She was kind, always trying to make him eat, and fussing at his father, and Kendall's, for traveling so much. A boy needed to be home where he could play, she said. Bea loved Kendall too. Kendall didn't have a grandmother either. Adam saw Bea watching him and Kendall sometimes and her eyes looked sad.

"You need to make the gift look nice," Bea had said. "Kendall's turning into a young lady now."

Adam had grinned. "Kendall, a lady?" She could run almost as fast as him. She was tougher than most boys he knew. Then he remembered that he really didn't know any boys.

Adam felt his smile growing goofier as he walked to the table Bea had prepared with girly ribbons and balloons. It was only the four of them, and the staff. Adam and Kendall didn't have other close friends.

Adam put his gift with the others. Kendall was smiling, happy. Her father hadn't expected to make it back in time for the party. He'd had to stay behind and finish up some things on the dig. But he had rushed back. His gift was the first she opened. It was a new pair of boots and a cool backpack loaded with clothes and things to pull back her hair. Maybe Bea was right about her becoming a lady. Usually Kendall just used rubber bands.

Her Aunt Edna had sent some bracelets and a diary. Adam smiled and handed Kendall his gift. She tore off the paper and looked at the box.

"Open it," Adam said.

Kendall opened it, and her eyes widened like green marbles. "Wow."

"Where did you get that?" Adam's father demanded.

Kendall looked startled.

"I found it in your study," Adam said. "In a crate. The cup wasn't fancy, and it had a nick on the top, so I didn't think you would mind since it wasn't on the shelf."

"Kendall, give John the cup," her father said quietly.

"I'm sorry," Adam said. He'd wanted the gift to be special, but all he'd done was embarrass her.

His father's face relaxed a bit. "I understand, but you must ask before you take any of my things."

"Here, Uncle John." Kendall handed him the box.

"I'm sorry, Kendall. It's very old. Let's go find you something else. Come along. You too, Adam."

Adam pressed his lips together and shook his head. His father spent almost every waking minute building his collection. He spent more time with those old things than he did with his own son. He could give up one stupid relic for a little girl who was almost like a daughter.

Kendall's father left, muttering that he had something to do. When Adam's father and Kendall came back, she held up a turquoise necklace. "Look. This is the one we found in New Mexico."

He and Kendall had both been there when their fathers discovered the Pueblo dwelling.

"I'm going to find a mirror," Kendall said and ran off.

Adam watched her go but didn't follow.

"You're angry," his father said.

Adam hunched his shoulders. "You care more about your bloody artifacts than you do me."

A strange look came over his father's face. "That's not true."

"You spend more time with them."

His father rubbed his hands over his face and for a moment, he looked old. "You must know that I love you more than anyone. You're all I have left. But you're always busy with Kendall. I thought you were happy hanging out with her. I know she's younger, but she's always been your best friend."

"She's my only friend. No other kids live in the deserts and jungles. Her father spends more time looking for relics than he does with her too. We don't have anything but each other."

"I thought you liked this life. You said it was like a treasure hunt."

It was, but sometimes he missed normal things that other boys his age did. Baseball, football, girls.

"Bloody hell."

Kendall was awoken from her sleep by Nathan's cry. She jumped up and ran from her room. The couch was empty, so she hurried toward Nathan's room, half expecting to see him and Jake fighting the Reaper's men. She bumped into Nathan, just inside his door.

"Are you OK?"

"Better than OK." He smiled and grabbed her in a hug.

Startled, she put her arms around his waist and returned the hug. He leaned back and his eyes locked on her mouth. Still smiling, he lowered his head and gave her a quick kiss. He lifted his head slightly, lips still hovering over hers, and then kissed her again, this time not as quick. His hands cradled her face, and the kiss became more demanding. The sensations caught her breath. His body pressed closer, hands sliding down her back to her hips, pulling her tighter against him until she felt like she was coming out of her skin. Her head started to swim and she felt the room change.

The heavy fabric of her gown brushed her legs. His hands were firm on her back, working the catch of her gown. He had been waiting for this all day. She had seen the longing in his eyes, felt it in his touch, the casual stroke of a finger along the inside of her wrist as she handed him a cup of wine. She let him pull her closer and his mouth teased hers. His lips were sweet from the honey he'd eaten earlier. His hips pressed closer, and she felt the promise there. There was a fleeting moment of guilt as she envisioned another face and another set of lips, just as dear. She brushed the feeling aside and let herself revel in the warmth of her lover. Her champion. Her husband. Her king.

A presence crashed into her like a gale, and Kendall knew Jake had entered the room. By the time she disentangled herself, she heard Nathan's bedroom door close. Kendall's head was spinning. She wasn't sure where she was. But she knew who had left the room.

Oh, Jake.

Nathan was panting, his lips still parted, eyes amber. "I'm sorry."

"I'll go talk to him." She caught up to Jake in the living room. He was standing in the middle of the room as if he wasn't sure where to go. "Jake."

He turned, face set into a mask.

"I'm sorry. I'm not sure what happened."

"You were kissing him." There was no sarcasm in his voice.

"It just happened. He was happy. He's not often happy. He remembered something." She didn't even know what it was. "Before I knew what was happening, we were . . . kissing." More than kissing. What was that? A daydream? A memory? Kendall touched Jake's arm, wrapping her fingers around the smooth muscle. "I'm sorry."

"I don't know what you feel for him," Jake said. "But I know something's there."

"I do feel something for him," Kendall said. "He's Adam." And King Arthur. Her . . . husband . . . Crap.

"Do you want to sleep with him?"

"No . . ." Did she?

Jake shook his head and turned away. His shoulders were slumped in defeat. "I can't do this."

"Jake, I . . ." *Love?* "I care for you. A lot."

"You care for him a lot too," Jake said and walked out the door.

Nathan walked in. "Where is he?"

"He went out."

An undercurrent of excitement rolled off Nathan. He couldn't be that happy that Jake was upset.

"I'm sorry, Kendall."

"It's not your fault," she said, searching dark eyes, thick lashes, and strong bones for some resemblance to the man in her vision or whatever that had been. But she hadn't seen the man's face. She had known his touch, though. Double crap.

"If you want to hit me, go ahead."

"No. It's not that." She blinked, trying to clear her head. "Why are you so happy?"

"I know who has the Holy Grail. You."

"Me?" Kendall frowned.

"You had it. A long time ago. I gave it to you."

"You gave me the Holy Grail? Where did you get the Holy Grail?"

"Remember the chalice I gave you for your tenth birthday? My father took it back and gave you a necklace instead."

"Yes, he said the chalice was too old."

"It was old all right. I don't know how he got it," Nathan said. "But it was the same cup in this painting."

"You're sure?"

"I am. I remembered it from a dream."

"Uncle John had an incredible collection. If the Holy Grail was on the black market, he would have known. But I didn't get it. He took it back and gave me the necklace."

"I was mad at him. It was just an old cup, I thought, but there was something about it that felt special to me. He had lots of old cups, so I put it in your suitcase before you left for Aunt Edna's."

"I had the Holy Grail! That was just before the plane crash. I never saw any of you again." Kendall searched her mind, pushing through the memories of grief and pain as she tried to remember the suitcase. It was brown leather, like Indiana Jones might carry. "I remember the suitcase, but I don't remember the chalice. Maybe Aunt Edna will know."

"I guess it's time to visit your aunt," Nathan said.

"We can't leave without Marco and Raphael."

"I'll try him again," Nathan said. "He doesn't like cell phones, but I'm sure under the circumstances he has it turned on."

They reached Raphael. He hadn't found Marco yet, but he was still searching the other floors of the château. He told them to go find the chalice. He would find Marco and bring him home.

"I'll go find Jake," Kendall said. She was excited about the chalice but confused about her vision. And dreadfully worried about Jake.

"I'll come with you," Nathan said.

"I should talk to him alone."

Nathan hesitated. "Kendall, I know you feel something for him." His lips thinned. "I don't want to mess things up . . . I . . . I care for you, but I want you to be happy. If that means with Jake . . ."

Kendall felt surprisingly miserable for someone who'd just found out where the Holy Grail was. "Thank you."

"Go find Jake. If you're not back in ten minutes, I'm coming after you."

Kendall nodded and hurried out the door. She didn't know where Jake was, but she figured she'd try the bar. She didn't get that far before she found him. He was on the first floor near the lobby, peeking around a corner. He turned and saw her and put his finger to his lips.

She eased toward him. "What are you doing?" she mouthed.

He nodded in the direction where he was watching. "The Reaper's guards," he whispered.

"How do you know they work for the Reaper?"

"I recognize one of them. You shouldn't have come down here."

"I have to tell you something. We know where the Holy Grail is."

He didn't hear her. Something had caught his attention in the lobby.

"Did you hear me? What are you looking at?"

"I just saw Marco."

"Here?"

"Go back to the room. I'm going after him." He looked down the hallway behind them and cursed. "There are more guards behind us," he whispered. "Follow me, and keep your head down."

She lowered her head, which made it hard to see, but she

relied on Jake to lead her. "Are you certain it was Marco?" she asked when they exited the hotel.

"Yes. Come on. He went this way."

"We have to let Nathan know where we're going." Kendall took out her cell phone and dialed him. "We have a problem," she said when he answered.

"I know. I'm right behind you."

Kendall turned and saw Nathan hurrying toward them, his expression dark.

"What the hell are you doing?" Nathan asked when he got near.

"Jake saw Marco in the lobby."

"Maybe Raphael found him."

"I didn't see Raphael, and he's kind of hard to miss. But the Reaper has four guards here." Jake motioned for Kendall and Nathan to hurry. "Come on, we're going to lose Marco."

Marco was scurrying down the street at a fast pace. "I didn't know he could move that quick," Kendall said. "Maybe he's been drinking the water."

They followed Marco as he hurried down a wide street and then darted into a narrow, curved side street lined with shops that were closed for the night. With each footstep Kendall felt herself stepping back in time, feeling the lives of the people who had lived and died there. The loves, fears, and wars. Shadows and voices pulled at her, making her feel sick. Drinking the water at the castle had made her senses more intense, but they were still erratic.

"Where did he go?" Jake muttered, scanning the streets and buildings.

"He must have gone into one of the doors," Nathan said. "Unless he can walk through walls like Raphael." He glanced at Kendall and put a hand on her back. "You don't look good."

Of all times, why did her senses have to kick in now? "I'm just a little . . . sensitive."

Jake walked back to them. He held her chin and looked at her face. "It's too much for you. We need to get her out of here," he said to Nathan. "I think we're chasing ghosts anyway. No way that old man could evade all three of us. The Reaper might be playing tricks with our minds."

"We can't leave without making sure it isn't him," Kendall said.

"We'll call Raphael and tell him where we saw Marco," Nathan said. "Finding the chalice is the most important thing right now."

While Jake went inside to look for the guards, Nathan called Raphael's phone and left a message.

"Are the guards still there?" Kendall asked when Jake returned.

"Yes, but I took care of them."

"What did you do?" Kendall asked.

"What I had to. They spotted me." He tossed Nathan the car keys. "I grabbed these from the room. Let's get out of here before more of the Reaper's men show up."

They hurried to the car, but Jake didn't get in. His face was a mask of gloom. "I'm not going."

"Why?" Kendall asked.

"I have some things to do."

"If this is about being the Reaper's son, I don't care."

"I have to think. Nathan will take care of you." His jaw tightened. He seemed unsure. "Stay close to him."

Kendall swallowed. "I'm sorry," she whispered, her heart breaking.

Jake nodded and walked away.

They left the hotel and drove to the airport, passing glorious sights that held no appeal. Her senses felt dead. Even the prospect of finding the chalice didn't help. And after all this time, would it still be there?

They bought clothes and toiletries in the airport before their flight to Aunt Edna's. Nathan was also distracted. Kendall knew he felt bad about kissing her, and neither of them wanted to talk about it. She had no idea if he had seen any part of the vision. If so, he hadn't mentioned it. She didn't know what she felt. Guilt. Pleasure. She loved Jake, but she loved Nathan too. Was it the same feeling for both men? She didn't know. She'd never felt anything like it. But the woman in the vision had also loved two men.

Had Nathan been Kendall's husband in a past life? Had she cheated on him with Jake? If they were truly reincarnations or doppelgangers, and if the legends had gotten that part of the tale right, then they had. Her head hurt just thinking about it, because she knew there weren't any clear answers.

She slept throughout most of the long flight to Virginia. When she wasn't sleeping, she was worrying. Mostly about Jake. He had just found out he may be the Reaper's son. He'd remembered finding his mother murdered. And now, after he'd softened his brittle heart and fallen for her, she had betrayed him too.

Jake stood at the front door of his house in Charlottesville, Virginia. He unlocked the door, but his hand hesitated on the knob. He'd enjoyed the house, what little time he spent here. The woman he'd called his grandmother had left it to him. She wasn't really his grandmother, as far as he knew. She'd found him when she was searching for her missing grandson. Turned out it wasn't Jake, but neither of them had family, and she was lonely, so he'd started visiting her. Just a few times at first, then more often, staying for dinner, helping her with odd jobs around the house. Maybe he was the lonely one, because for a while he'd felt like he had a family. Even after her mind started slipping, he still came, and it became a private joke between them, calling each other grandmother and grandson. She even told her neighbors that she'd found her missing grandson. There at the end, Jake was sure she believed it. And if Kendall was right about his mother's ghost being here, maybe the woman he'd called grandmother really was related to him. Family or not, he'd loved her.

Bracing himself, he opened the door and went inside. The house held none of the coldness that Clint had felt. It felt welcoming. Was there a presence here trying to ward off strangers and protect Jake? He sat down at the kitchen table and closed his eyes. He had a mother, a mother who had loved him. After years of trying to remember something from his childhood, and only coming up with that damned grave, finally he knew that she hadn't abandoned him on the doorstep of an orphanage in India. He'd never known how he got there. No one had. But he still had so many questions.

How had she gotten involved with the Reaper? Had she loved him? Had he kidnapped her? If she was the woman whose room Kendall had been held in, that didn't jive. Kendall had sensed that the Reaper loved the woman. What had happened? He needed to know who she really was before he could deal with who his father was.

He went to the spot where Kendall had seen her, and he stood, eyes closed. When that didn't work, he sat down on the floor, legs crossed like when he was a kid—was that a memory?—and he waited. He tried to clear his mind of everything but the grave and the blond hair against raw dirt, the woman's lifeless pale cheeks, eyes that had been so afraid and so kind, now closed—and the memories that had been locked away in a frightened little boy's mind finally returned.

Jake crouched behind the trees, waiting for his mother to come back. He didn't know where he was. He'd fallen asleep on his mother's lap on the way here. She'd told him she had to meet someone. He could hear her talking to a man. They were arguing. The man was angry, yelling at her, asking how she could do it, how she could leave. Jake didn't know what he was talking about, but his mother sounded frightened. He heard another voice, and then his mother cried out. Was she hurt? He wanted to go to her, but he'd promised he wouldn't leave until the man was gone. He always kept his promises.

The man said his mother's name, Maryanne. He kept saying it, over and over, his voice getting higher and louder. He sounded really mad. Or maybe scared. Jake was scared because his mother didn't answer. Had she run away and forgotten about him? She wouldn't leave him. Every day she promised him that she would never leave him. Sometimes it made her cry. Once she'd hugged him and said she was sorry for leaving him, that she would make it right. He'd never understood that, because she hadn't left him. She almost never let him out of his sight. Someone started crying, and Jake wanted to come out, but he'd promised. She had told him he must never break his promises, so he stayed there listening to the man sob. Or was it a child? Two voices? The man said a name, but Jake couldn't hear it clearly, and he couldn't see through the trees. Terrified, he waited until the sounds faded. When he knew his mother wasn't coming back, he slipped from his hiding place and moved toward where he had heard the voices.

His mother was lying in a grave. He shook her arm and patted her cheeks, but she didn't wake up. He held her hand and cried until he heard someone coming back. He wanted to stay with her, because he didn't know where to go, but she'd made him promise he would run if bad men ever came after him. Knights never broke their promises. So he got up and ran.

A touch on his shoulder brought Jake out of the memory. Startled, he turned, hoping it was Kendall. But she was with Nathan. He didn't see anyone. A shiver moved across his skin, and the hair on his arms stood. A lump settled in his throat as he looked around the room for his mother. If she was there, he couldn't see her.

Disturbed by the dream and the touch, wondering if he'd imagined it, he rose and went to get a drink. The fridge was stocked, thanks to Clint. Jake grabbed a Pepsi and sat at the table again, thinking, wishing. Wishing Kendall were here to be his eyes into a world he couldn't see. Wishing she were here anyway. After just hours without her, he felt like part of himself was gone. How had she worked her way into his heart in such a short time? He'd thought he was immune to love. He only bonded with the men on his team. He'd known women, accepted what they offered, and kept moving without giving them another thought. But he couldn't get Kendall out of his head, and the thought of her with Nathan made it worse.

"Don't be an ass," he said to himself. Nathan would protect her. He would give his life for Kendall. That was some solace, but not enough to ease the ache in his heart.

When he finally slept, he was tormented by dreams of his mother telling him to find something. He saw her face clearly, her beautiful eyes pleading, afraid. Then his dreams turned to Kendall and Nathan kissing. But his dream didn't stop with a kiss. He saw them touching, bodies pressing close and finally coming together as one. He saw Kendall's eyes flare as Nathan entered her and her hands gripping his shoulders, pulling him closer.

Jake woke in a sweat. He stripped off his underwear—he couldn't sleep without them if his mother could be in the house, moving through the walls like Raphael—and climbed under the cold spray of the shower. Kendall and Nathan. Kendall and Nathan. Even the rushing water seemed to taunt him with their names. Tense with frustration, he got out and dressed. He wouldn't leave her. He didn't care who his father was, Kendall belonged with him. He wasn't going to give her up. Nathan would have to settle for her friendship.

He dressed, packed a bag, and jumped into his Jeep. He'd wasted enough time.

The trip from the airport to Aunt Edna's seemed to take forever. Kendall and Nathan alternated between bouts of silence and talking. Kendall kept thinking about Jake, wondering if he was all right, and though Nathan wouldn't have admitted it, she knew he was worried about Jake too.

"He'll be OK," Nathan said after a long silence.

"I don't know. I've never seen him like this."

Nathan stared out the window of the rental car they had picked up at the airport. "I have."

She had forgotten that Nathan had known Jake longer than she had. "After you rescued him from that Iraqi jail? I'm sure that wasn't fun for either of you."

"He looked half dead. They had beaten the shit out of him."

"You really did save him." The little boy she had loved and thought she'd lost had saved the man who would end up being her lover. And if that wasn't confusing enough, they had all known and betrayed each other many lifetimes ago. *Stop it, Kendall.* She had determined that she wouldn't keep thinking about that damned vision until the chalice was safe.

Nathan rubbed a hand over his short hair and gave an empty laugh. "I saved the Reaper's son."

"We don't know for certain that the Reaper was his father."

"He is." Nathan said it without anger. "I was right the first time. He was connected to the Reaper. Jake just didn't know it."

"Just because Jake's mother knew the Reaper, that doesn't mean he's his father." But she knew deep down that he was. So did Jake. "Is that the only reason you rescued him? Because you thought he would lead you to the Reaper?"

Nathan seemed to be searching for an answer. "I don't really know. I just needed to do it." He swerved to avoid a dead animal in the road.

Kendall was certain there was more behind Nathan's motive than just spying on an enemy. He'd felt something for Jake. Maybe he'd sensed that they were both alone, and if Raphael was right about King Arthur, Nathan and Jake were connected on a deeper level. Her mind started going there, but she pulled it back. "I think you sensed a kindred spirit. Neither of you remembered your parents, you both had blank spots in your pasts, you both put up walls to keep people at a distance. Other than all your money, you're both a lot alike."

"If that's why you—" He clenched his hands on the wheel.

She didn't ask him to finish. She knew what he was going to say. That it was the reason she had feelings for Nathan and Jake.

"You're alone too," he said, interrupting her musing. "Your father is dead. You didn't know your mother. We're all sort of dysfunctional."

"But we're not alone now." Kendall patted his shoulder. "We found each other again." Now if she just had Jake. They would be complete.

They rode in silence for a while, and Kendall searched through her memories for any hint of the chalice. But she had nothing. "What will we do with the chalice if it is at Aunt Edna's?"

"Put it somewhere so that it's safe from the Reaper."

"With the Spear of Destiny? Wherever you hid it?"

"I'm not trying to hide it from you. I figured you're better off not knowing until the Reaper is out of the way."

"Now that I'm the keeper, you'll have to tell me."

"Are you pulling rank?" he asked with a hint of a smile.

"If you don't show me, I will."

"I will. Let's just hope we can find the chalice." He shook his head. "To think everyone's been looking for the Holy Grail, and I was the one who took it. I'm a bloody relic thief."

Kendall smiled. "You didn't really steal it. It belonged to your father, and you didn't know what you were taking. You haven't stolen anything since. Have you?"

"No, I got my collection legally. For the most part. I brushed the line a few times."

"You always had an adventurous streak," Kendall said, smiling as she remembered. "You never cheated, but you knew how to push the envelope. I guess that's what made you a good businessman."

"My father's money made me a good businessman. He left me a lot of money. It's one thing to succeed when you have to start from nothing. I had a helping hand."

"How much do you remember about your father?"

"More than I did, but there are still a lot of holes."

"His collection was magnificent. Everyone wanted it."

"Did we ever see it?"

"A few times. We weren't allowed to go inside the room unless he was with us. He didn't really like anyone looking at it. But we sneaked in a couple of times."

Nathan smiled. "Did we get caught?"

"No. We were very good at sneaking." She smiled. "He kept it in a secret room off his study. There was an old lock, ancient, probably a relic itself, but nothing like we'd seen. You were fascinated with it."

Nathan's gaze had left the road and steadied on her. "Your eyes light up when you talk about it."

"We had fun. It was an exciting life, if a little odd. Uncle John knew everyone in the antiquities community," Kendall said. "Sometimes we went to big cities to attend museum openings or some fund-raiser where the men wore tuxes and women dressed in lovely gowns. Do you remember that?"

"I remember hiding upstairs and looking over a balcony."

Kendall laughed. "That was in Amsterdam. Uncle John was there for some big fund-raiser." She turned to Nathan. "I'm sorry. I still feel like it's my fault that he died. I never dreamed that my trespassing could cause so much grief."

"It's not your fault," Nathan said.

"You heard Marco talk about the curse, and they died right after I broke into the chapel and took the vow."

"You didn't know you were taking a vow—"

"You did," Kendall said. "You tried to stop me. You knew something bad was going to happen, didn't you?"

Nathan shrugged one shoulder. "I didn't know anything for sure, but it felt off."

"That should have been my clue. You were never scared of anything. I'm sorry. It is my fault."

"It's the Reaper's fault. He's the one who killed them. He must have known my father had the chalice. If you want to assign blame to someone else, look at me. The Reaper killed my father for something he never had. I had already stolen the Holy Grail. Maybe if he'd found it, he would have left him alive."

Kendall touched Nathan's hand. "That's not likely. He killed other collectors besides your father. Look at Brandi and Thomas's parents. He killed them and they didn't have the Holy Grail."

He sighed. "None of us can change the past. We just have to

accept it and go on. Besides, if we're who Raphael thinks we are, reincarnations of King Arthur and Guinevere, then there must be a reason why they came back now. You taking the vow could have been meant to be."

She ignored the troubling vision and concentrated on the safest part of the theory. "I hadn't thought of that. It's as if we were chosen. Doesn't that just blow your mind? You were once King Arthur. *The* King Arthur."

A slow smile started on Nathan's lips. "It's bloody insane. I always wanted to be King Arthur. I used to dream about it."

Kendall felt a bubble of excitement at his smile. "They were probably memories, not dreams."

"If this is true, you were there too. And Jake." Nathan's mouth twisted. "Lancelot."

And there she went, headfirst into the pit of guilt. The love triangle of all times, Kendall thought. History repeating itself with a twist. She changed the subject, hoping to put the smile back on Nathan's face and keep herself from going insane. "We'll have to be careful not to mention any of this to Aunt Edna. She's a gossip."

"I remember," Nathan said, with a hint of humor. "She knew everything about everyone."

"Still does. She sends me e-mails to keep me informed." And to offer the latest selection of potential bridegrooms. Kendall already had one too many men to choose from.

"If your father was born centuries ago, how can she be his sister?"

"She's not. She's my mom's distant cousin by marriage or something crazy. My mom and dad didn't have any real family—now I know why he didn't—so when he died, Aunt Edna stepped in and adopted me. I thought she was my real aunt until I was grown."

"She loves you like family. I'm sure she'll be happy to see you. Let's just hope the chalice is still there," Nathan said.

"Aunt Edna has every drawing I ever sent her when I was a kid. She never throws anything away."

Nathan frowned. "But doesn't she sell a lot of stuff in her antique shop?"

"Oh God. You don't think . . ."

Aunt Edna's house was a Victorian, like many others on this street. It looked just as it had when Kendall was a kid, like a gingerbread house with the fancy trim and bright colors.

Aunt Edna was waiting for them outside, face lit with a smile. Like the house, Aunt Edna never seemed to change much, but this time she looked all *fixed up*, as she would say. Her gray hair showed signs of a fresh perm, and instead of a plain, solid-colored dress, she wore one with flowers so bright it looked like a patch of spring.

"She looks different," Nathan said. He'd met her a few times.

"Maybe she's having a fling with old man Wilson."

"He's the one with the farm behind her house?"

"That's him. They're always bickering, but I think they're really flirting."

Aunt Edna's dress flapped like petunias in the breeze as she hurried toward the car, chattering away before Kendall could open the door.

". . . so long since you've been here." Aunt Edna wrapped Kendall in a hug, and the smell of White Shoulders wafted up her nose. Her aunt stepped back, smiling at Nathan. "And this must be your . . . boss." *Rich* was the missing word. Aunt Edna's hands were clasped in excitement, and Kendall knew her aunt was dreaming about weddings.

"Yes, this is Nathan Larraby."

"It's wonderful to meet you," Aunt Edna said. "I've heard such nice things about you. Well, come on inside now, and let's have a little visit. You can tell me what Kendall's been up to. I worry about her. She's always been a handful ever since she was little. You can't imagine."

Nathan grinned. "I think I can."

Kendall wished she could tell her aunt who Nathan was. Aunt Edna had been there for Kendall while she grieved for him, but as much as she loved her aunt, she wasn't the most discreet person. The last thing Nathan needed was the press getting wind that he had another identity, a boy who was supposed to be dead.

"Did you get a new car?" Kendall asked, looking at a sporty little Mazda.

"No, that belongs to one of my guests."

"Guests?"

"I'm taking in guests now." Aunt Edna glanced across the street at the Happy Hearth Bed-and-Breakfast, owned by her archrival, Doris Clune. "Doris's isn't the only bed-and-breakfast in town now."

"You turned your house into a bed-and-breakfast?"

"Why not? I have plenty of room, and it brings in some money."

Did she need money? Kendall had helped her out once when she was about to lose the shop. "Are things OK?"

Aunt Edna waved her hand in dismissal. "Oh yes. This is my cruise money, and having a bed-and-breakfast keeps me busy. Between that and the antique shop, I never get bored. Idle hands and all that."

Aunt Edna had never gotten bored. If she had a moment of spare time, she was visiting her friends to get the latest news, serving as Hillside's resident gossip.

Aunt Edna waved her hands. Her nails were bright pink. "Don't worry, it's just a couple of guests. I'm sure they won't trouble you."

"We can't stay long. Just a quick visit." Long enough to find the chalice and get it to a safe place.

"You're staying the night?"

"Maybe one night. We have a busy schedule."

"I'll be glad to have a strong man in the house," Aunt Edna said. "We've got a burglar on the loose."

"Here?"

"He's made two attempts. The sheriff's still looking for him. I think it's Doris trying to undermine my business. That's just the sort of thing she would do. But the sheriff won't listen to me."

"When did this happen?" Kendall asked.

"Night before last, but I scared him off with my cowbell. Oh, there's the phone. I'll be right back. Make yourselves at home."

"That's a bit strange," Nathan said. "We find out the chalice is here and someone tries to break in."

"Could the Reaper have found out?"

Aunt Edna came back and interrupted any further discussion. "Another man wanting a room, but I'm booked. Too bad. He sounded handsome. Now look at you, empty-handed. Let me get you a glass of tea and we can catch up."

They caught up for a long time, as Aunt Edna told Nathan every embarrassing story she knew about Kendall when she was a girl. Then she gave them a tour of the house to show them all the work she'd done. She'd done some painting, but the house still looked the same. Except for the number of pictures of Kendall as a girl. Kendall didn't remember all those. She was touched, and a little embarrassed. Aunt Edna was the only family she had left, maybe not blood relation, but she was still family. Kendall should have visited more often.

Nathan paused over each one, and Kendall knew he was comparing them to the girl he'd known. He smiled at Kendall. "It looks the same."

Aunt Edna frowned. "You've been here before? I don't recall Kendall bringing *you*."

Aunt Edna would never forget anyone so groomworthy. Kendall nudged Nathan's arm and he shot her a look of apology. "I showed him pictures. Aunt Edna, do you remember when I came here, just before my father died?"

Her aunt's eyes saddened. "I do. What a sad time." She turned to Nathan. "She lost her father and her best friend. I don't know if she's told you about Adam, but she adored that boy. I expected they'd grow up and marry, but you never know what life will throw at you. Instead of a wedding, she had to sit by his grave and cry. Poor little tyke. So young and heartbroken." She patted Kendall's shoulder. "It ripped my heart out as well. Oh, tsk, listen to me bringing up sad times. What were you saying?"

Nathan's face was shadowed, and Kendall had a feeling he was blocking her. "Do you remember the suitcase I brought?"

"The brown leather one, I do. We tried to get you a pink one, but you said it looked silly. You wanted the one that looked like something Indiana Jones would carry."

"I know it's been a long time, but do you remember what happened to the things in the suitcase? I've just remembered a cup that Adam gave me. It was very special, a wooden cup. I don't remember what happened to it."

"I'm sorry. I remember the suitcase, but I don't remember what happened to it. We can have a look around in the attic and the cellar. I don't get rid of much. Neither did your father. That man and his relics. Relics this, relics that. He had a one-track mind. It wasn't healthy for a young girl, but you loved him so much, and you were just like him. I offered to keep you here, but you threw a fit." She smiled. "Stamped your foot and said you were going wherever your daddy went, and no one was going to stop you."

"I don't remember."

"I do. I worried over you, but you seemed happy. And you had Adam. He always looked after you."

Kendall felt her cheeks warm. She looked at Nathan, and her stomach dipped at the sad look on his face.

"Come along now. Let me show you to your rooms. I'm glad I didn't put anyone in yours, Kendall."

Her room. After her father's death, Aunt Edna had made a home for Kendall. She had loved her and raised her as if she were her real family. A warm feeling gushed over her, and Kendall hugged her aunt.

"Now what was that for?" Aunt Edna asked.

"To thank you for being you."

Kendall's old room had been redecorated, but some of her things were still here. A favorite book, a drawing she'd made for Aunt Edna that may have been a bunny rabbit. Nathan's room was across the hall from Kendall's. It was the room her father had stayed in when he was here. After settling their bags, they went down for supper.

Throughout the meal she continued to prompt Aunt Edna about the suitcase, but she couldn't remember anything. If it were still here, and it was doubtful, they would have to find it on their own. After dinner, she and Nathan started the search. "I don't think it would be in the antique shop. We should start with the workshop," Kendall said. The old carriage house was used for storing things her aunt didn't need at the moment or that needed work.

The years rolled away as they crossed the yard. They'd walked this same path about sixteen years ago. At some point, Kendall realized their hands were linked.

"Remember this tree," Nathan said, stopping at a large oak. "We raced to the top, and you almost fell out."

"You caught my arm," Kendall said. "Nearly ripped it out of its socket." She smiled. "It hurt for days."

"And you didn't let me forget it. You made me wait on you, hand and foot. It feels like another lifetime."

"It was, in some ways," she said. "We were everything to each other."

She hadn't really intended to say that. It was true, but Nathan wasn't that little boy now, and it made things feel awkward when there was Jake to consider.

"I know," Nathan said. "I knew that even before I remembered anything about those lost years. The first time I saw you, I knew you." Nathan's fingers stroked hers. "I couldn't explain it since I'd never met you. But somehow I knew we were connected. Then I started to get glimpses of you when you were younger. That was disturbing. I thought I was losing my mind. Then the other things started happening more frequently, the curse, and I knew something was wrong with me."

"That's why you blocked me from reading anything about you. Not that I tried to read you," she quickly added. "I just couldn't sense the things I would normally sense about someone."

"It was bad enough that I thought I was crazy. I didn't want you to think I was too."

"Now you know you're not crazy."

"Right. I just acquired some paranormal super ninja skills."

Kendall looked at him in surprise and saw a smile. He didn't often joke. Adam had, and it was good to see that side of him. "You're not alone," she said, smiling in return. "I have some crazy ninja skills too."

His expression turned serious. "I'm glad I'm not alone. I need you with me." He looked away, his jaw tight. "I don't mean to mess up what you have with Jake. I just mean . . . hell, I don't know what I mean."

The vision reared its head. She didn't know what to say, but she knew one thing for sure: she was glad she'd found Adam again. "I'm glad you're here," she said, and they left it at that. Hands still joined, they walked to the workshop to see if the chalice was there.

"You're not wincing now when you remember things. Maybe you're getting past the weird effect it's having on your head."

"It was probably the portal screwing me up," he said.

"Then we'll have to stay away from portals. Leave that to Raphael."

"I wonder if he's found Marco yet."

"If anyone can, it's Raphael."

Raphael searched the château from top to bottom, and after he got Nathan's message, he searched the area near the hotel in vain, wearing himself out with the travel. He knew Marco well. They had been brothers and shared a lifetime of secrets. If he had come here to find the Reaper, he wouldn't stop until he succeeded. Raphael went back to the château, focusing on the grounds.

There were several buildings on the property, including a small stone chapel that looked foreboding, resembling a large family burial vault more than a place of worship. The wood-and-iron door stood ajar. Raphael stepped inside, his chest tight with dread. He found Marco lying facedown near the altar, lifeless.

Raphael gave a soul-wrenching cry as he gathered his old friend in his arms and wept.

CHAPTER EIGHTEEN

THE CHALICE WASN'T IN THE WORKSHOP. THEY HAD searched through all the boxes and trunks, with no luck.

"What about all that stuff she kept in the attic?" Nathan said.

They'd explored it together when Adam was here, spending hours searching for pieces of the past. Kendall brushed the dust off her hands. "She used to keep a lot of stuff up there. It's probably too late to look tonight. Her guests might think the attic is crawling with rats."

They started back inside, when he stopped and looked at the house. "I think we're being watched."

"What?"

"I saw someone at the window," he said. "I think it's yours."

"It's probably Aunt Edna in there fluffing the pillows and doing a little spying. She's hoping you're Mr. Right."

He glanced at her, but didn't say anything. She wished she hadn't either. He didn't try to hug her or kiss her, but she couldn't help remembering the hotel kiss. He must have been thinking the same, because the air between them grew tense. "I'll see you in the morning," he said.

Kendall nodded. "If we don't find the chalice in the house,

tomorrow we'll go to the antique shop." They had to find it quickly before the Reaper figured out where they were. "Good night." She stepped inside her room and turned on the light, closing the door behind her.

"Hi."

Kendall let out a squeal and whirled. "Jake! What are you doing here?" She grabbed her heart, which felt like it might leap out of her chest.

"I needed to see you."

His steel-gray eyes had a soft look that made her legs wobbly. His dark hair was touching the collar of his shirt, and the expression on his handsome face was serious. She'd missed him terribly since Prague. "You did?"

He rubbed his palms on the pockets of his faded jeans. "Sorry I didn't tell you I was coming. I wasn't sure what to say, and by the time I figured it out, I was already here."

"What did you want to say?"

"I'm not letting you go. I don't care if he's Adam. I don't care if you've been in love with him most of your life. I don't care if he's King Arthur and you're Guinevere. I'm not going to let you get away from me without a fight."

Kendall stood rooted to the spot while her stomach did a sequence of flips. "OK," she replied a little breathlessly.

He pulled her to him and kissed her. It was a hot, possessive kiss, and she felt him from head to toe. His arms, chest, hips, and thighs. Part of her knew she belonged with him, and her fingers pressed into the muscles of his back to hold him there.

The door burst open and Nathan rushed inside, his eyes glowing. Kendall pushed away from Jake. "Nathan! It's Jake."

He had recognized Jake, but Nathan still looked frightening. "What the hell are you doing here?"

"I needed to talk to Kendall."

"You just show up in her room in the middle of the night?"

"There weren't any other rooms available. I called."

"What did you tell Aunt Edna?" Kendall asked.

"I didn't see her."

"You sneaked in?"

"Kendall, dear? Is everything all right? I thought I heard you cry out." Aunt Edna peeked inside. Her eyes widened when she saw Jake. She fumbled in her pocket and pulled out a small handgun. "Kendall, call the sheriff. Stay right there and don't move, you burglaring bastard. I'll shoot you right in the balls."

"Aunt Edna, he's not a burglar. This is my friend, Jake," Kendall said. "He was supposed to come with us, but he was delayed."

"Oh," Aunt Edna said, lowering her gun. "I'm sorry. I thought you were the burglar."

"Burglar?" Jake asked.

"There've been a couple of attempted break-ins," Kendall explained.

"Forgive me, Jake. I just assumed you were him." Aunt Edna stuck out her hand. "It's very nice to meet you."

"Aunt Edna, what are you doing with a gun?"

"It's protection. You can't be too careful." She dropped the gun into the pocket of her robe and smiled at Jake. "You say you're Kendall's friend?"

"Her bodyguard," Nathan said. "Jake works for me."

"You need a bodyguard, dear? That sounds dangerous."

"It's just a title to make him feel good," Nathan said, his lips tight. "He's really a boy Friday. Runs errands, that kind of thing."

"Like a secretary. My, times have changed."

Jake looked pissed for a moment, and then he smiled. "Nathan is joking, of course. I'm Kendall's fiancé."

Nathan's mouth dropped open, and Aunt Edna squealed. "Fiancé!" She grabbed Kendall in a hug, and then she stepped back and embraced Jake. She was so excited, she kept hugging, and ended with Nathan, pounding him on the back while he glowered at Jake. "Welcome to the family, Jake. Oh, Kendall. I'm so happy."

Kendall opened her mouth to explain that Jake was exaggerating, and then decided to do it later, in private. She didn't want a full-scale argument between Nathan and Jake now. On the bright side, if Aunt Edna thought Kendall was engaged, she couldn't keep bugging her to find a boyfriend.

"I've worried so much about Kendall being alone. I've been trying to help her find someone. She's so pretty and so adventurous, I'm always worried that she'll get into trouble."

"She is a little wild," Jake said, pinching Kendall's cheek.

Nathan looked mildly disgusted. "I'm going back to bed."

"Good night, Nathan," Aunt Edna said. Then after he had left the room, she turned to Kendall. "Is he all right? He didn't look very happy."

"He's bipolar," Jake said. "He'll be fine after he takes his meds."

"Oh dear, well, it's wonderful that you're here. I've tried so hard to get her to find a husband."

"You don't have to worry anymore," Jake said. He put his arm around Kendall and kissed the top of her head. "I'm here to stay."

This was getting a little much. She'd better put a stop to it now. "What a joker—"

Jake's mouth came down on hers, suffocating her words. Jake lifted his head and gave her three more quick kisses.

"How romantic," Aunt Edna said. "Oh, young love."

Kendall couldn't remember what she had been about to say, and Aunt Edna looked so happy. Tomorrow, Kendall thought. She'd explain it then. Let Aunt Edna revel in bliss for tonight.

"This is wonderful. Are you hungry? I can warm up some dinner."

"No, thank you," Jake said. "I'm just tired."

"Oh," Aunt Edna glanced at Kendall. "Will you be needing a separate room? I know things are different now, not like back in my day."

Again, Jake spoke up before Kendall could open her mouth. "If you don't mind, ma'am, I'll sleep in here. I like to keep a close eye on her. Especially with this burglar running around."

"Of course, well. I suppose it's a good thing seeing as how I'm out of rooms. I would have had to put you with Nathan."

"Who are your guests?" Jake asked.

"There's Tom. He's considering moving to the neighborhood and wanted to get a feel for the place. Then Charles, Charles Rutherford," Aunt Edna said, her cheeks warming. "He's here on business. Actually, he's interested in buying the antique shop."

"You're thinking of selling?" Kendall asked.

"No, I don't think so, but what's the harm in letting him look around." She chuckled. "He's right handsome."

"Aunt Edna, is this man the reason you looked so fixed up?"

"Maybe. I'm not too old to flirt." Aunt Edna had been married once, a long time ago. Her husband had died in the Vietnam War. For all her efforts to get Kendall married, Aunt Edna had never shown any interest in remarrying. After she was sure Jake didn't need food, drink, or anything else, Aunt Edna gave him a hug and left, looking pleased as could be.

A few seconds after the door closed, it opened again. Nathan stepped in. "You bastard."

"Boy Friday? You asked for it." His expression turned serious. "We have a problem. I followed someone in. Thomas."

Nathan was still upset, but he was in control. "You saw Thomas here?"

"Unless he has a doppelganger too," Jake said. "It looked just like the picture I saw of him at his town house."

Kendall perched on the rocking chair near the door. "He can't be alive. Can he?"

Jake lifted a shoulder in a shrug. "It's a little odd that someone who looks like him keeps showing up."

"And one of Aunt Edna's guests is named Tom," Nathan said. "Remember Thomas kept his first name even when he was pretending to work for the Reaper."

"Makes me wonder if he was really undercover," Jake said.

"Assuming that Thomas is still alive, you don't think he's working for the Reaper? He's spent years trying to find and kill him," Kendall said.

"He spent a lot of time undercover," Jake said. "Maybe the Reaper got to him. We know he's powerful, especially when it comes to mental tricks."

"How could he know we're here?" Kendall asked.

"I think he has some kind of connection with you," Nathan said. "He may be following you."

"Tracking me? Like a tracking device? I haven't seen anything."

"It might not be visible," Jake said.

Kendall gaped. "Where . . . you mean in me?"

"Under your skin. He could have done it while you were sleeping."

"Oh my God." A shiver rippled over her skin as she remembered him sitting there watching her sleep. She started feeling her arms and neck. "Where would he put it? Wouldn't I feel it?"

"It could be anywhere," Jake said. "I'll check you over tonight."

Nathan made a dismissive sound. "It's more likely he's reading your mind."

"That's worse." She felt violated. This was why she didn't read other people's minds.

"We need to take a look at this guy's room," Nathan said. "Did you see where he went?"

"The one next to Kendall's."

"I saw someone watching us earlier," Nathan said. "I thought it was from this window. It could have been the next one."

"Or was it you?" Kendall asked Jake.

"Wasn't me," Jake said. "I just got here."

"I say we confront him now."

"Exactly what I was thinking. You stay here," Jake said when Kendall stood to follow them.

"I'm not sitting here like a helpless damsel."

"You're far from helpless," Jake said, "but you're the target if Thomas or anyone working for the Reaper is here. They're not here to steal Aunt Edna's china. Even if they've figured out that the chalice was here, it's been years since you brought it. They'll still need you to find it."

Convinced, Kendall waited as they crept down the hall. The floors in the house had always creaked, but Jake and Nathan moved so quietly she couldn't hear them. After five long minutes, they returned.

"He's not there," Jake said.

"He must have left."

"Did you find anything in his room?" Kendall asked.

"Not even a toothbrush."

"No one travels that light," Nathan said. "Except in an emergency."

Kendall shook her head. "We need to ask Aunt Edna about him."

"We'll have to keep an eye on his room," Jake said. "I want to know who he is and what he's doing here."

Nathan nodded. "It's too much of a coincidence that he shows up just as we've traced the chalice here."

"Have you had any luck?" Jake asked.

"No. Aunt Edna remembers the suitcase but not what happened to it or the things inside. It's been so long. This is probably hopeless. She probably sold it."

Jake paled. "Do you think she could have?"

"I don't know. She sells some strange things in her antique shop. Some are really nice. Some oddball things. We'll search the place tomorrow. We really should get some sleep. Aunt Edna will be up bright and early pressing us with breakfast. And she won't take no for an answer."

Nathan and Jake stood in the middle of the room staring at each other. "Coming?" Nathan asked, but he said it in a way that sounded like a statement.

"I'm not leaving Kendall alone," Jake said. "So unless you're sleeping here with us . . ."

Nathan's eyes flickered. "Then I'll see you in the morning." Shoulders stiff, he turned and walked out.

When the door closed, Kendall looked at Jake.

"I told you I wasn't giving up," he said. "I know you have feelings for him too, but I think your body is confused. Your best friend who you loved, and you thought you lost, is all grown up, and he's rich and . . . handsome. I'm not confused. I know what I want, and I'm not going to stop until you tell me to leave." His gaze was steady on hers, not challenging, but determined.

He was admitting that Nathan was Adam, but he wasn't admitting defeat. Kendall smiled. "Let's get some sleep."

Jake looked at the bed. "I'll sleep on the floor if you want, but I'd like to sleep with you in the bed."

She should have said no, because he was right about her being confused, and the vision had made it worse. But she wasn't confused about her feelings for him, any more than she was confused about being glad Adam was back. She loved Jake. *In love?* She was still trying to figure that out. But the need to feel him close to her was stronger than any confusion or fear.

While he brushed his teeth in the bathroom down the hall, she gathered her things, not allowing herself to think too much about her decision. After he returned, she took her turn, and he watched as she walked to the bathroom door. She took a quick shower, brushed her teeth, and changed into a cami and yoga pants.

When she came back, he was sitting on the side of the bed waiting for her. His eyes were warm, full of promises and threats. Life with Jake would never be the same as before. It would be passionate, furious, demanding, but she wasn't sure she could live without him. Maybe she was in love. He stood and turned back the covers for her, and didn't try to touch her as she got in. He shut off the light, stripped off his pants, and climbed in beside her. She wasn't sure if she was glad that he'd left on his underwear, but it was nice that he showed her that consideration when she knew he preferred sleeping naked. He gathered her into his arms and pulled her tight against his chest.

"I missed you," he whispered, his breath warm at her ear.

She closed her eyes. "I missed you too."

They fell asleep wrapped in each other's arms. In the middle of the night she awoke to an empty bed and found Jake standing at the window looking out over the yard. "What's wrong?"

He turned, his body shadowed in the moonlight. "I heard something."

Kendall sat up. "Maybe the burglar is back."

"It's OK. It was just a fox." He walked back to bed and settled in next to her. His legs were intertwined with hers as he ran a finger down her nose and over her lips. "Are you sleepy?"

"Not anymore."

"Me neither." He shifted so that he was partially over her. "If you don't want this, say no." He kissed her softly once, and then leaned back to look at her face. He waited a few seconds and lowered his head again. He kissed her a little harder this time, and she buried her hand in his hair. They made love slowly, breath catching softly, bodies trembling in silence, and when they finished, she fell asleep to the sound of his heartbeat under her ear.

Morning came too soon. Nathan had just fallen asleep when sunlight filled his room. He tormented himself for a moment, thinking about Kendall and Jake across the hall. Then with a frustrated mutter, he dressed and started downstairs. The door opened and Jake stepped out. He had on jeans and no shirt. His hair was mussed, and his eyes sleepy. Through the crack in the door, Nathan saw Kendall in bed, still asleep. Her hair was draped over her naked shoulder, and he wondered if she was wearing anything. Bloody hell. "We need to get moving soon. We have a lot to do."

"You look like hell," Jake said.

"I feel like hell. I'll meet you downstairs." He walked toward the stairs but stopped at Jake's call. Nathan turned and looked back. "What?"

Jake looked like he wanted to say something, but then he shook his head. "Nothing."

The regret in Jake's eyes didn't help. Nathan didn't see anyone around, so he walked outside. The sun was shining, promising a nice day, but it couldn't banish the memory of the soft sounds he'd heard from Kendall and Jake's room in the middle of the night. What the hell was wrong with him?

He hopped the fence behind the house and walked to the adjoining farm. He started jogging along the field, just to put some distance between him and his torment. It didn't work, so he ran faster. He didn't realize how fast he was moving until he sped past a herd of cows that didn't even see him.

He stopped, heart pounding with exertion. The smell of cow shit helped erase the thought of Kendall and Jake naked in bed. He went back to the house, but they still weren't downstairs. A morning quickie? He poured a glass of orange juice and looked out the window. Aunt Edna was in the front yard, her arms flapping up and down. Another woman was there, and from the raised voices and wild gestures, they appeared to be arguing.

Nathan walked outside. The other woman looked about the same age as Aunt Edna, but her hair was auburn, and she was dressed quite elegantly for so early in the morning.

"I assure you it wasn't one of my guests," Aunt Edna was saying. "You need to check your own guests."

The woman clicked her red nails against her dress. "Edna, you know you opened this bed-and-breakfast to get back at me."

"I did no such thing," Aunt Edna said. "I needed cruise money."

"Well, you tell your guests to stay off my property." The woman walked stiffly back across the street.

"Well, I never," Aunt Edna said, huffing up to the porch.

"Trouble?" Nathan asked.

"The trouble is with that woman. She's a pain in my . . . backside."

"What's she accusing you of?"

"She thinks one of my guests was trespassing last night."

Jake? Nathan couldn't imagine him leaving the comfort of a big cozy bed with Kendall in it to go wandering in the neighbor's yard. "What time?"

"After midnight, she said. She's a madwoman."

They stepped inside, Aunt Edna still fuming, and met Kendall and Jake coming downstairs. "Did you sleep well?" Aunt Edna asked.

Kendall looked guilty. "Yes."

"Very good," Jake said, and even he looked a little guilty.

"Kendall, you can help me finish up breakfast."

"We'll take a look around outside," Jake said.

Kendall looked worried, and Nathan wondered what Jake was up to. They walked outside as Aunt Edna chattered on about breakfast being the most important meal of the day. Nathan followed Jake out of morbid curiosity, wondering if Jake was going to tell him to get the hell out of their lives.

"I'm sorry," Jake said.

That caught him off guard. "For?"

"You know what for. You're in love with her. I'm in love with her. I'm sorry for you, but we can't keep having this pissing match, or someone's going to get killed."

And it could be her. "You could leave," Nathan said.

"So could you, but I know you're not, and I know I'm sure as hell not."

"Even though you're the Reaper's son?"

"Neither one of us is exactly a catch," Jake said. "Even with all your billions of dollars, you've got some serious baggage."

"You don't?"

"Never said I didn't. But neither one of us is leaving, we both know that."

Nathan gave a raw laugh. "What are you suggesting, a fight to the death?"

Jake didn't laugh, but his eyes lit. "And let you do your Hulk thing and break all my bones? I'm smarter than that. I'm not asking you to leave, but don't make her feel guilty for choosing me."

"You're sure she's chosen you?"

A flash of uncertainty troubled Jake's eyes. "She slept with me, not you."

Bastard. "That's low."

"It wasn't the first time, and it won't be the last."

"I haven't really tried to stop you," Nathan said. Other than a few kisses and insults.

Jake's eyes narrowed. "You saying you're going to try?"

"I didn't get where I am by giving up."

"Is that a challenge?" Jake asked.

"No, I'm saying we should both leave her alone. She doesn't need this right now. None of us do. You've just found out you're the Reaper's son. I've found out I'm a dead kid named Adam. Hell, we probably all need therapy. We need to give Kendall some space to process everything."

"What if she doesn't want space?"

Nathan sighed. "We'll figure it out then. But we need to back off."

Jake frowned and looked irritated, but he rubbed his head. "So it's hands off for both of us?"

Nathan put out his hand. "Deal?"

Jake grunted, but stuck out his hand. "Deal. How about we try the other guest's room? We can shimmy up that balcony and get in."

Kendall was only half listening to Aunt Edna as they finished making breakfast. She kept looking out the window at Nathan and Jake, who appeared to be arguing, and then they shook hands. What the heck? Aunt Edna, whose distance vision wasn't so good, smiled as she watched them. "They're both handsome devils," she said. "I'll give you that. Of course your boss has all that money. You said he keeps a low profile, but he won't mind a little socializing, will he?"

Kendall felt a ball of apprehension forming in her stomach. She hadn't spent much time with Aunt Edna in recent years, but it had always been her aunt's goal to get Kendall married. Now that Jake had dropped his marriage bomb, Kendall worried what Aunt Edna might do. She would probably show up with the entire town in tow to celebrate. "What kind of socializing?"

"Oh, just a little get-together," Aunt Edna said. "I have a few friends who've been dying to see you."

Aunt Edna's little get-togethers could mean three or thirty. "Nathan's a very private man, and I'm not sure I'm up to company. I've been kind of stressed—"

"Oh, this is just what you need then. It'll take your mind off your worries. And Nathan will enjoy this. It's not like those big city parties."

Kendall looked out the window, which was offset from the main part of the house, and her eyes popped. Jake was standing on top of Nathan's shoulders on the balcony outside one of the bedrooms. Jake was doing something to the window, but it didn't seem to be working. Nathan was staggering, trying to steady him as he pushed. They were frighteningly close to the edge of the balcony. It wasn't terribly high, but one wrong move—there it was. The window Jake had been working on suddenly gave way and he toppled over. Nathan grabbed for him and they both dropped over the edge. Kendall ran toward the door.

"Are you all right, Kendall?"

"I just remembered something I forgot to do."

"If you happen to see the men, tell them to come eat."

She knew exactly where they were. Lying in the hedge after an unsuccessful attempt at breaking in. Hopefully not injured.

She heard them fussing before she rounded the corner. They were both climbing out of the overgrown boxwoods, one of which had a section broken out of the middle. "Are you OK?" she asked.

Nathan brushed a piece of greenery from his hair. "How did you manage to get behind enemy lines when you can't even get inside a window on a balcony?"

"You were supposed to stand still."

"How could I stand still with you dancing around on my shoulders?"

"What were you trying to do?" Kendall asked.

"We wanted to try to see who the other guest is," Nathan said.

"You're lucky you didn't break something." Kendall looked them over to see if they were injured. Other than a few pieces of boxwood stuck in their hair and clothing, they appeared OK.

"We'll have to try again later," Jake said.

"Come on, breakfast is ready. Aunt Edna will fuss if we're late."

They put aside their worries for the moment and tucked into a big country breakfast of eggs, bacon, sausage, and biscuits and gravy.

"You won't get a breakfast like this over at Doris's. She serves fruit and yogurt and granola. Have you seen how many calories are in granola? I might as well have a Snickers bar."

"You and Doris are still at it?" Kendall asked. Just like Aunt Edna and old man Wilson.

"That woman is a nuisance to this community."

Kendall hid a smile. "What are you fighting about now?"

"She had the nerve to accuse one of my guests of trespassing on her property."

"Maybe someone got lost," Jake said, his tone sounding a little guilty as he bent over his biscuits and gravy.

Kendall changed the subject and asked Aunt Edna about the man staying in the room next to Kendall's.

"Why, is he being noisy? I did think I heard some knocking around in the middle of the night."

Kendall blushed, knowing what her aunt had heard, and avoided both Nathan's and Jake's eyes.

"I could speak with him, if you like," Aunt Edna said, offering Jake more eggs.

"No," Kendall said. "I was just curious. I thought I saw him."

"I don't know much about him, other than he comes from somewhere in the Midwest, and his parents are dead."

Kendall met Jake's and Nathan's troubled gazes. Aunt Edna's description matched Thomas.

After breakfast, Aunt Edna refused to allow them to help. "You go on and look around for the suitcase. Lord knows where it could be in all this mess I have. I'll take care of cleaning up."

They went to Nathan's room, where Kendall's father had slept when they visited. Even after he'd died, Kendall had always thought of this as his room. There was a picture of him on a bookshelf. He was holding up an urn he'd found, his face dusty and beaming. Kendall picked it up and her eyes misted. She knew from sharing Nathan's memory of the crash that even though her father had been dying, he had managed to save Adam first. She touched the glass. *Thank you, Daddy.*

"I'm going to settle this," Nathan was saying.

"How? Camp out in his room?" Jake asked.

"I'm going to exhume Thomas's body and make sure he's dead."

"You can't do that," Kendall said, aghast. "It's illegal."

"I don't care. We need to know if this guy could be Thomas." He called and spoke to Hank. It was clear from Nathan's expression that Hank had his own objections to the request. "Do it," Nathan said. "I'll take responsibility."

"Brandi will kill you," Kendall said.

"She already wants to kill him," Jake said, but there was admiration in his eyes. "Good move. I'll check out Thomas's room again and see if he slipped in last night."

"Kendall and I can start searching for the chalice," Nathan said.

Jake started to protest, and then he shrugged. "Keep an eye on her."

"Just remember," she said, "I could put either one of you on your ass."

Both men smiled, and Kendall would have sold her soul to have them all live in peace. Maybe it would be better if they were all just friends, and forgot about attraction and romance.

Kendall and Nathan started in the attic. That's where Aunt Edna kept most of the family junk. They went through boxes of old things but didn't find the suitcase or its contents. Nathan was in a quiet mood. She felt kind of awkward being with him alone after spending the night with Jake.

She opened a box and saw the arrowheads she and her father had collected when she was so young she could barely walk. Her first foray into archaeology. She touched the notched edges, remembering his smile. What she wouldn't give to have him here. She covered a yawn and moved on to the next box.

"Didn't get enough sleep?" Nathan's voice was stiff, his message clear.

"Nathan . . ." She didn't know what to say.

He faced her, his eyes dark. "Are you sure about what you're doing? Or is this some kind of thrill ride? Women are always attracted to tough guys."

Kendall hadn't expected him to bring the subject up, and it annoyed her because she didn't have any good answers. "Is it really your business?" And her classy billionaire boss had an edge himself. Tattoos?

His eyes narrowed. "I've looked out for you all my life. You think I'm going to stop just because I lost some memories?" He stepped closer. "I know you feel something for me, more than just what you felt for Adam. I felt something when we kissed. Hell, I think I saw something."

He must have glimpsed something from the vision. Kendall touched his face. "Nathan, I think the world of you."

He trapped her hand against his jaw. "You kissed me back at the hotel. Me, not Jake. How do you explain that?"

"I don't . . ." She felt irritated, because she didn't know. "I don't have to explain everything I do to you."

"Don't be pissed at me because you can't decide which one of us you want."

Kendall clenched her fists, wishing she could hit him, partly because he was saying things she didn't want to hear. She did give him a good shove. "You didn't just say that."

Nathan cut her off by doing something completely uncharacteristic. He pulled her close and kissed her. Not a hesitant, wounded kiss, or one born of a spontaneous moment of joy. Not even one from a vision. This was hot. Kendall's lips responded, opening to his. Her legs wobbled like jelly and she clutched his shoulders just to stand up.

Nathan leaned back, his eyes glowing, teeth showing through panting lips. "See." He turned and walked off without a word.

Kendall sat down on the floor, thoughts and emotions still shooting through her head and body like electric shocks. "Well hell." After a minute she caught her breath and got up. She thought about checking on Jake to see if he'd seen the Thomas look-alike, but she was afraid he'd sense Nathan on her. That could refuel the war between them, and how could they effectively find the Holy Grail and evade the Reaper if they were fighting among themselves?

She walked downstairs and saw Aunt Edna peeking out the front window at Doris's bed-and-breakfast. "She's got another guest. A woman."

"Maybe if you actually put up a sign saying bed-and-breakfast, you'd get more guests. You have two storage rooms you could clear out." Kendall looked out the window, but Aunt Edna grabbed her arm.

"Close the curtain. We can't let her see us watching. She thinks I'm jealous because she has more rooms. Bimbo. Do you want to go to the shop with me?" Aunt Edna asked. "I need to check on a delivery."

And get away from Nathan and Jake? "Sure." And she would get to spend some time alone with her aunt.

"We should let Jake know where we're going. He's very protective of you," Aunt Edna said. "So is Nathan. There's something familiar about him. I feel as if I've seen him somewhere before. Perhaps in the newspapers. Oh, there he is now. Nathan."

Nathan was coming around the side of the house near the entrance to the cellar. He stopped when he saw Kendall.

"We're just going down to the antique shop," Aunt Edna said. "You'll tell Jake, won't you?"

Nathan's hands clenched against his thighs. He nodded.

While they were gone, Nathan and Jake searched the rest of the house. Nathan seemed distracted. "You're acting strange," Jake said as they finished up in the cellar.

"I kissed her."

Jake frowned. "I know. I saw you."

"Not at the hotel. Earlier, in the attic."

Jake gripped Nathan's shirt and shoved him against the wall. "We agreed hands off."

Nathan didn't fight back, but his eyes started to turn. "I know, and I honor my agreements. That's why I'm telling you I screwed up."

Jake let go and stepped away. "What kind of kiss?"

"It was hot," Nathan said.

"You bastard."

"I didn't mean for it to happen, but because we have an agreement, I'm telling you. It won't happen again." Nathan ran a hand over his head. "Unless she asks me to."

"Did she kiss you back—" Jake looked out the window and went completely still. "There's someone across the street watching the house."

Nathan hurried to the window and looked out. "Thomas?"

"I don't know. We're going to find out."

They slipped out the back door and ran through several backyards before crossing the street and working their way back down to Doris's bed-and-breakfast. "There, you see him?"

He was wearing dark clothing and hiding behind a van. Jake and Nathan circled around behind him and grabbed him, except he was a she, and she was Brandi.

"What the devil are you doing here?" Nathan asked.

"I came here to find you. There wasn't a room available over there, so I got one here."

"How did you know we were here?" Jake asked.

"I called the castle to check on everyone. Fergus said you were coming here. Is Kendall all right? I don't know what happened. I woke up in a closet in Thomas's town house. Everyone was gone. I thought the Reaper had killed you all."

"Would that have been a good thing or a bad thing?" Nathan asked.

"Are you crazy? I can't fight him alone."

"Kendall said you left the bathroom because you heard Thomas. When you came back, she passed out."

"I thought I heard him. I swear it was his voice."

"Did you see him?"

"No, but I saw someone. I'm sure it was the Reaper. He looked at me and it felt like he sucked all the life out of me."

"He's shown up here too," Jake said.

"The Reaper?"

"No, Thomas."

Brandi's eyes widened. "Here?"

"Or someone who looks like him," Jake said. "I followed him in."

"What's going on?" she asked.

"Are you sure he's dead? Maybe the Reaper did something to him. I mean, hell, we've got Raphael who was dead, and now he's not. Adam, who was supposed to be dead, and now he's not. A bunch of men who used to be statues, running around the castle. Seems to me nothing connected with the Protettori stays dead."

"I buried him," Brandi said.

"Did you see the body?" Nathan asked.

Brandi shook her head. "Not after I identified him. The casket was closed."

"We'll know for sure before long," Jake said.

"How?" Brandi asked.

"Nathan's opening Thomas's grave," Jake said.

It took a while to calm Brandi down. Nathan was afraid Doris was going to hear Brandi yelling and think they were attacking her. He was about to put his hand over her mouth to shut her up when Jake hit a pressure point in her neck and she dropped like the guards had at the Reaper's château. Nathan caught her. "You don't need Raphael's ability to put people to sleep," Nathan said.

"This only works close up," Jake said. "It's not as cool. We need to get her out of sight. Can you do your thing?"

"Run?"

"Like the wind."

Carrying Brandi, Nathan focused and felt the adrenaline kick in. He was able to control it more than before. He had Brandi at Aunt Edna's and inside the house before Jake hit the front yard.

He laid her on the sofa. When she woke up, she was angry. "What happened? How did I get here?"

"You passed out," Jake said.

Brandi frowned and then put her head in her hands. "I know it's probably best. It's been driving me insane thinking he could be alive, that he faked his death. I need to know for certain."

"They say the Reaper is a master of disguise, and I saw him impersonate a historian. Who's to say he couldn't throw on a wig and some makeup and impersonate Thomas?"

"Why?" Brandi asked.

"We'll ask him when we find him. Jake and I need to get to the antique shop," Nathan said. "You could stay and keep watch while we help Aunt Edna. But if you see him, don't approach him. Even if he looks like your brother."

They positioned Brandi in Nathan's room with the door cracked so she would have a view of Thomas's room, and then they drove to the shop.

"Good move getting rid of Brandi," Jake said.

"The antique shop is the only place we haven't searched, and I don't want her there. She might sacrifice us all to destroy the chalice."

"You, anyway," Jake said. "I think she'd enjoy that."

The drive only took a minute. Jake tapped his fingers on his knee. "You didn't answer me."

"About?"

"Kendall. Did she kiss you back?"

"That's between me and her."

"Damn you."

Edna's antique shop was on Main Street, tucked between a bookstore and a bakery. A sign over the shop read "Aunt Edna's Antiques." Nathan and Jake parked around back—Nathan remembered the parking lot from when he was a kid—and went inside. The shop had everything from furniture to jewelry, but a lot of what she sold was junk, as in not really valuable or antique.

"She's got a lot of stuff here too," Jake said. He was still pissed about the kiss.

"Some of it's good, but most of it's junk," Nathan said, weaving through the displays that Kendall had loved helping set up when she visited.

"One man's junk is another man's treasure," Jake said. "Just give me the Holy Grail."

They found Kendall in a side room examining a small wooden bowl. Her face was lit with excitement.

"Is that it?" Nathan asked.

Kendall looked up and smiled. "No. Aunt Edna got it from a yard sale for a dollar. It's from the seventeenth century, probably worth five hundred."

"Where is she?" Jake asked.

"As soon as I told her, she ran off. Said she had something to do."

"We found something too," Nathan said. "Our least favorite redhead."

"Brandi? What's she doing here?"

"What she's always doing, checking on our whereabouts," Jake said. "She's worse than Raphael, showing up out of the blue. Maybe she's related to him. She sure gets around fast."

Kendall paused, eyes narrowed in thought. "If you and I are children of former Protettori, who's to say there aren't more?"

"Oh hell," Nathan said. "That's all we need. Another one."

"She was actually worried," Jake said. "She thought the Reaper had killed us. She called the castle and Fergus told her we were here."

"Did you ask her about the town house?" Kendall asked.

Jake nodded. "She thinks the Reaper knocked her out. She saw something dark and the next thing she knew, she was waking up in a closet."

"I don't have a good feeling about this," Kendall said. "Shhh, Aunt Edna's coming."

Aunt Edna was talking to someone. "I think you'll like it." She stepped into the room with an elderly man who was wearing a hat. "Oh, Jake and Nathan, you're here too. Well, everyone, this is Charles Rutherford. He's looking to buy the antique shop. He has a collection of antique cups and bowls. I knew he was down at the diner and I couldn't wait to tell him what Kendall found."

Everyone in the room was stunned, with the exception of Aunt Edna.

Marco covered his shock and smiled graciously at them from under his wide-brimmed hat. He had cut his hair and trimmed his beard. "It's a pleasure to meet you. Is that the bowl?" he asked, looking at the one in Kendall's hand.

"Yes, isn't it lovely? And very valuable."

"Yes, it is. Thank you for showing it to me, but I'll have to look at it later. I have some business to attend to."

"Oh, that's disappointing," Aunt Edna said. "I'll walk you to the door."

"Nice to meet you," Marco said stiffly. He scuttled out faster than Nathan had ever seen the old man move.

"What's he doing here?" Kendall asked as soon as he and Aunt Edna left.

"Looking for the chalice, I guess." Nathan barked out a laugh. "An antique cup and bowl collection, huh? Sly old man. We're searching for him all over Prague, and he beat us here."

"How did he know the chalice was here?" Kendall asked.

"I told you that old man's more than what he seems. He probably has more tricks than Raphael. Maybe he really is Merlin," Jake said, remembering how Art had referred to Marco.

"Why run off if we're after the same thing?" she asked.

"Maybe he didn't want to admit it in front of Aunt Edna," Nathan said.

"I'll go catch up with him and find out what's going on," Jake said. "We'd better let Raphael know he's here."

Nathan's phone rang. It was Hank calling to say Thomas really was dead. "Then who did you and Brandi see?"

Jake frowned. "Maybe the Reaper is cloning his goons. You two keep searching for the chalice while I have a chat with Marco."

Nathan sighed. "I'll call Brandi and let her know her brother is really gone."

Brandi had just talked to Nathan when the doorbell rang. There wasn't anyone else here, so she walked downstairs and opened the door. Maybe it would be the imposter, and she would kick his ass. It was Fergus, and three men who looked like they were extras in a medieval movie.

"Brandi?" Fergus looked shocked. "What are you doing here?"

"Same as everyone else. Who are they?"

"Don't ask. It's a dreadful story. Where are Kendall, Nathan, and Jake?"

"They're helping Aunt Edna move some things, which means they're really searching for the chalice."

"Shhh," Fergus said, rolling his eyes toward the men in a way that made him look like he was having a seizure. He leaned closer and whispered, "Don't trust them."

The men, who looked a little lost, started asking about food. "Who are you?" Brandi asked.

"We're guardians," a rough-looking redhead said.

"I thought Raphael was the only guardian left."

A big blond man spoke up. "We were sleeping. Is there any food to be had?" He looked like he could eat a whole cow.

"Let's go inside," Fergus said. "Perhaps Kendall's Aunt Edna has some food. I'm sure she would be happy to feed you."

Brandi pointed to the refrigerator. "Help yourself."

They cautiously approached it and opened the door. "Look at this, will you," the bald man said.

The redhead looked suspicious. "It might be sorcery."

The blond stuck his head inside. "I'm so hungry I don't care."

"They're really guardians?" Brandi asked.

"They're statues."

"Statues?" Brandi looked at the men. Baldy was picking his nose.

"They were, until Marco awoke them."

Statues! Walking and breathing! It was true. "Should they be out here walking around? Shouldn't they be protected?" They were walking relics. Relics needed to be protected. *Or destroyed.* The first thought surprised her. This was the first time since her parents' deaths that she had thought of relics with any sense of preservation. She always focused on destruction. She thought about Nathan and his determination to protect them. Had she become so jaded she was blind?

"You try telling them that," Fergus said, managing to look snooty and exhaustedat the same time. "I tried, and they kidnapped me. The barbarians forced me into a portal, and we came out in Virginia."

"We're not barbarians," the blond said, gobbling down a pack of sliced turkey. "We're guardians. Or sentinels. I'm not sure which."

"A portal, like the one in the temple?" Brandi asked.

"Yes. It was terrifying. My head is still spinning, and then I had to rent a car and drive them here. And they make the most god-awful noises. Tell me *they've* found *it.*"

Assuming *they* meant Kendall, Nathan, and Jake and *it* meant the chalice, she told him no. "Not that they would tell me if they had. Did Marco come with you?"

"Marco?" Fergus's significant brows pulled together.

"Nathan called and said Marco showed up at the antique shop."

Fergus went pale as a dead Irishman. "Marco can't be here. He's dead."

Marco was moving so fast Jake was sure he must have been sipping from the fountain. The old man disappeared down a side street, and Jake followed. He felt a warning prickle a second before he heard words he'd never expected to hear in his lifetime. "Hello, Son."

In an instant, Jake was trapped in an invisible web against the wall, just like the one in the temple. Marco's wrinkles and white hair started melting and his faced changed into another face, a series of faces. The Reaper moved closer and studied Jake. "I'm sorry for this," he said, "but precautions are necessary. You're very strong. So like your mother. She was strong too."

Jake couldn't have moved even if he weren't frozen. The shock of hearing the Reaper admit that he was his son, hearing him speak of his mother in the way a normal father would speak of his child's mother, was like falling through a crack into an icy pond.

"Did you kill her?" Jake asked.

"Not in the way you think."

"I was there. I heard you arguing. You were angry with her."

The Reaper looked surprised, and his face stopped moving. Jake saw him clearly for the first time. Graying hair, middle-aged—he'd probably aged since drinking from the wrong chalice—and then Jake had a brief memory of the man smiling as he bent to tell Jake how much he was growing. How proud he was of him. Jake couldn't have been more than two or three at the time.

The Reaper reached through the invisible wall holding Jake and touched the side of his head as a father would caress his young son. Jake's throat worked, and the darkness that had swallowed his past faded. He remembered his mother, his father, the large home that he'd thought was a castle because it was so big. The secret rooms he hadn't been allowed to enter. His mother's love, and then her fear, always watching him and his father.

"I was angry with her. She had done a terrible thing. She stole something from me. But most importantly, she took you."

That rattled Jake. "I know you killed her. I saw her in a grave."

"She died, but not at my hand. Not directly."

"I don't understand."

"She was ill, already dying. She wouldn't have told you that; you were too young for such burdens." His face sagged. "But I think you were burdened nonetheless."

"She died of illness?"

"No. It was an accident."

"What, she fell? That's what they all say."

"No, she didn't fall, but it was truly an accident, for which I bear the guilt. If I hadn't tried to find her, it would not have happened. I had no idea you were there. If only I had known." His mouth thinned, and for a moment he looked old and frail. "I searched everywhere for you, but I couldn't find you. I thought she must have taken you to the . . . *there.*"

"Taken me where?"

"Where she lived. Where were you?"

"I was hiding in the trees. She made me promise not to come out."

"And you kept the promise. You adored her. You did whatever she asked." He smiled. "She called you her little knight in shining armor."

Knight. That threw Jake, as if he weren't already in a mind spin. Did all mothers think of their sons as knights, or could his have known about the reincarnation/doppelganger thing?

"She loved you very much." The Reaper's smile faded. "Loved me once too. A great love."

"Until she discovered that you're evil and really old?"

He smiled. "You had a brilliant wit even as a child. Evil isn't as simple as it seems. In fact, it can be quite complicated."

"You've killed people."

"Only when it was necessary."

"It was necessary to slaughter your own brotherhood?"

"I won't speak of that with you," he said, as if Jake was a child asking about grown-up things.

"Is she still buried there?"

"No. That wasn't a grave you saw, just a trench where she fell. I came back and moved her body."

"Where?" He felt angry that a whole part of his life had been lost, and he could never get it back.

"To my vault. I would like to show you sometime. I would like to get to know you again. You can't imagine my joy when I thought I'd found you again."

"That's why you hired me?"

"I needed to make sure."

"How did you find me?" Jake asked, thinking what an odd conversation this was.

"It was part luck. I had given up, and then I saw an article in a magazine about treasure hunters. You were in one of the pictures. I knew your face. I knew it was you, but I had to be sure."

"So you hired me to break into the prince's palace?"

"I killed two birds with one stone. I needed to see you in person, and I needed the best man for the job. I didn't know what the prince was about, or I wouldn't have involved you."

Jake looked down at his paralyzed body. "Strange fatherly sentiment for someone who has his son lashed to a wall."

"It's for your own good. I need you out of the way so I can find the chalice."

"You want eternal life."

"I want my life back."

That didn't make sense, but Jake was tiring from struggling against his bonds.

"I need the chalice. I'm going to leave you here while I locate Kendall. I hadn't expected to encounter you in the antique shop."

"Take me with you, and I'll convince her to give you the chalice."

"You love her enough to lie. But I'm not sure I could trust you there with her. She already lied to me once when she told me I had the Holy Grail in the temple. You can see the results of that. I'm older than I have ever been."

"Don't hurt her." It wasn't a demand. It was a plea.

"If she cooperates. But I must have the chalice. At all costs. I will see you soon."

The man who'd ruined Jake's life, a father he hadn't even remembered, walked away and left him pinned to a wall.

CHAPTER NINETEEN

KENDALL WAS SORTING THROUGH OLD DISHES, HER HEAD IN A trunk, when her phone rang. It was probably Aunt Edna calling to read them the menu. She'd gone down to the diner to get them lunch. Kendall banged her head as she grabbed the phone.

"Kendall, this is Fergus. Is Marco with you now?" Fergus's voice was trembling.

"No. Fergus, are you OK? Where are you?"

"Good. You must leave there immediately—you, Nathan, and Jake."

"Jake's not here. He went after Marco."

She heard Fergus's shocked indrawn breath. "He's not Marco."

"Fergus, what are you talking about?"

"Marco isn't really Marco."

Nathan had his face close to hers, listening to the conversation. He took the phone from Kendall and put it on speaker. "Fergus, have you been drinking?"

"I have not. You need to know, sir, that Marco is dead."

"We just saw him," Kendall said.

"That wasn't Marco. His body is at the castle. Raphael found him in Prague, dead."

Marco was dead. "No." Kendall clutched Nathan's arm. "Jake! He doesn't know."

Nathan put an arm around her shoulder. "Fergus, where are you?"

"On the way there. I have backup." There was a scratching noise and the phone disconnected.

"We have to find Jake," Kendall said.

"We will, but I've got to get you to safety first."

"No, we have to find Jake first."

"This is what Jake would want you to do. I'll find Jake."

"I don't care what he would want. I don't care what you want. We're finding Jake together."

The antique shop's bell rang and Marco stepped inside. He was Marco one second, and then he was Thomas, and then Brandi, the visitor's appearance changing like a holographic sign.

Nathan growled and shifted as he faced the Reaper—now Thomas again—and was immediately thrown against the wall, where he struggled and yanked against the air.

Kendall recovered from her shock and lifted her hands, but it was too late. Her body was frozen in place, feet stuck to the floor.

"I won't hurt you," the Reaper said. "I just need the chalice."

"I don't have it."

"You can find it. Your gifts are remarkable."

"I've tried to find it."

"Perhaps an incentive will help. You do remember our agreement? Your friends' lives in exchange for the chalice?"

She nodded. "Where is Jake?"

"He's unharmed. Angry, but unharmed. You still love him even though he's my son?" His eyes were sparking.

It was true. Poor Jake. "A son isn't responsible for his father's evil."

"I grow so tired of that word. As I just explained to Jake, evil is a complicated thing; not always what it seems."

"You've killed and destroyed for this chalice."

"For good reason. Now, I need you to concentrate and find it for me, and I won't hold you accountable for your trickery before."

Nathan's growls were more ferocious.

"Very impressive," the Reaper said, sparing a glance at Nathan. "You will be magnificent when you learn to control your gifts. I know the chalice must be here. I've been reading your thoughts."

"That's rude," she said.

The Reaper laughed. "It is, but we all must do things we don't like. Now focus, Kendall. Please. I am a desperate man."

What was she to do? Trick him again? She could lay a false trail or say anything was the Holy Grail. It wouldn't work for long, but she needed to get Nathan free. "I will make a deal with you. Take Nathan and Jake and leave them outside the castle. Leave them paralyzed. I'll have someone get them, and when they're safe, I will go with you and show you where the chalice is."

"What a tangled web you are caught in," the Reaper said. He was Brandi now. She had been telling the truth about what happened at the town house, as Kendall had already suspected. "You love them both. Love makes you vulnerable, you know. I have loved an incomparable love." Thomas smiled from the Reaper's face now. "I pity you. Two loves. I never recovered from one."

The shop's bell rang again. Fergus, Brandi, and three rogues rushed in, Gregor, the blond, and the bald one. Brandi stared at the Reaper in Thomas's body, her face flushed angry red and her fists clenched. Fergus tried to grab her, but she rushed at the Reaper with a scream. "How dare you use my brother's body!"

"You are a troublesome crew." The Reaper put up his hands and Brandi joined Nathan on the wall. "I did not want Thomas dead," the Reaper said. "I was upset with him for betraying me, but I understand the loyalty of family."

"You killed your own brothers," she spat out, flailing against the wall. "Don't talk about loyalty."

He shifted back into Marco, and flung the others against the wall. Except for one unfrozen sentinel. Gregor.

The rogue smiled. "That will not work on me, Luke. You know my gift is stronger than yours."

Fighting wasn't working. Jake was wild with fear. If he didn't clear his thoughts and find a way out of here, Kendall could die. He calmed his mind and tried to think his way out, but he was still trapped. He wished Raphael were here.

Just as last time, Raphael walked through the wall.

Jake didn't question it. "Get me out of here!"

Raphael had him down with the flick of a wrist. "Where are they?" the guardian asked.

"I think they're at the antique shop. How did you know where to find me?"

"I could see you from the street. I'm surprised he left you alive."

"I don't think he likes killing family. I'm his son."

Raphael's half-tattooed forehead rippled with surprise. "His son? Interesting. Very interesting. Come with me." Raphael wrapped his arms around Jake. Instinctively, Jake felt his eyes close. "Let's go rescue them."

Jake's eyes opened, maybe a minute later, maybe instantly, he didn't know. He and Raphael were in Aunt Edna's antique shop. Kendall was frozen in the middle of the floor, while Nathan, Fergus, Brandi, and two rogues were pinned to the wall. Only the redheaded one called Gregor was free, facing the Reaper. Nathan was so livid he looked like his skin would burst, but he couldn't get loose.

Jake's head was swirling. The spinning moved down his body until he felt like he was a vortex of energy. He thought he'd been struck by the Reaper until he saw the Reaper fall. They all fell to the ground. Except Gregor and Raphael.

What the hell had just happened?

Shocked faces stared at Jake. They could move their heads and speak, but couldn't move their bodies, just like it had happened with the rogues at the castle.

"It was you," Raphael said, surprised. "I told you to be careful what you wished for."

"Jake's the one who paralyzed us at the castle," Nathan said.

Jake was stunned. He'd done this? But how? He didn't have any special abilities. He hadn't taken the Protettori vow. He looked at the Reaper, who was watching him with a look of shock. And pride. Genetics. "I guess I've found my superpower," Jake hissed. "Thanks, Dad." He stalked over to the Reaper and bent down. "I should kill you."

The Reaper looked at Jake and his eyes saddened. "I know. I'm to blame for so much of your pain."

Gregor stepped forward. "I cannot allow that." The rogue opened his arms wide, and objects flew from the shelves, hurtling across the room. Jake dived for Kendall and felt something strike him in the head.

When the barrage was over, the Reaper and Gregor were gone.

"What in the world happened?" Brandi asked, slowly getting to her feet.

"I think Gregor kidnapped the Reaper," Fergus said, rising while straightening his jacket. "He's very good at it. That's what he did to me; kidnapped me and forced me into a portal."

Jake had wondered why Fergus and the rogues were here.

"It was not our idea," the blond rogue said. "Gregor insisted we help him. We will not answer for his transgressions."

"Why would Gregor take the Reaper?" Kendall asked.

"I don't know, but I don't think it's good." Raphael's eyes looked like a tiger's. "I wish I'd never turned Gregor to stone. I should have had him killed."

Nathan was helping Jake check Kendall over for injuries. "I thought you couldn't."

"I can't. But Marco can." Raphael's face darkened. "Or he could."

"Marco could kill another one of the Protettori?" Jake asked. "How?"

Raphael's voice was hushed with awe. "Marco was special."

"I can't believe he's dead. He saved my life." Kendall glanced at Jake, her expression almost apologetic. "The Reaper has to be destroyed."

Jake's mouth was hard. "I know. I'll be the one to do it."

"You can't kill your own father," Kendall said.

Jake shrugged. "Why not?"

"I'll go after Gregor and the Reaper," Raphael said.

"What good will that do if you can't kill them?" Jake asked.

Raphael's face darkened, his expression deadly. "I can't kill them, but I can turn them to stone and smash them into pieces."

"You can't travel now," Kendall said. "Remember what happened the last time. You've been traveling too much since then."

"As soon as I'm rested, I'll go. We'd better find the chalice in case they come back to get it. The Reaper won't stop until he has the Holy Grail." Raphael's eyes hardened. "And God knows what Gregor is after."

"We've looked everywhere," Nathan said.

"You haven't looked hard enough," the guardian said. "I know it's here. I can feel it."

"You can sense the chalice?" Brandi asked.

"Yes."

"Well, that would have been nice to know," Jake said. "Why didn't you search for it?"

Raphael studied the antique shop like a dog looking for a rabbit. "I can only sense it if it's nearby."

"We need to do something about her," Nathan said, looking at Brandi. They all knew she wanted to destroy the Grail.

Brandi backed away. "Like what?"

Raphael shrugged, lifted his hand, and Brandi fell asleep. Nathan grabbed her as she dropped. "A little warning would be nice." He laid her on one of Aunt Edna's nicer pieces, an antique sofa.

Kendall gave Jake a hug. "I was so afraid he would hurt you. How did you get away?"

"Raphael? He's like a big genie. I wished he was there and there he was."

"That's not possible, is it?" Kendall said, looking at Raphael, who was moving around the room.

"None of this is possible," Jake said.

"How did you do the paralyzing thing?" she asked.

"I don't know. It just happened."

"I thought the gifts came by the vow," Kendall said, knowing Jake hadn't taken it.

"Don't ask me," Jake said. "Ask Raphael."

Raphael frowned. "So did I. But it would appear you can also inherit them," he said, and vanished through the wall, only to reappear again a minute later.

"That's unnerving," Jake said.

Nathan eyed Jake. "So you've got a gift too."

"It would seem so. Do you want to be my guinea pig? We can test it again."

Nathan shook his head and walked off. "I'm going to check the shop again."

"You don't have any idea where the things in the suitcase went?" Kendall asked Aunt Edna again. She had shown up just in time to miss the action, thank God.

"I don't recall," Aunt Edna said. "There were some old things I just gave to Goodwill."

Nathan blanched. "Don't tell me the Holy Grail is at Goodwill."

Jake looked at his watch. "I guess we're going thrift-shopping."

"Wait," Aunt Edna said. "If you're going anyway, I have a few more things to donate." She went to the basket of grab bags on the counter. "These haven't sold, and they're just taking up space. I can't believe no one wants a surprise antique for three dollars."

Jake picked up the basket, and one of the bags fell out. Kendall picked it up and a bolt of energy shot up her arm. "Oh my God."

"It's all right, dear," Aunt Edna said. "They're just really old junk that's been collecting dust."

Kendall started ripping the bag.

"What are you doing?" Aunt Edna asked.

Kendall let the paper drop and held up a wooden cup. "It's old, but it's not junk."

"Bloody hell," Nathan said. "It's the Holy Grail."

CHAPTER TWENTY

KENDALL'S HANDS TINGLED AS SHE HELD THE CHALICE.
Everyone gathered around her, including the rogues, and
stared in awe at the simple cup. She felt the life of the man who
had made it, a poor carpenter who'd never realized his creation
would become a legend, the most sought-after object in the world,
the cup used by Christ himself at the Last Supper. Its existence
would stir imaginations and greed, and bring both death and
healing. There were cracks in the cup from use and dark stains
that Kendall knew were blood. She'd watched as the cup was
filled. Swallowing, she handed it to Nathan. He held it for several
moments, his throat working, his eyes glistening. And then Jake
took a turn, his strong hands trembling as he looked inside. His
misty eyes met Kendall's. They handed it around the circle, one
person at a time, allowing each to hold the cup that Christ himself had held.

"I don't know how it could have gotten into my shop," Aunt
Edna said, frowning at it. "I do remember that cup now, though.
You had it with you. I thought your father had given it to you
for your birthday. Such a terrible gift for a little girl. Your father
was a good man, but he was always thinking about relics, so I

switched it for a ring. That little silver one with a daisy. Oh my. I had no idea this was the Holy Grail. No wonder that man was trying to steal it. Rotten bastard. He took up two of my best rooms pretending to be two different people so he could snoop around." Aunt Edna's eyes brightened. "On the other hand, Doris Clune can't say she had the Holy Grail at her bed-and-breakfast."

Kendall shot Nathan and Jake an alarmed glance. "Aunt Edna, you can't mention this. Not a word. This is life and death." Kendall wondered if Raphael could temporarily erase someone's memory. The rogues knew about the discovery, which made Kendall nervous, since they were troublemakers. But she suspected they wouldn't be awake long enough to tell anyone about the Holy Grail.

Aunt Edna patted Kendall's arm. "I won't dear. But what will you do with it?"

"We'll hide it," Kendall said.

"What should I do with her when she wakes up?" Aunt Edna asked, looking at Brandi.

"Keep her here until we have time to get back to the castle," Nathan said. "That'll give us time to hide the chalice."

"You mean for you to hide it," Jake said, a sarcastic scowl forming on his face.

"I'll hide it," Raphael said. He took the chalice from Kendall and stared at it, his eyes darkening with memories. Kendall felt his grief, still raw after two thousand years, and knew that even now he agonized over his role in the crucifixion.

After they gathered up the chalice, which they'd hidden in a plain cardboard box, they said their good-byes to Aunt Edna and left Brandi asleep on the sofa. They had decided to travel to the airport together, where a jet would be waiting. Nathan didn't want the chalice out of his sight. He was taking his role as a guardian seriously, although technically, he wasn't one yet.

Kendall was too, even more so since she was the only keeper now that Marco was dead. She couldn't bring herself to be away from the chalice. Raphael would have taken the chalice and transported himself back to the castle, but he wasn't well enough, so Nathan exchanged his rental for a large SUV, and they all loaded up as Aunt Edna waved, yelling out something about a wedding.

Nathan drove. Raphael sat in the front passenger seat, his eyes closed. Kendall wasn't sure if he was resting or sleeping. He must be grieving for Marco. The two of them had been part of this brotherhood for so many centuries. Kendall sat next to Jake and Fergus, while the rogues were in the third-row seats. The trip was both hellish and hilarious. Fergus kept glancing back as if one of the rogues might stick a dagger in his back through the seat.

"You do realize Aunt Edna almost sold the Holy Grail for three dollars," Nathan said.

"You're the one who sent it there," Jake said.

"I had no idea what it was," Nathan said. "I just wanted to give Kendall something nice." He gave her a shuttered glance. "There was something about it that drew me, but I thought it was just another old cup. He had dozens."

"What are we going to do with them?" Jake whispered, motioning with his head toward the rogues. Even though they were dressed in modern clothing, borrowed from Nathan and Jake, they didn't appear to belong in this time.

"You're not planning to do anything with us," the blond rogue said. "We'll make our own decisions."

The other one nodded in agreement.

When Fergus seemed sure they weren't going to stab or mutilate him—basically, when they'd fallen asleep and were snoring—he grew quiet. Kendall felt the sadness surrounding him.

"Fergus, are you OK?" she asked.

"I was just thinking about Marco. I'm going to miss him."

"Me too," Kendall said. "I can't believe he's gone."

"If he was the one who hired you to take care of me, you must have seen him over the years," Nathan said.

"No. Only when he hired me. Everything else was handled anonymously. Money, reports."

"Reports?" Nathan asked. "What reports?"

"I sent him reports on you. He wanted to know how you were progressing."

"You didn't tell me that."

"I couldn't then. You had to be protected. Though now I don't believe your father was in the witness protection program as I was told. His lie was for your own good. He cared for you very much and he needed me to make sure you were safe."

"And you did," Kendall said. "I hope Nathan realizes that you've dedicated your life to protecting him."

Fergus blinked rapidly and sniffed. "Thank you, Kendall."

He didn't call her Miss Kendall now. They had been through too many dangerous adventures for any kind of formality.

"I do realize," Nathan said. "Thank you, Fergus."

More sniffles. "You're quite welcome. You should be grateful to Marco. He's the one who made sure you lived."

"And I guess Marco didn't try to protect Kendall the same way because he believed Adam was the one who'd taken the vow, when it was really the other way around."

"Yes, I believe so," Fergus said. "The Protettori may have known that she was there, but Nathan—Adam—took the blame and said he took the vow, so the brotherhood wouldn't have been as upset with her."

"Seems odd," Jake said. "Marco went to such lengths to protect Adam. I'm surprised he didn't do something to make sure Kendall was protected."

"What do you mean?" Kendall asked.

"I wonder if Marco didn't have another reason for his actions."

"I guess we'll never know now," Nathan said.

"Are you OK?" Kendall asked Jake after everyone had drifted into silence.

"You mean how does it make me feel to know my father is a monster? That he killed my mother, even if indirectly?" Jake's mouth twisted. "Peachy."

Kendall slipped her hand into his. "You're not responsible for his actions, any more than he's responsible for yours. We can't help who our parents are."

They drove to the airport and boarded the waiting jet. No flight attendants were allowed on board since Nathan couldn't trust anyone with their secrets.

The rogues had to be persuaded, with a few threats from Raphael, to climb aboard the *bird from hell*. Later, the blond got airsick and vomited all over the floor. Fergus swore he was not cleaning it up, but ended up doing it anyway because he said the rogue wasn't doing it right.

"Couldn't you have made him fall asleep?" Nathan grumbled to Raphael.

"No," Raphael hissed. "I keep trying, and it doesn't work."

The bald rogue stayed glued to the window, exclaiming at the impossible sights until he finally fell asleep without Raphael's help.

"He travels through portals, yet he's amazed at an airplane," Jake said.

It was a long journey back to the castle. The jet landed on the private airstrip just as darkness was falling. The place was hardly recognizable from the first time they'd seen it. Raphael and Marco had lived here in solitude, protecting the Protettori's relics and treasures. Now the place was crawling with guards. A necessity, Kendall thought, but it must be troubling to Raphael. And now he was alone.

"It won't be the same without Marco," Kendall said. She hadn't known him that long, but she had grown terribly fond of the old man. "He shouldn't have gone after the Reaper without us."

Jake mourned the old keeper too. He may have been a little loony, but he had been a good man. "I don't know why he felt so responsible for the problems the Reaper has caused."

Nathan rubbed his arm where the tattoo was hidden. "He didn't tell the other members of the brotherhood about Kendall and me taking the vow, but I don't see why that would make him feel so guilty that he would take on the Reaper himself."

"I think Marco had a lot of secrets," Kendall said. "Some we'll probably never understand."

"He was a very private man," Raphael said.

Hank and two other guards met them. Hank gave Nathan an update on security at the castle and Nathan's mansion. The other rogues had been rounded up and sedated, and were being held in a secure room. One without a bolt-hole.

"We need to prepare for a funeral," Nathan told Hank.

"Where will we bury him?" Kendall asked.

"The catacombs, I suppose," Nathan said. "Is that agreeable with you?" He glanced at Kendall and Raphael.

Kendall nodded. "He needs a place of honor."

"No one wants to know what I think? Is this a Protettori thing?" Jake asked.

Nathan rolled his eyes. "What do you think, Jake?"

Hank interrupted before Jake could answer. "Bury whom?"

"Marco. The Reaper killed him in Prague. Didn't you tell them?" he asked Raphael.

"I told no one," Raphael said. "I didn't want you to find out and be distracted by grief."

"I don't understand," Hank said. "Marco is here. I saw him not five minutes ago headed for the chapel."

Kendall gasped. "The Reaper!"

Raphael and Nathan's eyes had already lit. "He must be able to get past the statues if he's disguised as someone else," Nathan said.

"Get Kendall out of here," Jake ordered. "Nathan, take her."

"No, I'll go with you. You can't handle him alone. Hank, get her inside the castle and hide her. Call for backup." Nathan and Jake took off running. Raphael was already out of sight.

Kendall waited a second, and then followed.

"Come back," Hank called. "You have to stay with me."

"I'm not letting them face the Reaper alone. We have to help them."

"They'll kill me," Hank said, running after her. "Dammit. You are stubborn." He called for the other guards to follow. They all hurried past the garden wall that housed the maze. Ahead of them, Kendall saw a light coming from the chapel. She caught up with them outside the old church.

"What the hell are you doing here?" Jake asked when he saw her.

"I'm not leaving you to face him alone."

"Stay behind me," Nathan said, frowning at her.

"He may be here for the treasure," Jake said. "Raphael said he didn't really move it."

When they caught up to the guardian, he was staring at the Reaper, who was still disguised as Marco.

"Bloody hell!" Nathan said. "Why isn't he doing something? Kendall, get out of here."

Raphael and the Reaper turned as the trio approached. Raphael wore a stunned expression, but the Reaper just smiled. "Ah, you've returned. I must say I'm very glad to see you."

Nathan and Jake came together, forming a wall between Marco and Kendall. "What are you doing here?" Jake asked.

"I came to visit the stones," Marco said. "We need to complete the vow soon. Not now, of course, but perhaps tomorrow."

Kendall's senses were sparking like fireworks. She saw Marco as a child, as a young man, a father—that was a shock—and as an old man. She took a step closer. "Marco?"

"What are you doing?" Jake yelled, grabbing her arm. "He's not Marco."

Raphael reached out and touched his wrist to Marco's. "He is. But how? I saw you dead."

Marco smiled. "I still have a few tricks up my old sleeve. Some that even you don't know about."

"You're not dead." Kendall's eyes grew damp.

"Let me guess," Nathan said. "You drank the fountain water from the Holy Grail and you're eternal."

"No," Raphael said. "He's just very powerful. I assume you've all heard of Merlin."

CHAPTER TWENTY-ONE

I TOLD YOU," JAKE SAID, AFTER THEY HAD DISMISSED THE guards. He, Kendall, Nathan, Raphael, and Marco were still in the chapel. "I knew he was Merlin."

"That's how he got past the statues without a cross," Kendall said. "Remember, the Reaper took Marco and Brandi to the temple together? I didn't realize it until later, but he didn't have a cross."

"He didn't need one," Jake said. "He's Merlin."

"So he's not a reincarnation like us?" Nathan asked Raphael. He and Kendall had been firing questions at Marco. Jake was curious, but he was more worried about the consequences of all this.

"No, he's the original," Raphael said.

"Like you," Jake said, looking at the engraved standing stones in front of the chapel. This was where it had all started, where Kendall and Nathan had taken the vow. They were Protettori now, or would be officially after they finished the vow in the ceremony tomorrow. The gnawing worry that Jake had been facing for days was turning into a monster. Kendall and Nathan were growing closer. The bond they already had from childhood and from their past lives as Arthur and Guinevere—if you believed

Raphael—would only grow stronger now that they were part of a secret brotherhood whose members lived for centuries, and even longer.

Jake knew Kendall cared for him, and he hoped that she more than cared, but what would happen to them? Even if Kendall chose to spend her life with him, eventually he would die. She would keep on living. So would Nathan. No doubt Nathan would eventually end up with her. Jake was torn with relief and jealousy. He knew Nathan loved Kendall, and she would need someone to watch over her if she lived for centuries . . . or longer.

But he wanted it to be him.

Was it better for him to get out now and leave her to Nathan? She loved Nathan too, or some part of her did, and Nathan would look after her in the same way Jake would.

Jake became aware of Marco speaking in low tones. "I didn't realize Gregor was one of the statues or I would never have awakened them. I shouldn't have anyway, but I was desperate to save you."

"Gregor must be powerful if he can kidnap the Reaper," Kendall said. "And the Reaper's gifts didn't affect him."

"All the brotherhood were powerful to some degree, but Gregor was special. Very intelligent, strong, and determined. If only I had known Raphael put those vagabonds to rest. I thought they had died."

"I apologize for not telling you," Raphael said. "I didn't know what else to do with them. I couldn't kill them, and I didn't think you would. I certainly didn't expect you to try to wake them."

Marco stroked his beard, thinking, his blue eyes more alert than Jake had seen before. "I hope Gregor is weakened since he just emerged from his resting state."

Nathan frowned. "He didn't say what he wanted. I assume it was the chalice."

"Perhaps," Raphael said.

Marco froze, hand still clutching his beard. "You don't think..."

"I'm afraid so," Raphael said.

"Afraid what?" Jake asked. "What aren't you telling us now?"

"The fourth relic," Marco said. "Gregor protected the fourth relic for many years."

Kendall's eyes flashed. "What's the fourth relic?"

"The Tree of Knowledge," Nathan said.

Marco frowned. "How did you know?"

"Raphael told us. He doesn't want us to destroy the Reaper until Raphael finds out where the tree is."

"The Reaper has it?" Kendall asked.

"At one time, he did," Raphael said. "I believe Gregor thinks he still does. They were always rivals, each trying to find the rarest relics first. I don't think we've seen the last of them."

"You don't think they would work together?" Kendall asked.

"Let's pray not," Marco said. "If either of them were to get the other three relics, this final piece would be devastating in their hands."

"So we've got two supervillains looking for the relics now, not just my evil father?" Jake said.

Marco looked so pale Jake thought he might pass out. "Your father?"

"Would you believe the Reaper is my father?" Jake gave a dry laugh. "I've remembered my past."

"But how can that be?" Marco asked.

"He claims he loved my mother, but she was frightened of him. She took me and ran away. I think she found out what he was. I was there when she died. I was just a little kid, terrified, so I blocked most of the memory. I still don't remember it all."

"Welcome to the club," Nathan said.

Marco seemed shaken. "Are you certain?"

"He must be," Nathan said. "Jake didn't take the Protettori vow, but he's discovered a wicked gift. He can paralyze people and stop objects somewhat like the Reaper can. That should be proof."

"The gift of telekinesis. Like Luke had." Marco looked troubled. "So he killed your mother?"

"He says he didn't, not himself, that it was some accident. He feels guilty over it." Which troubled Jake. It didn't fit the picture he'd built of the Reaper.

"This is a shocking turn," Marco said. "I would like to hear more about it later, but I'm afraid I need to rest." As he left, he stopped and took Jake's hands in his wrinkled ones. "I'm so sorry for your trouble, but you aren't responsible for your father's actions." He held on to Jake's hand for a moment longer. "We should all get some sleep. It's getting late, and we've had quite an adventure. Tomorrow at sunrise we will complete the vow. You are embarking on a long and dangerous journey."

"Will we be"—Kendall swallowed—"like you and Raphael?"

"She means how long will they live?" Jake blurted out.

"A lifespan varies, even in the Protettori," Marco said. "It depends on many things. Danger, battles, how much water you drink, your mental and physical condition, and some of it is controlled by genetics." He paused, and his eyes swept over Jake. "But it could be assumed that you will live a very long time. I will say good night." Marco patted Jake's hand again, and then walked away.

Kendall watched Jake, her green eyes somber. He was certain she was thinking the same disturbing thoughts.

"Would you like to see where I moved the treasure?" Raphael's question was directed at Jake.

He felt like a kid who'd been offered a consolation ice cream cone because he hadn't won the prize. Raphael used his key and opened the stone doorway in the floor. They followed him down the steps. At the bottom, he pushed the switch, and the torches flared to life, lighting the empty room.

"Stand back." Raphael put his key into an opening in the floor, one Jake hadn't noticed. He turned it and the room began to move. It rotated counterclockwise until another room appeared. It looked the same, except it was filled with treasure.

"The treasure was here all the time," Jake said.

"It never left," Raphael said. "It was just hidden."

"A revolving room," Nathan said. "That's bloody brilliant."

When they had rotated the room back so that it appeared empty again, they filed up the steps and quietly left the chapel. Nathan and Kendall were standing near each other, talking. Jake stopped at the door and looked back at the stones, his thoughts in turmoil. They walked back to the castle in silence, each contemplating what tomorrow would mean. When they reached Nathan and Jake's door, the three of them stopped. Kendall gave Jake an awkward glance. Jake even glimpsed a hint of pity in Nathan's eyes. Nathan understood what this meant too.

Jake might have her now, but Nathan would have her for eternity.

"I'm going to bed," Kendall said, searching his face.

"Then I'll say good night," he said, ignoring the invitation in her voice, and with Nathan watching, Jake kissed Kendall softly on the lips and left. He had some thinking to do.

Kendall didn't see Jake that night. Or the next morning. She dressed, wearing a skirt and blouse, since she didn't know what was expected for such an occasion. Not that there was a precedent. There had never been a female keeper in the Protettori. Three cheers for the female race, she thought. She kept waiting for a tap on the door. She didn't want to go through this without

Jake's support. This was hard for him. Hard for her. She was torn. One part wanted to run away with him and forget about the Protettori. But the other part couldn't leave Adam. Nathan. Arthur. And she couldn't walk away from protecting the relics. She wouldn't. Deep down, Jake wouldn't want her to.

The sun was almost up now. She couldn't wait any longer. With a glance at the bed where she'd first spent the night with Jake, she left the tower and walked down to meet Nathan. He was waiting for her, dressed in khakis and a dark-blue shirt. They stared at each other wordlessly. Then he reached for her hand. "Are you ready for this?"

"No."

"Me neither, but we'll be all right. We did it before." He smiled, Adam's smile, and she felt a ray of comfort. He'd always looked out for her, and he would now. But this was going to be for a long, long time.

They walked to the chapel together, passing her parents' lonely graves. She wondered if her father's ghost would be there to witness her carrying on in his footsteps. Like father, like daughter. And the mother she'd never known, would she know what Kendall had become? And Jake, was he going to miss the ceremony? She glanced over her shoulder.

"He'll come if he wants to," Nathan said.

Kendall nodded but didn't say anything. They reached the chapel and found Marco waiting. His eyes looked bright. He was wearing his robe, and he did indeed look like Merlin.

She had so many questions for him, but now only one thing was on her mind. Where on earth was Jake?

"Take your places before the stones," Marco said.

Kendall and Nathan moved into place as if they were a bride and groom at a wedding. She remembered standing here before, reading the words on the stones, hearing Adam begging her to stop. But she hadn't, and now he was involved in this too. A guardian of the Protettori, and she was the new keeper.

"Are you ready?" Marco asked. The old man looked happy to be relinquishing his title. "You remember how it goes. Repeat the words on the stone."

"Are you starting without me?"

Kendall turned and saw Jake standing in the door of the chapel. Raphael appeared behind Jake, his face grim. "You won't believe what he did," the guardian said. "The damned fool took the Protettori vow."

"Bloody hell."

Marco's eyes twinkled, and Kendall thought he hid a smile. "When?"

"Last night," Jake said with a grin.

"You're sure he took the vow?" Marco asked Raphael.

Raphael nodded. "I read his memories."

Kendall was so overjoyed she wanted to cry. Jake had just taken the oath that she and Nathan had taken in their youth. They would all be together now. For a long time.

Nathan looked conflicted. Kendall could feel his anger, but also a sense of relief.

"Well then," Marco said. "Jake, take your place next to Kendall so we can make this official. Raphael, you will witness."

Jake stood on the other side of Kendall and slipped his hand in hers. "Ready."

"You bloody bastard," Nathan said, and took Kendall's other hand.

"You think I was going to let you two do this without me?" Jake's eyes narrowed. "Hell no! We've got two villains and another relic to find."

Dear Reader,

Thank you for taking the time to read this book. If you enjoyed it, you can find other books in this series (The Relic Seekers) and my Highland Warrior series on my website at www.anitaclenney.com. You can sign up for my newsletter to get updates and to enter contests. My books can also be found on my Amazon author page at www.amazon.com/author/AnitaClenney. Connect with me on Facebook at www.facebook. com/anitaclenneyauthor and my street team, Anita Clenney's Book Warriors, at www.facebook.com/groups/ AnitaClenneyWarriors.

Thank you!
Anita

ACKNOWLEDGMENTS

THERE ARE SO MANY PEOPLE I NEED TO THANK FOR HELPING me bring this book to life. My family, who is always so understanding and supportive. Writer friend Dana Rodgers for her support. My beta readers Beth, Rhonda, Becca, Teri, Mel, Sandie, Lynn, Lori, Tamie, Fawn, Ann, Patty, and Jaria for their excellent feedback. My street team, Anita Clenney's Book Warriors, and Goodreads group, Anita Clenney's Book Clan, for their help spreading the word about my stories. My agent, Christine Witthohn, for her guidance. My developmental editor, Clarence Haynes, for his help. My editor, Helen Cattaneo, and the entire staff at Montlake Romance. And most of all, I thank my readers. Without you, my stories would not have a home. Thank you!

ABOUT THE AUTHOR

N EW YORK TIMES AND USA TODAY bestselling author Anita Clenney has penned some of the hottest paranormal romantic suspense books on the market, including the Highland Warrior series and the Relic Seekers series. Before becoming a writer, she worked as a secretary, a realtor, a teacher's assistant, a booking agent, and—briefly—a pickle factory worker. Today, she lives in Louisiana with her husband and children.